Woven into
the Fabric

Woven into the Fabric

Into the Very Fabric of Our Lives, God Has Woven Spun Gold

Tsehai Essiebea Farrell

AuraTales
Publications

Cover photo artwork: Angela Perkins
© 2017 Essiebea Tsehai Farrell
All rights reserved.
ISBN: 0963369318
ISBN-13: 9780963369314
Library of Congress Control Number: 2017949783
AuraTales Publications, Inglewood, CA

I am with the Creator from the beginning;
I am given patterns and sets of living strings;
I am Destiny,
the Weaver.

Prologue

Ethiopia: A Beginning

The ancient people lived simple lives along the shores of Lake Tana until, one day, a tall wet woman emerged from the sea. Her limbs were longer and more slender than the people had ever seen before. So too were her hands, feet, and neck. She ambled along like a slowly swaying palm. Her eyes, her most startling feature, were elongated across her face, nearly temple to temple. It seemed her forehead widened a bit to accommodate them, thus making her face a softly edged inverted triangle. When she finally looked up, they could see that the width of her eyes spanned fully a third of her face. The irises, of the deepest emerald green, sat in pearly, opaque orbs shadowed under lavishly fringed lashes. Her dolphin-textured skin was turquoise brown.

She wore sea grass and flowers, and the children followed as she walked the village, stopping often to examine, smell, touch, and taste her new surroundings. The men gathered near when she came down to the shore, because schools of fish had fluttered in to glide across her silky legs as she stood in the water. The men came to catch the plentiful fish—or so they said—but just as the sea creatures had, they too longed to touch her flesh.

Over the weeks, her curly down hair grew into soft black ringlets. She did not speak, though at night her humming sweetened the whistling wind. In the silence of their souls, the villagers came to love her. They could not explain why, but surely they did.

One man, Tegene, gathered the courage to approach her to be his wife. The villagers did not approve: it was as if he were trying to mate with one of the gods. Tegene cared what they thought, but he could not divert his heart. So he married Yeshi, the woman from the sea, with his solemn pronouncement to her. The only guests at the modest celebration were the animals that had gathered in their name.

The years creased by seasons, then folded one into the next. When the time of the Great Sleep came, the children were the first to succumb. First, lethargy slowed their pace; then, in a few days, they passed away in their sleep. It was only Taferit, the child of Tegene and Yeshi, who continued to awaken each day wide-eyed and full of vigor. Surely, the villagers speculated, she took after her mother—her strange mother. Perhaps it was she who had brought this curse from the sea.

The people drove them out. After the family disappeared beyond the boundaries of the world, the lake began to foam and churn. The earth rumbled and mounted into a deafening quake. With an explosive crack, the most distant end of the lake fell from the surface of the earth.

Day and night, the villagers heard the mournful cry of the remaining waters and the distant thunderous roar of its family falling into oblivion. Thick plumes of smoky mist bellowed from the cliff. No one fished. No one dared cross.

Years passed, and the lake did not calm nor nourish them anymore, so they turned to the land and toiled hard for food. Soon, the beauty of the women and the vitality of the men gave way to the strain; even love lost its sweetness to labor.

⚬⚬⚬

Then, one evening in the pink of a summer sunset, standing in silhouette against the horizon, was a too-tall woman and her sinuous daughter. After a while, they proceeded to walk toward the village. Everyone immediately recognized them and gathered at the campfire to await Yeshi and her daughter, Taferit.

"Pack up your things and follow us," said the chimes from the younger woman's mouth. "We will take you to the land of thunder and everlasting plenty."

Was it the voice, their eyes, or the patience in their willowy frames that compelled them? Without hesitation, the people packed their belongings and the next morning followed them beyond the edge of the world, way down below where the water falls.

There, night and day, rainbows and a turquoise mist shielded them from the direct heat of the sun, and their hearts beat with renewed vigor to the rhythm of the thunder.

Tis Issat Falls became the source of the Blue Nile, which courses down to the south before heading north to wed the White Nile in Khartoum. Where they meet and flow side by side, the rivers' personalities remain distinct—one rapid and effervescing, the other slow and meandering. Married, they flow on to their honeymoon in Cairo.

The old ways passed into the new as the villagers learned to live beyond fishing and farming. Yeshi showed the people how to construct canoes (*tankwas*) from the abundant papyrus lining the Blue Nile. So they took their rich spices, coffee, and cloth and set out to trade with other lands. Yeshi became their first queen, because that is what she was.

With eyes and flesh that echoed the fecundity of the lush forest and the promise of the Blue Nile, Queen Yeshi gave Ethiopia to the world.

Chapter 1

──────◇◇◇◇──────

Timkat Epiphany

Ethiopia, 1954

Without speaking, Brehane's uncles and her mother stepped to the duty of their father. Sirak and Iskender carried three-year-old Brehane's grandfather down the hill upon the seat they were making with their crossed hands and arms, while he, sitting upright, clasped their necks. At the bottom, they placed him in the oxcart already fitted with his padded chair and two built-in wooden benches along the sides. Uncle Sirak drove, while her mother, Saba, sat in the back to assist their aging father. Gondar's roads were paved, but not smoothly, so Brehane rode high upon the shoulders of Uncle Tedros as he and Uncle Iskender walked alongside, keeping pace with the cart.

When Saba felt the coolness of the highland morning yielding to the heat of the Ethiopian sun, she opened and placed her father's huge umbrella securely into the tall reed brace mounted to the cart. After a time, Uncle Tedros placed Brehane in the shade of her mother's lap. Before the child drifted off to sleep, the little girl saw many families and whole villages converging at the crossroads and walking in unison up the mountain. There at the top was the huge church: Medhane Alem, Savior of the World, site of the Timkat ceremonies. Eager but overwhelmed by anticipation, heat, and the rickety lull of the cart, Brehane could no longer hold open her eyes.

By and by, the rising passion of the sistrum, lyre, and drums drove Brehane from her nap. She heard the songs of the dozens of gathering priests and the trilling ululations of the women. When the wagon paused again along the crowded road, her mother climbed off first, then lifted her daughter down. Uncle Tedros took the cart seat next to his father.

Clasping Brehane's small hand and pulling her close, Saba wedged their way through the congregation, finally reaching a lively cluster of women. The women immediately enveloped Saba in smiles, hugs, and traditional three-cheek kisses.

Seeking her out, Aunt Aster pulled Brehane into her kissing, cooing, hot embrace and placed her on the fleshy protuberance of her ample hip. Now relieved from the press of crowding legs, the child felt far more comfortable and secure on this new seat—better able to grip her knees over her aunt's buttocks and stomach and rest her body against a soft breast or well-padded shoulder. This was not at all like the loving but bony frame of her mother.

The huge sanctuary cast elongated shadows from its towers like arms of welcome to the throngs of highland faithful parading in unbroken lines of men, women, and children. The gloriously brazen jewel-toned umbrellas shielding the priests sailed high above the white sea of the traditional garb of the masses.

The pilgrims vied for the shady spots in the church courtyard. Others dipped from the fountain and edged their way forward, seeking a good vantage point to view the impending pageant. The priest and elders gathered under a canopy, where young men fanned them and served them cool water.

The scores of priests arrayed in robes of the richest purples, plums, emerald greens, and royal blues embroidered with golden threads represented all the churches in this and neighboring provinces. Their heads donned ancient and elaborately filigreed gold or silver crowns.

Even more stunning to the eye and spirit were the high priests who carried upon their heads the sacred Ark. The Tabot, the Ark of the Covenant, consisted of two stone tablets wrapped in magnificent fabrics of velvets, satins, and silks. These sacred coverings had taken the holy weavers years to complete. Woven into the fabric of each cloth was spun gold. Tradition, and an effort to keep the location of the true Ark secret, required that every church have a replica of the original tablets of the Ten Commandments in its Holy of Holies. The elder priests balanced these large stone tablets on their heads with the erect bearing of much younger men and with the dignity befitting the high honor of bearing the holy relic.

Timkat epiphany had begun. Priests clustered in a circle surrounding the musicians. The younger priests, garbed in pure white, had occasionally erupted in loud songs and holy dances along the procession. But now, in the heat of the day, they all came together in the courtyard near the outer door leading to the Holy of Holies to prepare for the full measure of their dance offering.

The drummers and sistrum and horn players began in earnest a rhythm so deep, haunting, and full of longing that the women wept and the elder men stood staring misty-eyed. The music carried beneath it a lull and roll like the sea gathering itself for a tempest.

Time receded as their spirits mounted the music, which transported them back to Mount Sinai. Again they gathered with Moshe and the original souls of ancient times to receive the Tabot of the Holy Commandments from the Most High. Again, they soared to the Tabernacle in Jerusalem to watch King David dance before the Ark.

A handsome young priest named Mikael stepped into the center. Fresh butter and sweat gleaming in his curly locks, he raised and lowered his head and undulated his shoulders to the rhythm of the drummers. Fluid, graceful, powerful—rocking, swaying, churning—he moved above the braced stance of his parted feet. Then the tempo escalated, and Mikael was everywhere. Encompassing the ring of the sacred space, he skittered and leaped, twirled and genuflected.

The blare of the horns seared the mind and broke open the heart. Weeping and trembling, Mikael pleaded with his every sinew to the God of Creation to receive this song and dance in praise of His Glory on behalf of His people.

No longer a mere man, Mikael was a sound, a streak of light, an utterance of awe, a portal of prayer—the spirit of sweet surrender. Then, released by the elders, the other young priests joined Mikael in the tranced possession of David's spirit dancing before the Ark. They became the primordial movement of all Creation—the stampede of the bison, the grace of the gazelle, the magnificence of the peacocks, the soaring silences of the dove, the posturing of the winds, the passion of fire, the steadfast rhythm of the sea—all the earth alive, glorifying the presence of the Lord. Hallelujah!

Finally, swept up in the whirlwind, the high priests and elders joined the flurry. Possessed by the Holy Spirit, they moved fiercely beyond their years and infirmities. They soared, screamed, and cried out in ecstasy to heaven: Hallelujah!

The able-bodied women danced, while others lifted their gauzy shamas from their shoulders, draped them over their heads and faces, and wept-their voices piercing the sky with the incense of ululations.

Brehane, whom Aunt Aster held beside her on a ledge, was stunned by the complete spectacle. Frozen by the penetrating sounds of spirit, she felt a light tingling inside her body, dancing and quaking along her spine. The child was smiling as she followed the eyes of the priests in their skyward stares. The cloudless sky was gathering upon itself in varying shades of blue, creating formations of heavenly hosts and jubilant angels.

Brehane was a child without the words to describe or explain her epiphany. But the memory in her heart of this holy day in the Ethiopian highlands when her soul caught fire would haunt her and forever call her home.

Chapter 2

At Her Mother's Loom

*T*all and serene, Saba was a weaver of fine fabrics. Her long, graceful fingers danced between the thin white cotton threads. On many afternoons, the clacking of the wooden loom receded as the whispering strings lulled Brehane to sleep.

Brehane, always alongside her mother, had a small basket of her own filled with new cotton puffs into which she pressed her face closely to find and remove every seed, stick, or speck of dirt. She also had strands of spun cotton threads, ranging from coarse and thick to the fineness of cocoons, and short strands of colored threads—purples, deep reds, greens, blues. Brehane's favorites were turquoise like the sea or pink as a bright smile. But the treasures of her basket were the short threads of spun gold no longer than her small fingernails. They were magic in the sunlight. She bundled the strands over and over into a tiny ball, which she now held out on the center of her palm and presented to her mother.

Saba noticed her daughter, paused her work, smiled, and accepted the gift. "How pretty," she said as she held it to the window. "See how it catches the light? It's like you, Yenni Brehane. You are my little light. You are talented, Brehane. One day you'll be a weaver just like me." She kissed both of her daughter's cheeks and placed the ball on her table near the scissors, needles, and hooks.

Brehane stood behind her mother's seat leaning against her, listening. Her mother quietly hummed and sang as she worked, inch after inch and yard after yard of gauzy white fabric. She would always begin a shama in the evening and would work well into the night. This left her free in the early mornings to accompany Brehane down the hill to the shore. The three-year-old knew her way down the rocky path and refused her mother's assistance. Her mother smiled behind her hand at the determined set of her daughter's pursed baby lips and the scramble of her tiny feet. Brehane was eager to meet the sunrise as it cast its bright rays across the water. Once she and her mother reached the shoreline, they both lifted their hands and greeted the morning peace, "Selam,"

Brehane spent hours with her nurse, Rut, playing by the sea but would return throughout the day to watch her mother work and see the growth of the fabric as the modest threads of white cotton gave way to vibrant jewel tones. Purple string, woven stiff with sparkling golden threads, provided the broad border for the festival robes. Brehane was not permitted to touch the string, and even her mother herself was prohibited on certain days. Brehane's beautiful mother did not often speak with her lips, yet she had raised her daughter on the poetry of her heart nimbling its way through her hands. Into the cloth, she formed the delicate, intricate patterns that paraded across her mind.

To her child it seemed all the same—the way her mother loved her hair into sculpted row after row of braids. The way she orchestrated the cotton, woolen, silken, and golden threads through the chorus of her loom. The songs she hummed and sang that perfumed the air around them. The spongy *injera* and savory *doro wat* that she prepared to feed her family. All the same mother love.

Brehane learned early that love becomes everything. She would grow to be a woman beckoned by the puff of a cotton ball, the wool on a sheep's back, the whisper of songs, patterns, and memories blowing in her mind. Then, would she too answer the call to shape and give voice to a festival robe of great splendor, to weave the fabric of an ancient and imminent destiny, to clothe the people's spirit in glittering gossamer raiment? Would she answer the call to weave a seamless word?

Chapter 3

Confusion

*L*oud voices penetrated Brehane's nap. Normally, the rise and fall of her family's movement and talk were not of much concern to Brehane. She would continue to eat, play, or rest without being disturbed. But this time, the pitch and the urgency were different. Then her uncle came, wrapped her in her thick *gabi*, and carried her to her mother. Once in her arms, Brehane could hear her mother's sobs and feel her chest quaking. Brehane quickly removed the blanket from over her head and searched her mother's tearful eyes.

Her relatives and a strange man and woman were standing opposite her mother, who was clasping her so tight it almost hurt. She and her mother stood alone, both crying. Saba, struggling with her own brothers, refused to hand over her daughter. Brehane noticed her mother calling the man by name; he was not a stranger to her.

Saba turned her back to the men and lifted her daughter's chin to see her face. Her large wet eyes seeped into the child's heart as she desperately whispered, "Yenni Brehane—my light. My sweet Brehane, I am your mother. Look at me, remember my face.

Remember me, daughter, remember me. I love you. My sweet girl. You are Yenni Brehane. Don't forget who you are." She smothered her with clutching kisses.

The stranger gently tugged at her mother's shoulder. Saba spun around, clutching and shouting, "Don't take my baby! Father, help me. Don't let him take my baby!" she shrieked with empty arms.

"Release her. She is also his child," her father spoke softly, but firm. "Let him take her to America. He will make her a better life."

The strange man had Brehane now. He briskly wrapping her back in her blanket and, saying a few parting words to her grandfather, he and the woman left with the child.

"Anat, Anat!" Brehane screamed for her mother and struggled to free herself from the prison of her gabi. Secured in the back seat of the moving car, wedged between the man and the large woman, she was still free enough to stand and turn around to look through the back window in time to see her mother break free from her brothers and run down the path from the house, only to be recaptured. She bucked, heaved, tore, kicked, screamed, and spit curses at them, but they held her back. Just before the car's descent down the hill snatched mother and daughter from each other's view, Brehane saw her mother collapse to her knees in the dust.

As if by emotional relay, suddenly Brehane bucked and kicked, mimicking her mother's wild resistance, only to be held tightly by the man while the woman swaddled her entire body like an infant in the thick blanket. She screamed, cried, and pleaded until her swollen eyes and face dripped with tears, snot, and drool.

Then, just as the night enveloped the dusk, her mother was finally overwhelmed by the strength of her uncles. Alas, to the looming and potent unknown, Brehane too succumbed.

—※—

Nothing was right. The few words she had begun to mutter with confidence beside her mother's loom, *Mendeno*, the first song she learned to sing—a song that was sung to her each morning—none of these words mattered anymore.

Brehane missed the soft whine of Amharic on her ears and the tugging plea behind the music. She missed the aspirant echoes of the known sound—the comfortable and familiar sound of her own language—the known life. It was exchanged now for a foreign language, a language that cut and spit each word apart with hard, harsh sounds that provided no respite for a child. This new language did not embrace the heart; rather, it scurried over the edges of the mind and scratched at tender skin. She kept silent in English.

"Brenna," they called her now. But she remembered Brehane. She did not answer. Long after she understood that the name was meant for her, she did not answer to Brenna. It was not her name.

Her new father, suspecting she understood but was being obstinate, withheld the sweet candies he would sometimes give her. She loved the candy. It was her only certain sweetness now—now that she no longer had Anat's smiles, cooing words, and snuggling warmth. Candy, that's all, which was now being denied her because she would not submit to the name.

"Brenna!"

"Yes," she finally uttered, and she received her treat. It tasted a little bitter this time.

She had three big sisters and a brother now—Catherine, Alice, Sharon, and Nathan—and Mommy. There was no more talk of Anat, or the sea outsider her old home, or the temple. No more language. Just words. Just being told what to do, but mainly, "Don't!"

With each A-B-C and 1-2-3—*un, uhlet, soist*—Ethiopia faded away like smoke, along with her young past. She was finally left with only one lingering sentiment: she did not belong here. She was forgetting why, but any day things would change, be made right again.

Over time, she came to love her "mommy" in the way a small child with no options clings to real and imagined affection. She learned to love sugar, in everything. "She's got a sweet tooth," they all said. When really, she had a rotten tooth and a sugarcoated life.

Chapter 4

8762 Maple Avenue

Los Angeles, 1955

*B*renna's new home was in a four-family apartment building. It had a living room, a dining room, a bathroom, a kitchen, and a back porch. There were no bedrooms, but her mother slept on a Murphy bed in the living room, and the five children slept in the dining room: Catherine and Alice on the second Murphy bed, Sharon and Brenna on the green letdown couch, and Nathan in the crib.

It was morning, and as usual, Brenna heard the crackle of the plastic under the sheet as she turned over and landed in a cold wet spot. She sneaked out of bed in her soaked pajamas and headed for the bathroom. *I'm so cold*, she thought as the linoleum floor licked the soles of her small feet.

She climbed up the step stool and turned on both faucets. She threw her face rag into the sink and hoped the water would mix to make it warm. She turned off the water and cautiously tested the rag with one finger. She couldn't wring it out very well, but she used the somewhat warm towel to remove the sting and smell of pee from her legs.

By then, Catherine and Alice had raced in for the toilet, so Brenna clutched the yellow towel hoping her older sisters wouldn't snatch it from her.

"Oo-woo, you peed in the bed, you peed in the bed!" they chanted. "You're a l'il pee pot!"

"No, I didn't. I didn't. I'm not a pee pot!" Brenna said, dashing out the door and rushing to her drawer in the hall closet for clean panties. She pulled on pants and a T-shirt. She slipped back to the hall to put her wet pajamas and undershirt in the hamper outside the bathroom.

By then, all three of her big sisters had taken over the bathroom—tub, sink, mirror, and toilet—getting ready for school. When she walked back through the dining room, her sisters had already turned the big Murphy bed back into a mirrored wall.

She laid a pink towel over the pee spot and climbed on the bed to enjoy some peace, free of five-year-old Sharon's nightly warning to "stay on your side" and her frequent kicks to enforce it. Then she noticed her baby brother NaNa sitting on the potty chair in the corner. She knew he had to dookie, but she just hated to smell it. She didn't want him to feel bad, so she smiled and said, "Rise and shine, monkey time!" He tried to smile back through his pushing face. Brenna turned toward the wall and pulled the cover over her nose.

She awoke from her doze by the rustle of her sisters passing on their way to the kitchen. She jumped up for breakfast. Mommy put Malt-O-Meal in blue, green, yellow, pink, and white plastic bowls. Each child took the usual place around the kitchen. Cathy and Alice squeezed onto the bench on the other side of the table,

Sharon sat on the tall kitchen chair / step stool with the pullout cutting board for her table, Nathan sat in the old high chair, while Brenna pulled down the oven-door table and sat on the floor while Mommy quickly mixed the PET milk, sugar, and butter into her hot Malt-O-Meal. This was her favorite cereal, but she was a little disappointed to have the blue bowl, because the plastic on the rim was jagged from getting melted. Sometimes it scratched her finger or lip if she put her mouth too close. Of course she didn't say anything and tried not to look any kind of way. She scooped a spoonful, brought it to her mouth, and started blowing.

"Brenna, go around the edges like this." Sharon skimmed the circumference of the cereal in her own bowl to demonstrate. She added, "It's the coolest part." Brenna watched and then turned to her own bowl, trying to decide if she should believe Sharon or if this was just another little-sister trick. She didn't do anything until they all looked away and returned to eating. Then, slowly she spooned the cereal around the edge of her bowl and cautiously tasted it. It worked. "Yeah, it's the coolest part," she parroted back.

"Told you so, stupid," Sharon said with a laugh.

Brenna watched her sisters as they ate. She looked from head to head. From the oldest to the youngest: a flip, a ponytail, and two braids. Brenna thought, *when I go to school, I won't have to wear these three baby braids no more. I can wear two braids with barrettes on the ends, and curled bangs.*

Mommy was at the kitchen sink fussing about something. Brenna was relieved to find that she was not looking at her. She noticed her sisters getting up, so she snatched her bowl from the oven door and closed it so they could pass through the doorway.

She reached up and placed her own bowl on the counter and hurried to the front door.

The sisters were already rushing down the steps with their jackets halfway on, clutching their books and lunches and racing to the gate. Brenna stood watching them through the screen door, staying on to watch all the other kids pass. School. To go to school was her biggest dream. Saturday, February 11, would be her fourth birthday. Next year, she would be going to school. For now, she could hardly wait for after school, when her sister Alice would teach her the treasures from her school day. She started humming one of the songs Alice had taught her: "A-B-C-D E-F-G, H-I-J-K LMNO-P..."

Chapter 5

A Suitable and Worthy Heir

Ancient Ethiopia

The queen summoned her daughter to a private audience. The formality of the summons and the ornate dress Makeda had been requested to wear made her feel uncharacteristically timid as she approached both her parents. They smiled and followed her with their eyes as she took the seat her father had indicated across from them. Makeda's father was regent, not ruler. It was the time before the notion of the ruling of kings. The natural order was that the dominion of the lands passed through a lineage of women, down from Yeshi of the Sea. And the men who married the beautiful queens, such as her father, held honorable positions according to their inclination and gifts. It was he who orchestrated the affairs of state—indispensable to the erection and maintenance of the majesty, wealth, and splendor that was Ethiopia. Even more so, he was the trunk of the tree of life for his wife and child.

He stood and leaned to kiss his daughter's forehead, relieved that she had finally come of age and that they were now permitted to assist her with the tangled skein of dreams, voices, premonitions, and fancy that had rocked and assailed her otherwise blissful childhood.

"Dearest Makeda," her father greeted her warmly, "it's time that we speak to you specifically about the legacy you have inherited and the responsibility you will soon shoulder." He sat. "To be queen means far more than ensuring the protection and care of our sacred land and people. Unlike your age peers, your initiation began at your birth."

The queen joined in. "Daughter, even when you were a girl, we watched you grapple with this world and saw your strivings because your head was in the clouds and your heart sailed the sky. That is as it should be."

Behind Makeda's questioning eyes, recognition was dawning as she listened to her parents.

"Do you recall the beautiful stories Sophia wove for you? They were not only intended to soothe you from your strange dreams but also to accustom you to other realms of reality. Sophia was chosen to be your nurse because she is one of our most gifted priestesses. According to tradition, as your parents, we were permitted to love you and protect you but never to interfere or even explain—until now.

"You see, beloved, our throne is a spiritual throne. We are couched here on this throne of gold, and we reign from a place of privilege. But our power, our principles, and our perpetuity of dominion is not from here. It is from beyond and above this realm." The queen was silent for a moment, reaching for the place inside to speak more of the truth while allowing her daughter time to eat and digest her words.

Her husband served the next portion. "I know what we say is new, yet I'm certain it is familiar now that you are emerging from your solitary initiation with an understanding—and, Sophia reports, great facility—with other realms. I confess, it was torment, my child, to see you tossed by the spirits all these years, especially since the onset of your flow. The Way seems brutal at times. Your two elder sisters fled to the ancestors during their childhood; they did not stay to survive, as you have. As your father, I longed to rescue you from those harsh and lonely battles but I could not. It is a requirement."

Her mother then continues. "I, your own mother, my mother, and all the queens before in this lineage have mounted and met our various ordeals. So you were in the secret company of all of us who have ever been hailed to this throne. My hand was stayed by the eternal forces and my lips sealed to even acknowledge your ordeal until now. Come." She stood and opened her arms; Makeda scurried into them like a child. "This is a joyous day. We are free to speak openly to you of the mysteries. We are permitted to answer any of your questions."

Makeda's and her mother's eyes glistened with tears that salted their smiles. Her father extended his arms to cradle them both. After a time, the queen stood and walked to her throne with her husband and daughter. Standing with Makeda before them, she pronounced: "Welcome, Makeda, heir to this throne of Sheba and bearer of the legacy of this house. You were tried by the gods and found suitable. You were initiated into their realm and navigated a solitary path that now deems you worthy. Although this physical throne will soon be yours, tonight you will receive the first emblem of your reign. We are very proud, because we know for a certainty that you will carry this emblem of sovereignty with dignity and preserve it in wisdom and care. We know that you will deliver it unto the fulfillment of the wider vision, which shall be given only to you for the sake of our people. No parents could be more satisfied, no queen more confident in her heir than I. Following your coronation, you shall reign on the throne, and I will stand behind you as Mother Queen Witness until my death."

With that, the queen removed the bracelet from her own wrist and slipped it over her daughter's hand. She continued her pronouncement. "This bracelet is our sign and seal. It is also an instrument of marvelous power in times of need. Remove it only to place on your successor."

Makeda accepted the bracelet and kneeled before her mother, bowing in supplication. In turn, the queen lifted her daughter's chin and blessed her with a kiss on the sacred clearing between her brows.

―――

Several weeks later, the queen and her entourage arrived at her daughter's door. "Come, Makeda; it is time." These were the final hours before her coronation, and there were other rituals to satisfy. The chambers below the Temple were prepared.

The queen walked hand in hand with her daughter down the long corridors of the palace and through the side entrance to the Temple; then they descended the narrow winding stairway. Thirteen priestesses accompanied them through the passages, including Sophia, the high priestess who would remain with them in the inner chambers for the duration. A complete staff of chambermaids and attendants awaited them.

Makeda replicated her mother's beauty, yet she carried the quiet serenity of her father in her delicate frame. The queen was powerful, decisive, and severe. Her intellect and tongue were quickened by keen spiritual insight, so she swiftly scanned, discerned, and dispensed precise justice. She was a powerful war strategist, yet she spent no sleepless nights. She was of the lineage refined and fashioned by the hand of fate, destined, prepared, initiated, and ordained to rule. She was queen as her mother and her mother's mother before her throughout the generations had been queens. Now the mantle would be passed to her only surviving daughter, Makeda.

As the queen walked the ancient corridors, she recalled the eve of her own rite of passage, when she had walked as the daughter and the queen yet to be. Her own mother's words remained in her as a branding: "Queenship is not parenting the people, and it is more than governing. Although you will lead rituals, like the Holy Ones, queenship is more than the housing of traditions." Her mother had spoken to what it was not. Now, what final wise and useful words could she feed her daughter about what it *is* to reign? Anxiously she searched to secure the voice for that which she had wrestled from her twenty years of ruling. What is the pivotal, essential core? This she would pass on to her child. Then she felt a cool breeze inside her racing heart and knew it to be her husband's steadfast love tempering its quickened pace. She relaxed. Time. There is time.

They emerged from a narrow staircase into the hub of a network of corridors. They chose the center path and moved with their retinue through a heavy veil of frankincense that muted the odors from the family burial tombs far up the catacombs. They entered a large chamber with a huge stone-hewn altar in the center. In the far corner, visible through draped layers of sheer fabrics, were two elaborately prepared sleeping areas.

From the opposite direction, Makeda heard baaing lambs and turned to see them hemmed into a sturdy wooden pen. A young attendant sang gently as she walked among them, closely scanning for her choice. Sacrificial lambs.

Perhaps five feet from the altar were two wooden thrones with three smaller seats beside them. Designs and symbols were crudely carved over the legs, arms, and the top of the back, but the family seal was engraved in fine detail on the top of the larger chair and overlaid with gold. Purple and beige tapestry-covered stuffed cushions were on the seats, with padded upholstery on the back. One was her mother's Temple seat, accompanied by one that had been freshly carved and finished for Makeda.

Tonight the queen would not be sitting in judgment but would be called upon to possess the Spirit of the ancestors and the gods of Ethiopia—to be a vessel and a conduit of their Will. And somewhere amid all the ritual and water, fire and prayer, the queen would exhale the spirit of her reign; simultaneously her daughter would inhale to receive the passage of power as the fresh breeze of a great new beginning.

Makeda and her mother were first taken to the bathing chamber, where two deep stone baths jutted side by side above the floor. The heavy incense cast hypnotic halos around the candlelight. The fire cracking in the compact fireplace provided ample warmth for the small room.

Makeda was familiar with the Temple rituals into which they now entered. Ablutions, cleansing, bathing, and water were essential. Following the queen's nod, Makeda was disrobed and supported by an attendant as she stepped up two steps, then over the ledge of the bath.

Her foot touched the warm shelf on the inside of the bath, and she felt her leg tingle from the sea salt, flowers, and herbs of the saturated waters. When she was seated inside the tub, the waters rose perfectly. Everything below her collarbone was submerged, and her thighs and back rested against soft heavy cushions. Makeda's neck fit into the well-worn neck rest, and she settled her head back upon a firm, damp pillow. Earlier that afternoon, her groomer had released her many braids. Now her face wore her hair in a plumed crescent. Priestess Sophia stepped forward to perform the ritual of the hair.

From a large gold pitcher, Sophia poured warm scented water over Makeda's hair. Makeda closed her eyes as she readily surrendered to the comfort of these living waters and Sophia's holy and able hands. Sophia thoroughly washed Makeda's hair seven times, each time with a different blend of selected herbs and flowers; every item and movement was blessed with quiet prayer. Another priestess in the bathing chamber stood alone intoning a continuous hum of sacred chants and prayers.

Finally, Sophia poured warm fragrant oil and massaged Makeda's hair and scalp. Her head was then wrapped in a thick cloth. Two young priestesses disrobed and joined Makeda in the bath. They helped her move to the carved stone stool in the center of the tub. They proceeded with the ritual bath. They washed either side of her body, simultaneously coordinating strokes of each body part for harmony of spirit circulation. They used grasses and great sea sponges to rub, massage, and exfoliate her silken skin. They rubbed her narrow, delicate feet with pumice and used hand tools to cut and shape her fingernails and toenails.

Soft music wafted into the baths. By the end of the third washing, Makeda had gently drifted into a state of fluid receptivity and had moved into the beckoning sway of the dimension between worlds.

The queen was bathed simultaneously in the adjacent tub with prayers and skill to coax the spirit of queenship to the fore and release it from her vessel; the spirit was then to be guided into the young awaiting queen-to-be, Makeda.

Through the entire night, the rites were performed with such devoted precision that eventually everyone fell into the ease of the well-worn groove of ritual practice designed to bridge a way for the Ancients to cross. The Ancients then came and performed in timeless alliance. As required, before the new dawn, they had accomplished the inner workings of the transfer of the reign. Makeda was now the Queen of Sheba. The coronation would be the public manifestation and confirmation of that fact.

Chapter 6

Hannah and the Heart of the King

Ancient Israel

Hiram of Tyre was the only remaining son of a wealthy family. The sea had provided his family the access that allowed them, over the generations, to become the most renowned merchants in the land. His father, a worker in bronze, had died when Hiram was a young man, and his mother soon followed. His brothers, now too deceased, were never blessed with children, but he himself had two beautiful daughters, Rahel and Hannah. It was to the wedding of his eldest that Hiram had invited King Solomon, who had been sojourning in their city for several weeks. It was for his reputation of excellence in the art of gold, silver, and bronze work that the king had first summoned Hiram some years before. It was he who had fashioned the intricate, extensive, and elaborate gold pieces that were the foundation of the Holy of Holies in the Temple in Jerusalem. The Ark of the Covenant itself was placed in his strong and meticulous hands. His spirit, vision, craft, and humility allowed for the strict implementation of divine design and architecture. Over the years, the two men's mutual love of God, beauty, and horses had drawn Solomon and Hiram together in an otherwise unlikely friendship. King Solomon accepted the invitation.

Fortuitously, Sarah, Hiram's wife, was so agile with needlework that she did not leave the delicate stitching of her daughter's bridal garments entirely in the hands of her servants. King Solomon was so impressed that he personally complimented her handiwork. But it was Hannah—their youngest, thin and long-limbed even at the age of eight—who stood in awe of the pomp and spectacle that accompanied the presence of the king in their village and in their home. She and her dearest friend, Nathan, managed to sneak, peer, gawk, and mimic the movements of the king and his retinue. Later, Nathan, who had always been her betrothed, would don his elder brother's discarded and frayed once-fine robes and secretly imitate every detail of the king he could recall or embellish. Hannah thrilled in her part as his favorite queen and would always manage to get old jewelry and dresses from her mother's wardrobe to flaunt her gangly stature. The vision in Nathan's young eyes was of Hannah—not the girl before him, but, the woman and queen— standing beside his imagined self, the mighty king of Israel.

There had never been a more glorious affair in this city; the people would dine and drink over tales of the wedding for generations to come. Months later, in his workroom, Hiram of Tyre suddenly collapsed and died. Many held that his earthly body could no longer contain the heavenly joy of seeing such a perfect marriage for his beautiful firstborn, Rahel, crowned by the presence of King Solomon himself. In truth, he had died before his greatest wish had been fulfilled. That was to secure his wild and mysterious daughter Hannah in marriage to Nathan, the son of his lifelong friend. So a trace of her father lingered. It is said that when such love and care exists, the soul is compelled to hover close to the earth, breathing whispers into the influence of fate.

Following Hiram's death, his men discovered that he had made large investments and purchases that would certainly have yielded great return under his meticulous and scrupulous hand; without him, however, the bounty unraveled and was eventually lost. Finally, a shame-faced Baruch, Hiram's manager of affairs, confessed the predicament to Hiram's wife. Her husband had trusted his men to each do their individual service, but only Hiram himself held all the pieces necessary to access their vast wealth. An early death had not ever entered his plan. His merchants failed to puzzle together all the family resources. In just a few years, most of the money and the men had just disappeared.

Sarah's needlework, once made only for special gifts, had now become fervent, late-night labor to sell for money to sustain them. One evening, Sarah retired to her husband's old workroom and sat in her familiar chair. She recalled, when he yet had lived, that she had so often sat here crocheting, shielded from the fires but still near him as he wrought his golden treasures. She now spoke quietly to his absence. "Beloved, I know you did not intend to leave us bereft of resources. But so we are. What shall we do? I implore you to intercede with God on our behalf. Send me guidance. A message. A dream. I miss you with all my heart and beg that you stay near me as I feel you now. I need your comfort and strength. I cannot do this alone. Is it selfish of me to hold you so close to the earth when you no longer have a form? Am I keeping you from eternity, beloved?" Tears clouded her eyes, and she could not see her stitching. She stood and moved over to his workbench and caressed his well-worn tools. "I am selfish for you, Hiram. Yes, stay with me a while longer until I can face this. Stay, beloved. I'm sorry to ask, but please stay."

A few days later, nearing wits' and money's end, Sarah received a messenger from King Solomon. Only recently hearing of her husband's death and the family's predicament, the king had immediately dispatched an emissary, who told Sarah to prepare herself and her young daughter to move into the king's palace. "King Solomon extends his protection and security to the family of his dear friend Hiram of Tyre."

Her prayers were answered. Sarah and Hannah were moved into exquisite quarters in the palace among the women of the king's own family. Sarah found immediate comfort and friendship among the women of the house. She spent her days in lively conversation with others who also did fine needlework. Her superb work became quite popular among the company of wives and concubines of King Solomon. Hannah was moved into the chamber that connected to the rooms of Yehudit, Solomon's daughter with Ruth. Hannah and she were born in the same year, and very soon it was clear to all that they had become sisters and inseparable best friends.

Yehudit and Hannah were the king's favorites. He treasured the happy time spent walking and talking with his girls, and they doted over their beloved father. They would sing and dance for him and keep their ears open for funny stories to share. Everyone knew that when the king was in a rare foul mood, a visit from Yehudit and Hannah could sweeten his mind.

So Hannah's loss had become a great gain, and the life of elegance and pomp that she had once admired and mimicked had become her own. She grew up with every opportunity, grace, and privilege that being the daughter of the king of Judah afforded her. She came to love her new family and her new life.

Years passed, and the pattering feet of giggling girls gave way to the soft scuff of slippers along the palace floor; their awkwardness yielded to the smoothly curved grace of fine gowns on refined young women.

Chapter 7

Yehudit to Wed

Ancient Israel

The day had finally come, and Hannah watched as the dressers carefully made minute adjustments to Yehudit's wedding garments and marveled at how her once-heavy and boyish sister had become this poised, confident woman before her now. She recalled her elder sister Rahel's wedding, so long ago, before her father died. But thinking of her aba made Hannah sad, so she turned away.

Gazing out the window, she let her mind journey back to the time when her world was pristine, sweet, and innocent, when she experienced and expected endless evenings of walks and stories and laughs with her aba in their home in Tyre. She relished her father's satisfied sighs as she massaged the swollen flesh between his thumb and forefinger, stiff and sore, after he had wrought the obdurate gold all day. He would dislodge specks of dirt and gold dust from beneath his nails then touch her dimpled cheek. She would hug him. He called her "My sunshine." Then suddenly he was gone, and she was lost. For whom would she sing her new songs? And who would listen with such delight? No longer did their neighbors greet her with smiles and nods or chatter in her wake, "Hiram of Tyre's beautiful child, how she grows!" They began to huddle and whisper, "Hiram of Tyre's…peace be unto him, daughter."

Gradually she and her mother became poor and desperate. Then a miracle happened. They came to live here in the palace of King Solomon. The deep loss of her father was cushioned by the fatherly attention and affection that now grew between Hannah and the king. He was a great light in her life. When her father had died without warning, her devastated heart had retreated. The world, she discovered, was filled with both shocks and miracles. Then the king himself came and made Hannah his daughter, and she gained another sister and best friend in Yehudit. Best of all, she was told that His Majesty was immortal. He would never die; she would never have to lose a father again. So she bonded with him deeply and completely, for she was also driven by the belief that if only she had loved her Aba more, maybe…

Today as she glanced out the window, she knew that those were just the hopes of a very young girl. The king may one day die, as he was in fact aging. And, just as Yehudit was now preparing to do, she too must someday marry and leave her beloved father's house. Hannah recalled when Nathan, her betrothed from childhood, had come to claim her the year before. Much to her mother's and his parents' dismay, she would not go. It was beyond her own understanding, but she could not go. She felt wretched for the grief she was causing and shamed at the fall of the glistening longing in Nathan's eyes. But her love for him, for all its purity, had never grown to contain her vociferous heart and rainbow mind. To

Hannah, he felt too much like one of the tall cedars she had seen on the hillsides in the north firm, stable, rooted, and growing daily toward its inevitable death.

Hannah left her recollections and turned back toward her sister. They were alone now for one of the last times before Yehudit would be transformed into a wife. Suddenly the reality of her own obligatory wedding day sent a bolt of panic through her chest. She too must marry; she too must leave. A wave of sorrow enveloped her, and she turned back to the window. Looking out over the courtyard only reconfirmed that this beautiful palace was her home. Life here was complete in every way.

Abruptly, she turned and asked her sister, "Yehudit, how can you leave? How can you leave home?"

"What are you talking about, Hannah?" she asked. "I'm getting married."

"I know, I know. But how can you just go and leave us? Isn't it hard for you?"

"Well, I guess so," she replied and touched the back of her sensitive younger sister's hand. "I love you, and you don't need to be sad. You will come visit us often. One day you'll have your own family, and our children will be cousins and great friends, like us." They hugged.

"Yehudit," Hannah began hesitantly; then she blurted out, "I don't think I can ever leave home!" She crumbled and cried into her sister's shoulder. Yehudit held her for a long time, rubbing her hair, touching her face, and whispering appeasements.

After a while, Hannah straightened. "I'm sorry." She saw the concern on her sister's flawless brow and added, "Let's focus on your wedding day. Don't worry about me. I'll be fine." She pulled away.

"You know how unpredictable my heart is. I just need time." Hannah offered a weak smile and returned to the window. She stood, gazing beyond the courtyard to her future, which loomed in the distance like the steady gathering of an impending storm. Then flint struck her mind, and her silent pensive mood fled. *No.* Her thoughts quickened. *I do not have to go. I do not have to leave this house!* Everything convened at one resolution. Smiling and beaming, Hannah rushed over to Yehudit, who was busy in the mirror with her jewels. She grabbed both her sister's hands and pulled her to her feet. Eye to eye, she spoke her joy into Yehudit's surprised face.

"I have a solution," Hannah said in a gush. "I don't have to leave home!"

"But how? How can you stay?"

"Yehudit, it's really so simple." Hannah paused before delivering her great news: "I will marry Father!"

Horror flooded Yehudit's eyes, and words rushed from her lips. "How can you speak such words? How can you marry our father? It isn't possible, it is forbidden!" Instantly, she snatched her hands and her heart from Hannah. Yehudit did not and would never understand this betrayal. Hannah's expectation of her adopted sister's mirrored support shattered on the floor between them. Reflecting their friendship now in shards, Hannah saw the jagged possibility that gaining the king might well mean losing her dearest sister.

The news spread like a sandstorm throughout the palace. Yehudit loved Hannah, so when compared with the response of the rest of the household, Yehudit's reaction paled. Even Hannah's own mother seemed suddenly enfeebled by the realization of the determination in her daughter's eye. For the first time, her mother wished that she had endured the poverty and never come to this house.

The king—after finally making sense of what Yehudit wailed though her tears and what his wives confirmed—summoned Hannah to stay her intransigent heart. King Solomon confronted her gently but directly. "Hannah, what is this nonsense? You have the entire household in an uproar." He spoke sternly but with a slightly amused tone.

"I cannot see another way," Hannah uttered softly. "I only see this." She lowered her eyes.

"My sweet child, my wind-song daughter, this will never be," he proclaimed. "Go now and set all of your mothers' and your sister's hearts at ease."

When he kissed her forehead to dismiss her, she looked up and lingered before him. He recognized in her eyes that he had become Solomon, no longer father; she saw the faintest flicker in his resolve. It was enough. He did not move until he heard the door close behind her. Instinctively, he massaged the dampness from his palms and sighed as he smoothed his hand up his forehead and over his hair.

Chapter 8

A Jordan Downs' Christmas

Watts, California, 1964

Christmas in the Jordan Downs Projects meant two must-haves for teenagers: a pair of Levi's jeans and a new set of Roller Derby Street King Outdoor Shoe Skates. That's exactly what Brenna and her siblings received. She also got a soft pink sweatshirt. Being the two youngest, Brenna and Nathan were up early to open their gifts. They heard their neighbors and friends outside talking and laughing as their voices whizzed by on new skates and bikes. But they knew Mommy would not let them out of the house before 10:00 a.m., even on Christmas. "You're not going to grow up to be *common*," she always told her children. Meaning: no being out early, or out late; no eating on the front porch; no overly short dresses; no loud talking; no walking with a boy's arm around you; no smacking gum or smoking; no makeup…

At exactly ten o'clock, Brenna and Nathan bolted out the back door, plopped down on the step, and laced up their new skates. Brenna tilted her skates, spun the wheels, and applied the first dose of 3-IN-ONE oil. She passed the can to Nathan and zipped off, disappearing around her friend FeFe's building. She was trying to lose her little brother. She was thirteen, and her little brother was not going to hang around her today.

Just as she got to the corner, FeFe sped by on the crossing sidewalk. Those Jones kids could play harder and skate faster than any other kids in the neighborhood. There they went: FeFe, Glen, Gregory, and Marsha, with the two oldest, the twins (Ronald and Channel) chasing them. Was it jail tag or monster tag? Really, they played too rough for Brenna. Ronald made scary sounds whenever he was the monster, and when he caught someone, he actually bit. Hard. Brenna waved and watched them pass.

She caught up with Beverly and Linda, and they skated the long way around to go through the hole in the fence behind the bleachers at Jordan High. Beverly immediately started scavenging for long cigarette butts under the stands. She brushed off the dirt and showed off a butt that was at least a half a cigarette. Then, challenged by her find, Brenna continued scavenging until she found a longer one. It was partially brown, like it had been wet, spit on, or something worst. Well, it was dry now, so she showed it off for the length. Beverly frowned then said, "OK, bring it. The smoke will kill the germs."

They hid under the far end of the bleachers, and Beverly took out a fresh book of matches. Linda, Beverly, Gail, and Brenna puffed away on the butts. They coughed, spit, retched, got dizzy, and laughed till their stomachs hurt until, in the distance, they heard the speakers from the Activity Room blasting the Miracles' latest hit, "Shop Around." Immediately, they extinguished their butts and headed for the music.

Still in their new skates, they ran across the track and field until they reached the asphalt. They were gliding across the campus when they saw Peola rolling toward them. He was wearing old skates fastened to raggedy tennis shoes. His family was new to the projects. They had escaped from somewhere down South. Peola had told them, "The white folks didn't like my daddy, so they run us out." Brenna was glad Peola and his family had escaped those mean white people she'd seen on the TV attacking Negroes with fire hoses, burning crosses, lynching boys, and bombing little girls in church. But still, Peola and his siblings were entirely too big, too loud, and way too country. To her personal shame, Peola had declared that he liked her. Now here he comes with that big bowl haircut, big gapped-tooth smile, and those shinning eyes. She could not skate away fast enough. He had almost reached them when suddenly his skate came off. Didn't he know you can't attach a skate to a tennis shoe? Good, he was heading back. He'd probably forgotten his skate key.

When the girls rounded the benches of the cafeteria area, there they all were: hundreds of teenagers from all over the projects dressed in Levi's jeans and brand-new skates. They were already grooving in a huge circle—most skating forward, some backward, a few hugging couples. They were all dancing on skates in perfect rhythm. They all looked so smooth, so fast, and so beautiful. Brenna and her girlfriends sped along the outside of the ring until they caught up speed and were enveloped in the wave of circling youth. Now they too were floating on the voice of Smoky Robinson: "My momma told me…you better shop around." It was a great Christmas, because they got everything they knew to want.

Chapter 9

Other Ways of Knowing

Stanford University, 1969

The two girlfriends had their own rite of spring. Their acknowledgment of the vernal equinox and the final slide into summer vacation lay not in the lushness of the ivy-covered buildings, nor the campus in full blossom—rather, it was the first time Tresidder Union Cafeteria listed strawberry shortcake on the menu. Yesterday, as they rushed past each other on their way to class, Debbie said the only two necessary words: "Strawberry shortcake!" This meant that the very next day, they had an automatic date to meet in the cafeteria for their first dessert lunch of the year.

Nearly noon the next day, Brenna headed across the quad in front of Memorial Church en route to Debbie and the strawberry shortcake. She was glancing up to the grand mosaic facade above the arched church entrance when a bright glint of the sunlight flashed off the gold-leaf tiles and blinded her for a few seconds. She halted briefly. When she continued walking, she noticed an idea nudging at the corner of her mind. Then she heard a simple pronouncement: *You are going to Africa.*

Lost in their dessert lunch, she and Debbie sat spooning sweet ripe strawberries with silky mounds of melting vanilla ice cream over their gleeful taste buds and savoring the cool glide down their throats. "Mmmmm." Giggling and rolling their eyes in exaggerated delight, they scraped the juice-soaked cake remnants from the bottom of their dishes.

Just then, Brenna recalled the odd moment she had earlier and told Debbie about the flashing light at the church. "So, by the time I got to the Old Union, my eyes were fine, but I had an eerie feeling."

"OK. Tell me about this eerie feeling. Like what?"

"I don't know, but when I calmed down, I had one thought: 'You are going to Africa.' No. It wasn't just a thought; I heard a voice. It was so clear I thought someone was talking to me, but no one was there."

"So, how do you feel now?"

"Fine," Brenna said with a smile. "The funny thing is—I know I'm going to Africa."

"Wow, that's deep!" Debbie said.

"Yeah, that's why I wanted to tell you. You know about strange things."

Debbie leaned forward. "Are you calling me strange?"

"Absolutely."

"Oh, just checking." Debbie smiled and settled back into her seat, "So, did that voice happen to say how or when you would go?"

"No, not a peep about that."

"Well, there's only one thing to do, then."

"Yeah. What?"

"Wait. Just wait and see. If this is really a premonition, forenotice, or something like that, it will develop on its own. Just wait and watch. And be ready to act. On the other hand, if this is just you degenerating into personal insanity—then please leave your books and suede jacket to me. You won't need them in the asylum."

They laughed, finished their strawberry shortcake lunch, and rushed off to afternoon classes.

———

Later that evening, though Brenna chose not to share the mysterious aspect of the earlier incident, she simply said to her sweet and decidedly more practical boyfriend, Chip, "I've had a strong feeling lately that I'm going to Africa."

"Yeah, I really want to go to Africa too," Chip replied.

"It's not a feeling that I want to go Africa," she said, somewhat defensively. "I do, but the feeling is: I *am* going to Africa."

"Sugar, sugar, of course, of course I believe you're going," he cooed. "We just need a plan." He became quiet and thoughtful for several minutes. "OK, what about this? We'll take Italian our sophomore year and then go to Stanford in Italy for our junior year. I've heard there are some really cheap flights from Florence to Sierra Leone. So we'll go to Freetown on our spring break." Before responding, Brenna checked inside, like a prayer, for confirmation. There was nothing, no response. During the normal course of things, this nothing response was her usual internal response. Occasionally, she inquired about something and received an absolute *No*. Even more rarely, a feeling would echo back a resounding *Yes*. Her basic interpretations were: *no (leave it alone) or yes (proceed without question); no response suggested either do it or don't do it—it doesn't matter.* In other words, most things she asked about received no response at all. She felt that this lack of response meant it was her choice. There was no response to Chip's idea, and he looked very eager. She replied, "OK, then, sounds like a plan. Let's do it!"

⚒

They took a year of Italian in preparation for the campus abroad. By the summer preceding their junior year, however, they were no longer a steady couple although they remained friends. More important, Brenna's initial internal *No response* to his plan had become a decided *No!*

For Chip, things proceeded precisely according to his plan. He attended Stanford in Italy. By spring break, he was in fact in West Africa for the whole two weeks. And he sent her gifts.

Delighted, Brenna open the box and consumed the African images on the postcards he sent. She was in awe of the structure and character of the landscape and wildlife and how they indisputably echoed the distinctive features of Africa's indigenous people. There is a word for this, she knew. She thought, and then there it was— *autochthonous*. "Of the land itself." She smiled, satisfied in her first experience of the meaning as she continued for hours, wrapping and rewrapping herself in traditional African styles with the yards of vibrant hand-printed and hand-dyed fabrics that Chip had also sent.

To her surprise, she noticed that she had no feelings of regret or envy that Chip was in Africa now and she was not. Actually, she admired how Chip was able to make a plan, stick to it, and get what he wanted. Yet, it felt to her like that just wasn't her trip. Although nothing specific about her trip was on the horizon, she didn't mind. She carefully placed the last piece of fabric in her drawer and set the envelope of postcards on top. Then she heard it, the same voice from two years ago repeating itself: *You are going to Africa.* But then it added: *Soon.*

Brenna had thumbed through the mail from her PO Box and was headed for the door when the desk clerk at the campus post office called out her name and beckoned her over. The clerk rummaged under the counter. "I got a letter here; I think it's for you." Brenna went over to examine the envelope. "It doesn't have your box number," the clerk added. "Is it yours?"

"Yeah, I think so, thanks." She walked out into an overcast spring day and sat on a nearby bench. She smiled at the linen-fiber stationery, the small scratchy handwriting, and the pink glob of stamped sealing wax on the back flap: Mrs. Betty Clifton had tracked her down.

Hi Brenna,

I couldn't find your mom's number, so I thought I'd try just sending this note to Stanford. (I hope you're reading it right now.) How are you? We're doing fine. Mr. Clifton's still complaining about his arthritis, but the old man's doing OK. Anyway I read an article in the Sentinel about the upcoming Watts Festival. All the while I was reading I kept thinking of you. I really don't know why.

I think maybe this year you should run for Miss Watts. Wasn't one of your older sisters a Miss Watts before? The first Miss Watts, right after the riots? Anyway I think this would be a great year for you to be Miss Watts. The pageant is in the summer, so you'll be home from school. A Stanford girl for Miss Watts! Won't that be something? What do you think?

I'm enclosing an application for the pageant. I think this is your year: Miss Watts 1971. Has a nice ring to it, huh? Are you coming home for spring break? Call me. I'm still at LO4-3736, I mean 564-3736. I hear there's a fabulous new tea room in the West Adams Historic District. Would you like to join me for tea? I want to hear all the news from school. Do you have a new beau? Mr. Clifton says hello and asks if you're still playing ping-pong. Take good care, dear.

See you soon,

Betty Clifton

PS. Don't forget to send in your application, Miss Watts.

Brenna smiled. Mrs. Betty Clifton had been in her corner ever since Brenna had had a summer job with her nonprofit, Youth Serving Youth, just out of high school. The Cliftons had no children of their own, so they kind of adopted Brenna. Mrs. Clifton would take her to plays, the opera, art galleries, and restaurants. Brenna remembered the spectacle of the Ramona Pageant in the amphitheater, with real horses galloping up the aisles.

Mrs. Clifton always told her that a young woman of her intellect needed cultural exposure and took such exposure on as a personal project to see to it herself. They'd had many memories and experiences together. Brenna appreciated it, but sometimes Mrs. Clifton was just a bit too nosy and opinionated about her life. But Miss Watts, Brenna wondered. *Is this the year?*

Enclosed was the two-page application. Brenna looked at it and thought the gesture was sweet but curious, because Mrs. Clifton knew it would be a while before her braces were removed. A beauty queen with braces? No way. She slipped the note, along with the application, back into the envelope and was ready to dismiss it when something made her pause and ask again: *Is this the year?* After all, she had planned to run for Miss Watts someday. Sharon, one of her older sisters, had won the pageant in 1967. And, like her sister, Brenna enjoyed serving her community; in her heart, she always felt it was her responsibility to serve. A scripture came to mind that bolstered the thought: "Him to which much is given, much is expected." Not money—definitely not money. But she had other gifts. This note was enough to provoke a simple prayer for guidance. "God, do you want me to run for Miss Watts now?"

Yes, was the inner answer.

Startled at the immediacy and the answer, Brenna tried barter-ing with the Spirit. *But I have braces on my teeth! What about next year?* Silence. The simple affirmation stood.

Brenna was not always immediately eager and willing to fol-low her inner guidance, but she was by no means stupid and was familiar with her own process enough to know that she would not be able to get around this *Yes*. When Brenna returned to her dorm, she sat down at her desk and with a sigh filled out the pageant ap-plication. By the next day, the application was in the mail, and with it an avenue of her destiny opened.

Chapter 10

---⊗⊗⊗⊗---

The Pageant

Los Angeles, 1971

The Watts Summer Festival was founded in 1966 to commemorate the Watts Rebellion of 1965. After four years as a small local festival, in 1971 things changed. Everything was on a grand scale that year. The money and resources of the whole city were brought to bear. Popular singers headlined the festival's concerts, along with top-notch entertainment. The opening event was the Miss Watts pageant, which received citywide media coverage.

Brenna's braces came as a surprise to the pageant committee and were a source of constant ridicule from the other contestants. Despite this fact, she was selected as one of the fifteen semifinalists who would participate in the pageant.

The contestants were introduced to each other at a brunch early in the summer. Although, Brenna did not know any of the girls, she did manage to chat with quite a few. Some of the contestants seemed to resent Brenna. How could she have the audacity to think she could compete against them with braces on? Brenna ignored their whispers and chuckles because, quite simply, she agreed. She would rather not be in a beauty contest with braces.

But, so be it. Acquiescence to her inner guidance did not necessarily provide emotional buffers—but it did make unexpected provisions.

On the day when the contestants met at the photographer's studio to take their official portraits for the pageant program, the teasing was relentless.

"Brenna, be sure to smile real big. We wouldn't want to miss your teeth!" The girls howled and shrieked in laughter that curled them over their vanity tables. Brenna shot a hurt, hot glance in their direction. Trying to ignore them, she continued putting on her makeup, taking much more care in highlighting her long lashes with Maybelline, emphasizing her shapely mouth with Posner's Ivory Coast Mahogany lipstick, and lifting and patting her natural hair into a perfect halo. These features she hoped would perhaps compensate for, or at the very least distract attention away from, her braces.

Finally, it was her turn, and the photographer, Mr. Valentine, called her in.

"Good luck, metal mouth!" Again, the girls' laughter peeled around the room.

Fine, Brenna thought. *We'll just see*. It wasn't with any sense of conviction.

It was simply hope.

When she took her seat on the tall stool before the backdrop, Mr. Valentine said, "I heard them giving you a hard time about your braces. Look this way; let me see your face. Hey, you're a pretty girl, don't worry about them. Just let me do my job. You'll have the best picture out of the whole bunch!"

Mr. Valentine's kind words made her break into a big happy smile. He took a few headshots, smiled, then added, "Now let's try a few with your mouth closed."

The photographer's proofs came a week later during a pageant rehearsal. The eight-by-ten headshots of each of the semifinalists were placed atop the grand piano on the auditorium stage. Excitedly the contestant gathered around the piano, shuffling through the stack. After a while, Gail said, "What does Brenna's picture look like?" They all giggled and shifted their focus to search for it.

Brenna didn't bother to rush over, believing that the braces would compromise her looks. She tried to look nonchalant as she adjusted her leotard, mopped her neck with a towel, and retied the toe string of her dance shoe. She felt her whole body tense as she waited for the next wave of ribbing and heckling, signaling that they had found her photo.

"Here it is!" one girl exclaimed. After the initial scuffling of feet, the girls grew silent. On of her tormentors, a young woman named Gwen said, "Humph!" and set off a chorus of grunts and shuffles. Brenna turned, wondering what pose could have prompted this reaction. Mary, another tormentor, tossed her picture to her like a Frisbee. She retrieved it and found a startling beauty gazing back from the portrait: serene, elegant, and innocent, with just a hint of mischief suggested by the tiny dimple at the corner of her mouth. It was her most beautiful picture. Magic. Shocked, vindicated, and relieved, she thanked God and Mr. Valentine for his confidence, skill, and above all his kindness. Although the headshot had not shown her braces, as Brenna walked off the stage, she instinctively turned to face her competitors and gave them the widest wiry grin she could muster.

—

The contestants' schedule was layered with guest appearances: TV, radio, amusement parks, festival fundraisers, luncheons, churches, dinners, grand openings, parades, nightclubs, extravagant parties, and more. They had so many obligations that it became like a second job for the young women, who also worked full-time jobs during the summer.

For all the time and energy the pageant demanded of the contestants, the prizes they would win had never been remarkable. When Brenna's older sister Sharon had won Miss Watts four years earlier, she received trips to New Orleans and San Diego as well as other small gifts. After one particularly exhausting day, Brenna knew that if it wasn't for her "inner guidance" directing her to run, she would have found something far less stressful to do for the summer.

Two weeks prior to the pageant, the contestants attended a weekend mountain retreat. After an eighteen-hour day of yoga, interviews, makeup, wardrobe classes, and dance and performance rehearsals, the contestants—most slumping over pillows, chairs, and couches—tried to stay awake long enough to at least hear, if not see, Bonnie, the prize coordinator, give her report. The monotonous drone of Bonnie's thin voice was barely audible and hardly registering in Brenna's slumbering mind until she heard these words: "…and the grand prize for Miss Watts is…an all-expense-paid trip to five African countries." Brenna jolted to full attention. Then the same inner voice returned and stated, *This is your trip.* She was now upright in her chair, with suddenly bright eyes and a broad smile.

Bonnie looked at her quizzically, "Brenna, do you have a question?"

"Yes. Which African countries?"

"Ethiopia, Kenya, Tanzania, Nigeria, and Ghana."

"Wow! That's great!" she replied.

Dismissed shortly thereafter, the girls went to bed, but Brenna could not sleep. Ethiopia, Kenya, Tanzania, Nigeria, and Ghana circled over and over in her mind like a mantra. The names of these countries seemed to call her, compel her, and entice her into their mysteries. "I'm going to Africa. I'm going home." Later, it dawned on her that she still had to actually win the pageant in order to get the trip.

With two weeks to improve, she knew, some of the girls could prove to be strong competition. In her mind, Brenna scanned the strengths and weaknesses of each contestant with a clear analytical eye. Most posed no real threat, but a few—maybe. Nevertheless, she concluded that if the pageant were to be held right now, she would likely win. So maybe she needed to stop helping them and just compete.

The pageant committee had encouraged "sisterhood" as an important principle to guide them in their interactions with one another. They said that this communal principle was what made the

Miss Watts Pageant so special. They were all supposed to be there to help, support, and above all care for one another, just like sisters. Brenna liked this idea. It allowed them the chance to disprove the stereotypes of women cat-fighting and Black people hating one another. Despite the teasing about her braces, she had already helped in every way she could. She had been in a dance troupe in Northern California, so she helped choreograph dance routines for other pageant teams who were struggling. She had also attended modeling school, so she helped with carriage and posture for any girl who asked. In addition, she had experience in public speaking, so she coached anyone who wanted her help.

A moral dilemma rarely announced itself, but it seemed to do so here. Brenna thought: What if she just stopped helping them? No one else would notice. They'd probably think she was too busy to help these last few weeks. The trouble was, she would know. She would have to alter her true nature in order to win a contest. What seed might she plant in herself that could grow into future personal deceptions for gain? She knew she would not like the consequences of putting that life pattern into play.

The inner voice had said that this was her trip. Wouldn't this require that she be her real self to claim it? Would the presence of the voice assure her that, no matter how much she helped and supported others, she would still win if she were true to herself? Brenna decided to believe this, although it required that she would have to work even harder toward her own excellence for the pageant.

Early the next morning, she was up rehearsing her poem and performance for the talent portion of the pageant. Over and over she practiced. When other girls joined her, she went

from group to group encouraging, assisting, and guiding as requested. She was happy with her decision, and things became
much clearer. This is what she knew: she really cared for the
other girls like sisters. This trip to Africa belonged to her. And
she would win.

———

The day had arrived, and Brenna was transported through the pageant in horizontal reality. The air was thinner. Time was suspended. The roar of the audience was muted. She no longer danced her
body; her body was dancing her. Everything she did was without
effort or contrivance—it was attuned, precise, and magical.

"Ladies and gentlemen, let's meet our fifteen lovely semifinalists now!"

Smiling broadly as she walked out on stage in the first parade
of the contestants, Brenna was startled at the harshness of the TV
camera lights, flashbulbs, and the blaring live sound of the H. B.
Barnum Orchestra. Her heart pounding, her legs wobbling, and
her whole body quaking, she felt overwhelmed and certain that
the audience could see how she was quivering. For one small thing
was she grateful: prior to coming on stage, she had remembered
that nonstop smiling often made the lips prone to snagging into
grotesque positions over dry teeth, so she had applied a protective
coating of Vaseline across her teeth. Finally free, she smiled broadly with her six newly de-braced top front teeth. Just enough—out
on early orthodontic release—for a pageant smile.

All the hard work was paying off; so far, the pageant was a great
show. They had made it through the parades, two rounds of individual

questions, the group dances, and the leotard display. The girls were backstage preparing for the talent portion. This pageant committee had taken a stand that, because so many talented girls usually participated, they did not want someone to win just because she was the best singer or actress. So, to ensure that this did not happen—especially this year, when the queen would serve as a real international goodwill ambassador—no points that a girl received for the Miss Grand Talent title would be applied to her points for Miss Watts.

Brenna was dressed in the fabric that Chip had sent her from Africa. All three pieces: one tightly wrapped under her arms, then around her slender body; another as a flowing shawl, draped over her shoulders; and finally, the last piece was wrapped again and again atop her head into an extraordinarily high *gele*. She had spent weeks memorizing and practicing her original poem, "The Nature of My Beauty—Black Beauty." Now she gracefully moved about the stage, incorporating subtle wrapping and restyling of the fabric into her performance, seamlessly transforming them into four different dress styles that matched the moods in her poem. She took her time and performed the poem for her people:

It is in the peaceful corridors
Of my soul
That I walk with grace
And have the strength to love.

Who says I have the right to proclaim beauty?
None less
than the brownness of mother earth
None less

than the ebb of the sea
As the swaying of my hips to its music.

I am a given.
Given to this earth, this planet, this time
I was given from the loins of my mother
To whom I attribute my
natural grace,
sensitive heart,
penetrating eyes and
soulful smile

I was given as a Sistah—
To share, to quarrel
To love
To teach, to learn, to build
To win.

I was given to Africa.
[She sings an *African song*]
Taken to America
Taken to Watts
Taken to Poverty
Taken to rape and degradation
Taken to church and the image of a white god
…who didn't even see me.

[*Song continues*]

We been had,
had, had, had
We been took,
Took, took, took

We been mislead
We been had...had...had

Black is truly beautiful
I awake in the mornings
Natural pillow flattened, or multi-braided
And I see your eyes gazing at me
Pleased

When your fingers find my hair and
Fumble through its cushioned soft strength
I just close my eyes with peace and confidence
There is no need
to get up
and
Rush to the mirror
to make up
For I am made from birth
Through life.

And the beauty of me is not only in a sculptured face
And sensuous body,
For there are depths to my beauty

That are peaceful and endless
Like the night

Mother Nature is my mirror—
I am reflected in the earth
In my people
And in the light
—and she looks after her own

Lover, sister, mother
Yeah it's kinda hard
To love a woman like me
Because I am reality
firm
brown
Reality

And we all know—
I just don't take no
half-steppin'
"Shit, you don't give a niggah no slack!"
"Naw, that's why you're still a niggah,
'cause you're always lookin' for some slack."

I guess I am what you might have to call Responsibility,
When a Brother
Looks into my eyes,
Touches my body

And loves me...
You see, love transforms, love fights, love protects
Love gets over

Then Brother starts to feeling inside and saying to himself:
"I don't want to see no hurt in these eyes
or pain felt by this body.
For this is my love
This is my woman
This is my life
And if freedom is to be,
Somebody's got to take the responsibility
And in you woman,
I can see,

One of them bodies has got to be me!"

Now...
that's love
that's beauty
that's strength.

Exhausted, she bowed and drank their applause like cool water. They gave her a standing ovation, so she returned and blew kisses. Finally, once she was backstage, someone offered her a glass of water, a towel, and a chair. She collected herself and waited for the others to finish.

Not a rule, but the tradition had always been that midway through the pageant—just before intermission—the Miss Grand Talent prize would be given to one of the two top contestants. The other would go on to be Miss Watts. The girl chosen for Miss Grand Talent never went on to win Miss Watts.

They called all the girls who had chosen to perform back on stage. The H. B. Barnum Orchestra gave a loud drumroll. Through a fog, Brenna heard her name being called. What?

"The winner of the Miss Grand Talent prize goes to...*Brenna Hayes!*" Surprised, she stepped up to receive her trophy and walked backstage as the curtains closed. While happy to have won the talent prize, she wondered if she could be the first one ever to win both titles. Quickly the contestants rushed to change into their African ball gowns. As they chattered in the dressing room, one girl remarked, "I heard Miss Grand Talent never wins Miss Watts."

"Well, I guess one of *us* will get it, then." They all nodded in agreement.

Then, LaDonna, another contestant and ally, spoke up. Loud and confident, she said, "Brenna's going to win both." Brenna turned to meet LaDonna's level gaze and returned her smile. She felt encouraged. The others continued to debate the point as they dressed.

The curtain opened to dramatic fanfare by the H. B. Barnum Orchestra revealing five stunning young women in African gowns of vibrant colors and audacious designs flowing across the stage, evoking awe and ancient ancestral memories from deep in the heart of the audience. Each contestant answered her question with simplicity and poise. Finally, by the end of the segment, the five finalists were selected: Linda, Gail, Brenna, Dorothy, and Lynn.

With the curtains closed, the other girls crowded around the finalists. Then one said, "If Brenna wins, I'm going to walk off." She heard echoes of "me too…me too…me too." Now, finally fed up, Brenna whispered to her naysayers, "*When* I win, no one will care what you do." Her statement silenced the group. The finalists had just enough time to powder their noses and compose their smiles before the brief musical interlude concluded and they were expected to be back in place for the rising curtain and rush of applause.

"Ladies and gentlemen, we have our five finalists!" the emcee bellowed above the crowd. Then he turned to the contestants and with a flourish of the hand said, "Ladies, please." This signaled the young women to parade down the catwalk one more time to the roar of the crowd. Finally, they wound up on their marks at center stage, where they knew they would be called on one at a time to answer a final question. Brenna was fourth in line. They called Dorothy first.

"Dorothy," the emcee prompted, "there are many keys to having a successful life. Name what you think one important key to success is, and explain why."

As soon as Brenna heard the questions, her mind raced for her own answer.

In the background of her own mental flurry, she heard Dorothy saying something about education being the key. Brenna was so nervous that she could barely breathe, so she focused on her breath, as they had instructed her to do in yoga class. *Concentrate on the breath as it passes the tip of your nose. Better.* She prayed the audience would not see the small tremors that jellied the pit of her stomach or the quivers at the corners of her smile.

Now it was her turn. She stepped to the mark near the emcee and turned to him for the question. Again the young model beside him reached into the basket on the podium and pulled out a question.

"OK, Brenna, here is your question," the emcee stated; then he opened and scanned the paper. "Do you think the Watts Riots of 1965 helped or hurt the people of Watts?"

"Thank you for the question," Brenna said. "First, I know some people think it was a riot here in 1965. But the people who actually live here feel and say that it was the Watts *Revolt* of 1965. It was not a mindless riot but a rebellion. (*Applause.*) A rebellion against police brutality. A rebellion against poverty and racism. (*Applause mounting.*) A rebellion against substandard schools and hospitals. A rebellion against stores with poor-quality food and goods and disrespectful service at the highest prices. (*"Tell it, baby! Say it like it is!"*)

"The burning of the stores in our community was not a signal of self-destruction but a signal that our people are not appeased. That we will no longer be silent in the face of injustice and inequality. Older people tell us that conditions in Los Angeles are so much better for Black people than in the South. But most of the people who threw rocks and burned buildings were young people. We were born here, and however bad somewhere else may be, we wanted the world to know that we too are oppressed and we didn't stand for it. We won't stand for it! And we will never stand for it!"

The audience was on its feet, and the whole auditorium was swept up in the passion of Brenna's righteous indignation. Brenna stopped and let the fervor of the people have the last say as she made her way back to her mark.

Then, only two were left. The announcer's voice broke the suspense: "The first runner-up is…Miss Gail Webb. That means Brenna Hayes is our Miss Watts 1971!"

In her peripheral vision, she could see several contestants, in fact, walk off the stage. As predicted, however, their presence was not missed, and photographers rushed in immediately to fill their vacancies. Tears fell from her eyes as she turned to receive her robe, staff, roses, and, of course, her crown. The audience erupted as she walked down the runway to greet them; the whole auditorium went wild. Brenna had displayed a grace and beauty they could admire, the grace and beauty of a queen. She had answered her question with the dignity and passion of their own voice. They went wild because she authored and performed "The Nature of My Beauty—Black Beauty," which told their truth. They felt that mother Africa needed to see them return home in their youth, beauty, intelligence, and prodigal glory—as embodied in her.

They chose Brenna because they had fallen in love with her essence. She made it easy for them to love themselves again as people of African descent. They chose her because she was a silent hope of vindication before their mother—Africa. They knew she would represent the very best in them and that Africa too would fall in love with her and in turn—through her—perhaps love them. One family once again united.

With smiles, tears, and kisses, Brenna loved them back. She gladly accepted the honor of their unspoken mandate: *Take us home with you.*

Chapter 11

~~~~~~~~~~

Before You Ask

*F*our days following the pageant, the runners-up demanded to see the official tally of the votes for Miss Watts. They were convinced that Brenna had somehow cheated. Tommy Jacquette, the Watts Summer Festival director, escorted them all back to his office and opened the safe. He already knew the results but didn't say a word; he just displayed the judges' tally sheets before them on the table, then stood back, folded his arms, and watched their faces. The girls scrambled for the documents, eyes scurrying over the sheets and then passing them on one to the other.

"Oh, here it is," said Gail as she grabbed the list and read aloud. "Third runner-up: ninety-two points. Second runner-up: ninety-three points. First runner-up: ninety-eight points. That's pretty close." She continued, "Now, where's the paper with Miss Watt's total?"

Tommy handed her a final sheet.

Brenna stepped up to view it over her shoulder.

"Miss Watts. Total points: ninety-six points! See, I told you!" she exclaimed to the other girls, shaking the paper at the director.

"She only got ninety-six, and I got ninety-*eight* points. See, I'm the real winner," she snorted.

"Read it again, Gail," Tommy said calmly, "Look close, and read it out loud."

"OK. Miss Watts total points for Brenna…ninety-six. I mean… one ninety-six."

"That's right; she got one hundred and ninety-six points to your ninety-eight." He took back the tally sheets. "You've seen it with your own eyes. She won fair and square. Let it go." He turned to Brenna as the girls shuffled out of the room.

"Sorry you had to go through this, but you won by a heap of points," he said to Brenna. But by then he was laughing. "They just needed to see it to put a stop to their mess. You OK?"

"Yeah, I'm fine."

"Yes you are, Miss Lady. You fine and smart and got a whole lot of class."

"Thanks."

"Brenna, how do you feel about your Africa trip?"

"I'm really excited. I can hardly believe that in six months, I'll be in Africa!" She paused and looked a little pensive.

"What's the matter?" he asked.

"Well, I am a little nervous about making the trip by myself," she confessed.

"How old are you? Twenty-one?"

"Not yet, but I will be in February, then we leave in March." She added, "Anyway, Bonnie said that I would have guest hosts in every country who'll be there to meet me and show me around. I'll be fine."

He looked at the flutter of her long lashes and the innocence of her wide eyes and shook his head. "Brenna, you're a pretty girl. Beautiful, really. I'm sure you're used to handling male attention. But I don't think you realize what happens to men when they meet a beautiful woman who's also a beauty queen. It's something about the title that sets men off. I'm afraid they might try to eat you alive."

"Really?" she asked.

"It drives them out of their minds." He shook his head again and chuckled. "I think you'd be OK, but I'm not willing to take the chance; so, you won't be traveling alone. You're too young."

"No, I'm not. I'm a senior in college."

"I've already decided. We're sending a companion with you. Let me take care of it." He looked at her and gave his wide smile.

"Well, OK then. That'd be great. Thank you," Brenna said, quickly agreeing.

"You feel better?"

"Yes, I do. Relieved," Brenna said with a smile.

"Remember, we're doing the radio show tomorrow at five p.m."

"Yes, I'll meet you there. Thanks again." She waved goodbye.

The following week, the five finalists gathered at Bonnie's house to collect their prizes. The entire dining table was full. Bonnie showed Brenna to a small guest room, which was filled with her Miss Grand Talent and Miss Watts prizes, and watched her enjoy the bounty.

Brenna set aside the prizes that she did not need: a scholarship to a state college, a modeling-school scholarship, a typewriter (she already had a new one), and a very good stereo. Brenna stacked these and a few other items on a separate table. She turned to Bonnie.

"Here, I don't need these," Brenna stated.

"Really? What would you like me to do with them?" Bonnie asked.

"Give them to my runners-up. They worked hard all summer too. Let them decide who gets what."

"Why? They were pretty mean to you."

"I know. But still, give them the prizes." She stayed in the room packing her things. Bonnie went out to tell the other girls and share the gifts. Brenna passed the girls with her boxes and bags on the way to her car. "There she is!" She heard Gail's rough voice and kept walking. "Wait, Brenna!" Brenna paused and watched Gail approach.

"I got the scholarship. I know you didn't have to do this," she said, with a question on her brow and a half smile on her lips.

"OK, then." Brenna turned with her packages.

"I mean…thanks, Brenna. Thank you."

Brenna turned back to face her. "You're welcome." Brenna surprised herself because she meant it. After the other girls left, Brenna met with Bonnie.

"I was looking over my Africa itinerary. There are so many fancy functions for me to attend—state dinners and actual balls. I'm just a student. I don't have the right clothes, and I really can't afford to buy all this by March."

"Oh, don't worry. You didn't look at all your prizes. It's already taken care of—look here." Bonnie showed her the prize list in the program. "Disneyland's costume department is making your wardrobe. Edith Head is designing you an outfit. The Hilton Hotel is providing you lodging, and TWA and Ethiopian Airlines will handle your flights. You'll have a companion with you. Also, the Mothers of Watts are having a series of fundraisers so you'll have spending money for the trip."

"Wow, that's impressive! I guess everything is taken care of. By the way, won't I need to come back and forth from school for wardrobe fittings and other Miss Watts duties?"

"Yes, you will, almost every other week." Bonnie went on to assure her not to worry. "PSA is providing you with unlimited free airfare for the whole year from school to home and back. Also, Hertz has given you free car rentals every time you're in town. Honey, it doesn't get any better than this. These are the best prizes in the history of this pageant."

"Bonnie, do you know who'll be my companion?"

"Well, the committee wants it to be Maya, Miss Watts from last year. The one who crowned you. See, last year she was supposed to get a prize trip to Germany, but it fell through. So, they were hoping to make it up to her by letting her go with you. But I don't know if that's a good idea.

"Why not?"

"Well, she's been getting all the attention this past year, and she may not be so willing to give it up, even though it's your trip. What do you think?"

"Um, I don't think I mind, and if it would help the pageant keep its word to her, then I guess it's OK with me. How old is Maya, anyway?

"If you're OK with it, I'll let the committee know. Just keep an eye out. I think she's around twenty-four. Why?"

"That's good. It'll be like having my big sister with me." Brenna smiled.

"Let's hope so," Bonnie said under her breath.

It seemed the resources came from everywhere. Nothing she required or desired for her trip was not provided. Brenna was learning something. Her inner voice had been precisely correct. She knew that, although it appeared things came from everywhere, they really came from only one place: God. The guidance, the support, the resources, and the opportunity all came from Him.

In her prayers that night, she thanked God. Before she fell asleep, she got a feeling that this trip was not the end of a promise, but just the beginning.

Chapter 12

Arrival in Africa

Addis Ababa, Ethiopia, 1972

After a day and a half of traveling, they finally landed in Africa. Their jet taxied toward the gate, and one of the Ethiopian Airlines hostesses came back to Brenna and Maya's row.

"Miss Hayes?" she asked. Brenna nodded. "A delegation and a group of reporters are waiting to meet you at the gate when we stop," she said with a smile.

"Really?" Brenna asked.

"Yes. You might want to freshen up." She left and returned with two additional fresh hot damp towels. "You have a few minutes. We'll deplane everyone else first."

"OK, thank you." Brenna peered through the small window, unable to see much but the tarmac and a few trucks and planes. She reached for her cosmetics bag in her purse, pulled down the tray, and begin touching up her makeup as the other passengers bustled down the aisle. Then she saw her traveling companion, Maya, stand to retrieve her bag from the overhead.

"Maya, wait a minute. I'm coming!" Brenna called.

"Oh, I'll be just outside. It's getting stuffy in here. I'll wait there." She hurried off.

By the time Brenna collected her things and started down the steps of the plane, she saw a small group of women and photographers moving toward Maya. Then two little girls stepped forward, each holding a bouquet of flowers, one large, one small. As Brenna approached the group, she noted that the girl with the large bouquet moved to Maya, made a small curtsy, and handed her the flowers. When Brenna wedged her way through and stood beside Maya, a woman ushered the other girl to present her with the smaller bouquet. The girl dipped and extended the flowers.

Brenna smiled and received the flowers from the shy child, but she was very aware that the larger bouquet was really meant for her and that the delegation was under the false impression that Maya was this year's Miss Watts. Puzzled as to how to make the correction, Brenna continued to shake hands and nod and smile at the people and flashing cameras.

Finally, a willowy stern-faced woman spoke to her in clipped English as she guided Brenna to the side by her elbow. "Please stand aside a moment so they can photograph Miss Watts alone."

Brenna paused and faced her. "I am Miss Watts."

The woman raised her severely arched brow and turned back toward Maya, who was grinning and posing for the sea of photographers.

"What should I do?" Brenna asked the older woman.

"Nothing. I'll handle this, my dear." She flashed a smile. "Just wait here." Their eyes locked for a second, then she was off.

Speaking rapidly in her native tongue, she herded the cameramen and photographers toward Brenna. Then, taking Maya by the arm, shaking her head and finger as she spoke, she led her off to the side. Brenna caught a glimpse of a contrite slump of Maya's neck as she was peppered with reproach.

Smoothly, their hostess, Marta, eased back into the small crowd and made a swift exchange of the bouquets with Brenna. She gave Brenna a brief now-that's-settled smile, curtsied, and stepped aside to let Brenna bask in her entitled attention.

Africans did not play. Vindicated, Brenna turned and obliged the cameras with her recently liberated, straight-toothed, lovely smile. Enjoying the royal treatment, the two young ladies cruised to the Addis Hilton in a black limousine. Brenna didn't say anything to her older companion about her stepping out first and taking her flowers. But she remembered Bonnie's warning to her that Maya might try to continue to act as if her own year as Miss Watts had not ended. Brenna would have to watch out for Maya.

The limo pulled in front of the hotel, and they stepped out to a flurry of bellhops scurrying for luggage and an ingratiating concierge attentively hovering. A man with a lion on a leash caught their attention. He beckoned. They looked at each other and walked over.

"Come on. Come on. Take the picture," the grinning tamer implored. "This is the Lion of Ethiopia."

The lion was large, with a billowing mane framing his huge face. He seemed calm and responded to his trainer's voice and manipulation of the leash by standing. The trainer positioned Brenna and Maya on either side of the lion and encouraged them with gestures to touch him. Eventually they touched the mane and smiled for the clicking cameras and popping flashes.

The Addis Hilton had a modern space-age design; their room was airy and bright, with a welcome basket of fruit and a large bouquet of flowers. Brenna and Maya swept through their suite, finally landing on their beds. "Now, this is living," Maya said with a sigh.

"Oh yes, I could get used to it!" Brenna said. She sloped about in exaggerated Hollywood style. The phone rang amid their giggles. It was Marta, inviting them to a late lunch at the hotel restaurant.

"Please settle in and meet us downstairs at one thirty p.m. Is that OK?"

"Yes, that's fine. Do you know if our friend Bessie has arrived?" Brenna asked.

"Yes, yes. She arrived last night. She will be joining us for lunch."

"OK. great. We'll see you soon," Brenna said happily.

The Hilton was a first-class hotel, at least from among the few they had seen. The restaurant was easy to find. There was Bessie, Brenna's second companion. Just a few weeks before the trip, Bonnie had told Brenna that Bessie, who was a member of the pageant committee, would also be joining her for the Africa trip. Bessie was a much older woman, so Brenna felt safer with her here. After hugs from Bessie and introductions, they joined the other men and women at the table. Maya and Brenna order standard American burgers and fries for lunch. Although Brenna had had her itinerary for several months, Marta provided them with their revised itineraries: museums, galleries, schools, concerts, receptions, tours, and dinners. It looked great.

"Look here at Thursday, two p.m.," Marta pointed out. "You will have a private audience with His Majesty."

Brenna scanned the itinerary. Yes, there it was. A meeting with His Imperial Majesty, Emperor Haile Selassie. An audience.

"Girls, can you believe we'll actually be meeting Emperor Haile Selassie! I've heard about him all my life," Bessie swooned in her melodramatic way. Everyone was excited. Not even one of the Ethiopian companions had ever had a private audience with their emperor.

Later in the lunch, Brenna informed Marta that they were each missing a piece of luggage, leaving them with their current outfit and only one other.

"Don't worry—we'll have your things as soon as possible. As for your meeting with His Majesty, I think both you ladies would look lovely in traditional Ethiopian clothing. Don't you think His Majesty would be surprised and pleased?"

"Well, yes. That would be nice," Brenna added with a nod to Maya.

"OK, let's see what we can arrange." Marta seemed delighted by her own idea.

"Thank you."

Lunch was served. After a while, people settled into the meal.

"Mr. Igegu," Maya began, "we took a picture with a lion in the front of the hotel. The tamer said he was the Lion of Ethiopia. Is the lion the country's symbol?"

"Well, yes and no," Mr. Igegu, our trip facilitator in Ethiopia, responded. "The lion is a symbol of the royal family. But the true Lion of Ethiopia is His Majesty. He is the Lion of Judah."

"The Lion of Judah?" Maya asked. "But I thought Judah was in Israel?"

"You're quite correct," said Mr. Igegu. "But we Ethiopians are also from the House of Judah. You are a scholar, yes?"

"Well, I'm working on my doctorate in history at UCLA."

"Very good, my dear," he said, clearly impressed. "Have you heard of the *Kebra Negast*?" Maya shook her head. Igegu proceeded thoughtfully and said, "It's an Ethiopian volume whose title means the 'glory of kings.' It traces our history down from our first king, King Menelik, who was the son of the Queen of Sheba and King Solomon. It tells of their love affair and marriage and how that marriage bound forever the destinies of Ethiopia and Israel. The book then chronicles the lineage of our kings down to the present, making His Majesty the two hundred thirty-fifth king down from our first king, Menelik."

"So the Queen of Sheba was from Ethiopia?" Bessie asked.

"Absolutely," he said proudly. "Our royal family is of that bloodline."

"We never knew about this!" Maya snapped. "So much of the glory of African history has been maligned, minimized, or claimed by Europeans or Americans as their own. In all the pictures of the Queen of Sheba, we've only seen her portrayed as a white woman."

"Oh no, no, no!" Mr. Igegu laughed and spoke to the others in Amharic. They responded with raised brows and short intakes of breath. "We find it hard to believe that you did not know the Queen of Sheba was Ethiopian. It's in the Bible."

"We're shocked too, but in a good way. How can we find out more about this story?" Brenna asked.

Marta spoke softly to the group members in Amharic, and then turned back to Brenna. "Later this week, you are scheduled to tour our National Museum. We'll alert the curator of your interest."

"Great. Thank you." Brenna's mind went over this connection between Ethiopia and Israel. *Didn't the Bible say something about when the Queen of Sheba heard about this great king in Jerusalem, she had to go up to test his wisdom with hard questions? I think she brought him gold and great treasures. But I'm sure the Bible didn't say she had a son with King Solomon who went on to become the first king of Ethiopia. Or did it?*

They all took a walk after lunch to a local marketplace filled with Black people. Black people everywhere. Only Black people, from the taxi drivers to the donkey-cart drivers. Men and women in Western clothing side by side those who wore the traditional white shamas with colorful borders. Away from the few city streets, the ground, the dirt itself, was a rich reddish brown. Some of the people who passed them caught Brenna's eye, nodded, and spoke a native greeting. It was strange for her to not be able to understand or speak to people who, much to her surprise, looked like they could be her family members.

They were in Africa. The air smelled of incense, smoke, spices, and food. People and animals bustled and bleated through the market. It was the rusty bare feet and the many missing teeth that most immediately spoke of Africa—basic and elemental. But the impact of the multitude of large almond eyes whispered mysteries and promises.

"Wait a minute, ladies," Bessie said, catching both Maya's and Brenna's hands. "We need to just stop a minute and take this all in." They stopped and joined her in just looking around the market, tears welling in their eyes. Bessie spoke, "We're really here. We're in Africa. We made it back!"

Tears streamed down all three of their faces, and they moved in to embrace one another. They wept for the millions of their ancestors stolen from Africa for the slave trade and the millions more who were born, lived, and died in captivity. They wept for the handicapped hearts of Black Americans today, still bearing the scars of deep unacknowledged and unresolved abuse. They wept for hope. The hope of a healing for their people.

"Yes. Against all odds, we...have...returned!" Bessie proclaimed triumphantly. "And with us, all our people have made it back. We're home!" And there, in the busy marketplace, she raised her clinched fist to the African sky. Maya and Brenna followed, despite the puzzled stares of the locals.

Chapter 13

Injera

Three days into their stay, Woizero Debre-Worq, the mayor's wife, invited the ladies to dinner at the Ghion, a restaurant known for its fine Ethiopian food and traditional decor. When they entered, the amber flicker of candles in torch-like sconces on the wood-paneled walls warmed the dark interior of the restaurant. Men, women, and families dressed in traditional white attire, and some men in suits, sat on low stools around colorful and round table-high baskets with pointed tops.

The maître d' showed them to a semiprivate round room with a thatched roof like a village hut. Their party of eight entered and sat on the low-back wooden chairs and stools covered with animal skins. Again, in the center was a tall basket woven with red triangular designs.

"This is beautiful," Maya commented as she rubbed her fingertips across the dome at the top.

"This is our dining table. It is a *messob*," Mr. Igegu commented. He reached over and lifted the large pointed top to reveal the interior, a flat, round, rimmed surface at least thirty inches in diameter. The party buzzed with chatter as the group settled in.

"Are you comfortable?" W. Debre-Worq asked Brenna.

"Yes, it's a little low, but I'm fine." Brenna adjusted herself on the wooden seat. "It smells great in here. I look forward to tasting the food." Aromas of spices, incense, brewing coffee, and roasting meat hung on the air.

Brenna noticed a young man kneeling at her side holding a large bowl before her in one hand and a matching water pitcher in the other. He nodded toward the bowl. Brenna looked around and saw that their hosts were washing their hands over the bowl. So, she took the soap from the basin, and the young man poured warm water as she lathered. He waited and then poured rinse water over her hands. He nodded, and she took the towel he had laid across his arm to dry her hands. She noticed these same ministrations around the table.

"It is traditional that we eat from a communal plate and we eat with our hands," W. Debre-Worq informed them. "Actually, we eat only with our right hand."

Waiters served a round of sodas and water, placing the glasses on small wooden tables beside each diner. They reviewed the adventures of the day, including the visit to the museum to the see the works of the laureate artist Afewerk Tekle. They also visited Africa Hall to see the seat of the Organization of African Unity and the beautiful stained-glass windows, also created by Afewerk Tekle. They spoke of visiting the marketplace and selecting exquisite formal Ethiopian gowns for their imminent audience with the emperor later in the week.

At last the food came. The waiter bore a huge round serving platter, which he agilely maneuvered over and around the diners to place in the center of the opened messob. The platter was heaping to the edges with small piles of various foods. Next, the waitress came around with a platter piled high. She placed a folded portion of flatbread in front of each diner. The guests simultaneously looked to W. Debre-Worq.

She smiled and said, "*Injera*. This is our bread." With her right fingers, she deftly unfolded her injera to reveal the gray spongy inside of the flatbread. "It's soft." She tore a small piece and slipped it into her mouth. "Try yours."

Each one lifted the folded pancake-like bread. Brenna tasted a small piece. It felt rubbery and had a sourdough flavor. She noticed her hosts using only one hand and quickly brought her left hand back to her lap. One of the men said a few words in Amharic, perhaps a prayer, and then everyone began eating.

W. Debre-Worq continued her instructions and demonstrations. "Here, just take a piece of the injera and use the spongy side to grasp whichever dishes you would like." She picked up a piece of meat in a red sauce and adroitly deposited the packet in her mouth.

"What is this?" Bessie asked, pointing to a pile of greens.

"*Gomen*. I think you call them collard greens?"

"Oh, yes. You all eat collard greens too?" Bessie took a piece of injera and scooped up some collards.

"How do you like them?" Marta asked.

"They're good. Taste some," Bessie said to her companions, who followed suit and nodded their approval. "Different spices, but really good." Bessie continued with the greens for a while.

Marta pointed and described the various dishes on the platter: *doro wot*, referring to the chicken leg with a boiled egg beside it; *sega wot*, the chunks of beef in a red sauce. "Wot means sauce or stew.

We have lots of wots." They chuckled at the rhyme. She described the *fit-fit*, a cold salad made of small pieces of injera tossed with tomatoes and sweet chilies in a vinaigrette dressing. "Try it."

They tried each dish she described. The doro wot had a spicy, somewhat sweet taste; it was a little awkward to wedge the meat off the bone without lifting the chicken leg. But Brenna noticed how her host pressed the injera against the bone until it surrendered meat. Sega wot, the beef cubes in red sauce, were not only spicy but were very hot and very peppery.

"Oh," Brenna said, "this is hot. The pepper."

"Here, try this." Marta quickly filled a small piece of injera with an off-white cottage cheese and fed it to Brenna. Brenna opened her mouth and received it. As she chewed, the curds quelled the heat of the pepper.

"Thanks, that is better."

By then, others around began filling injera with morsels and feeding Maya and Bessie.

"This is our tradition. *Gursha*. We sometimes feed each other during meals. It's a gesture of respect or affection."

"These are yellow split peas; this is…pumpkin," Marta said. She checked with the ladies to see if that was the right word in English. They nodded. "Pumpkin. This is lamb, these are red lentils, and this is cabbage and carrots."

"I love the flavor. What spices do you use?" Brenna asked.

"We have *berbere*. It's really a combination of local spices. Our injera is made of an Ethiopian grain called *teff*, which is our food staple."

"How do you make the injera?" Maya asked.

"Well, we mix the ingredients and then let the mixture sit to ferment for a few days. When it's ready, we pour it out onto a large hot grill. I think it's like your pancake, only about ten times bigger. Maybe it's more like a crepe. We only cook it on one side. That's why it's smooth on one side and spongy on the other."

"Would you like to visit one of our vocational schools for girls, to see them prepare injera and other traditional dishes?" W. Debre-Worq asked.

"Yes, we'd like that," Bessie said, and the other two agreed. Brenna approached the cottage cheese on the platter with her finger and a piece of injera, paused, and looked at Marta.

"That is *mitmita*. It's like your cottage cheese, but we blend it with spices. Take some and add meat." Brenna did and nodded her approval. It was the combination of injera, pumpkin, split peas, doro wot, and mitmita that sold Brenna on Ethiopian cuisine. Sweet, spicy, sour, textured, smooth. A festival of tastes, strange yet with a hint of the familiar.

Marta continued to explain, but Brenna's focus was now directly on savoring food. She was getting the hang of eating with the injera and her fingers. The pinching of the fingers reminded her of her grandmother sitting out on the porch eating *kush*, a greens and cornmeal mush, out of her cornflower-blue bowl with only her fingers. She noticed that Ato Kifle's wife was feeding herself and offering her husband gursha every other bite. He continued conversing, periodically turning his head to his wife to receive his food. It was natural and so sweet.

After the meal, when everything was cleared, a young woman stepped into their private dining room with a smoking long-handled pan. She lowered the roasting coffee beans into the center of the diners. The Ethiopians began sweeping their hands and gathering the smoky fragrance toward their noses. Brenna and her party joined in to whiff the pungent aroma of the roasting coffee beans.

In less than a minute, the coffee and the young woman were gone.

"She's going to perform the traditional coffee ceremony. Can you see from here?"

Brenna looked across the room to where the young woman was now seated on a stool on a raised platform. She watched her first arrange her tray with utensils and a metal coal burner and a black clay coffeepot. Then, before the entire restaurant, she ground the roasted beans with a mortar and pestle, heated water to boiling, brewed the coffee in the clay pot, and poured the thick liquid into twenty or so tiny cups. All the while, chunks of frankincense resin melted on hot charcoal disks, sending up plumes of smoke.

The young woman, adept in the art of the Ethiopian coffee ceremony, made the complex process seem leisurely and delightful to watch. It took nearly an hour to complete. Finally, she brought a tray over with the coffee and a red clay coal burner filled with smoldering frankincense to their table. They sipped the hot, thick, and surprisingly smooth drink, and the smoky aroma of the frankincense mingled through their nostrils to infuse the flavor of the coffee.

Brenna smiled and found herself opening to the sensory excursion that was Ethiopia. Yet, she watched the coffee ceremony with envy, wishing that she too could have such explicit and rehearsed skill that only comes from centuries of inherited traditions. Brenna wondered what it was about the whirr of the music, the smells in the air, the taste of the spices, and the eyes of these people that filled her with a longing that she did not comprehend.

Chapter 14

Audience

The black limousine moved smoothly through the streets of Addis. The three women sat quietly in the back, looking stunning in their African garb. Both Brenna and Maya wore formal Ethiopian attire. Not the gossamer fabric commonly seen in the marketplace; their formal gowns, gifts from the emperor's daughter, Princess Tenagne Worq, were of heavy natural cotton fabric that fit the upper body then fell into an A-line from the curve of the hip to the floor. The sleeves fitted to the elbow then dipped into an elongated angle beside their bodies. The bodice bore an intricate embroidered design, and matching borders ran along the neckline, sleeves, and hem of the garments. Brenna looked across at Maya in the facing seat. She looked beautiful in her matching gown, with Brenna in turquoise blue and Maya in bronze trim. Bessie, with her natural flare for the dramatic, was costumed in bold green, black, and red—a Ghanaian outfit with a gele wrapped so high and elaborately on her head that it almost touched the roof of the car. *Yes,* Brenna thought, *we are fit to meet a king.* And that was exactly what they were about to do.

After their car cleared the guard kiosk, they saw the commanding silhouette of the Jubilee Palace against the afternoon sky. The shadows cast deep prints over the gray stone facade, and the steps leading to the front doors summoned them like a passageway to an ancient world. Inside, two servants and a palace guard ushered them in to a waiting room, where they heard the accents of then saw a group of white Americans being led into a connecting room for their audience. They recognized their host, Dr. David Talbot, the minister of education, whom they met on the day of their arrival and saw at least once a day since. He came forward to greet them.

"Ladies, you look lovely in your Ethiopian attire." He grinned, and his eyes widened behind his thick glasses. "Come this way," he said; he then sequestered them in a private corner and commenced providing basic protocol instruction for their audience.

"When you address him, say 'Your Majesty.' Now, let me show you the proper way to curtsy before him." Dr. Talbot gave a brief and awkward demonstration. "Now you try. Good, Maya; Brenna, lower your head as you bow. Yes, that's it. Just lift your garment slightly as you do so. Good. Yes. Yes. You all seem have it now. Just spend a few more moments practicing."

Brenna was reminded of the hours she'd spent at Powers Modeling School learning the proper way to walk, sit, stand, and eat. Today she practiced in earnest because she didn't want to embarrass herself.

They heard the bustle then saw the American group being ushered back out.

"Hello," Bessie said. She glided toward them with extended hand and said, "We're from California."

"Pleasure to meet you, neighbors. We're from Texas," a large red-faced man, hat in hand, eagerly responded; he gave her a robust shake. The rest of the group made its way to them.

"Tell us," Bessie asked, "what was it like to have audience with the emperor? What happened?"

"It was great—I mean, like walking into history. The emperor was standing right in front of his throne. We walked over, and he shook our hands. He's a small guy. But quite impressive."

"They took our picture with him," a stout and pretty woman added.

"Amazing! Just being in the room with him was amazing," the other man commented.

"Excuse me," Dr. Talbot said, stepping in. "Ladies, it's time."

They thanked the group and excused themselves to accompany Dr. Talbot. Then a uniformed officer entered the room and stood at the other door. He announced: "His Majesty will see Miss Hayes, alone, first."

Brenna shot a questioning glance to Dr. Talbot, who nodded his consent. She proceeded to the officer and followed him in. Alone. She moved with directness and a sense of heightened awareness. She covered her anxiety with a thin veneer of poise. She did not know what to expect, because the everyday world had subsided into the background. Her focus shifted to the emperor himself and the throne looming behind him.

For his part, the emperor had already considered this young woman. After the pageant, they had sent a press kit with the information on this new Miss Watts, who'd been selected to be their goodwill ambassador. He recalled the photograph of Miss Hayes. It was her eyes that struck him; more specifically, the wise and knowing look that emanated from her lovely face. But he had seen this look before in the eyes of a queen and in the penetrating eyes of his own wife. This look could move inside a man and hold him upright in his standing. Eyes like these saw all that a man could be and called him forth. Eyes that strengthened and soothed simultaneously. Maybe a wife for his favored grandson, Yohannes? His grandson could rise to his full potential under this sustaining gaze. He had kept the photo out. *We will see*, he thought.

The emperor stood to receive her as she approached him. He smiled as she presented her recently rehearsed curtsy. She smiled back to acknowledge his kindness and to amend for any awkwardness. When their eyes met, it felt like a return, a familiarity.

"Welcome, Miss Hayes. How are you, and how have you enjoyed your stay in my country so far?" The emperor's voice was thin, and his eyes smiled.

"I'm well, thank you, Your Majesty. I'm honored to have this audience with you. I'm having a wonderful time in Ethiopia."

"Parlez-vous français? Do you speak French, Miss Hayes?"

"Un peu," she responded.

"Very well, then. I speak a little English myself, and so between the two, we should be able to communicate. So tell me about your studies at the university."

"I'd be happy to. I am an English/premed major at Stanford University. I haven't decided what—"

"Excuse me." He turned to address an attendant. "Bring a chair for Miss Hayes."

The emperor sat on his throne. After she settled in her chair, she chatted on about college highlights and told him about Watts. He smiled, even chuckled, and encouraged her to continue with small questions along the way. Without any effort, she was amusing to him.

"My dear," he quietly interrupted, "where are your people from?"

"Arkansas, Texas, Louisiana," Brenna said.

"No, I mean, where in Africa?"

She paused, a little confused and embarrassed.

"Well, Your Majesty, with slavery and all, we really don't know *where* in Africa we're from."

"Yes, I see. But I know. I know where you are from," he stated emphatically. Then he leaned forward toward her and rested his forearms on his knees. He held her eyes in his gaze. "Miss Hayes, you are a princess from the royal lineage of the House of Judah, my house, and I know my own anywhere!" he declared. After a pause, he added, "We just have to make the adjustments." He sat back in his throne.

With those words, Brenna's world altered. She felt the deep impact of what he said, though she did not yet understand what it meant. In an instant, the emperor was no longer just an emperor on his throne: beside him, there seemed a breach in reality, and a huge fan appeared and opened into a passageway. Suddenly, Brenna felt herself being jettisoned headlong down the giant accordion corridor with the emperor behind her, propelling her forward so fast that everything they passed was a blurry barrage of sights, sounds, smells, and sensations. She came to the end and halted so quickly that she felt a rebound as if she was tethered to a huge rubber band. Abruptly, she was snatched backward as the time corridor ratcheted shut in her wake. Then, *plunk*. She was back.

With the images still swirling in her mind, she knew she had traveled through history. She had peered down the sparkling corridors of time and had seen how one thing led to another and how everyone and everything were connected. She now knew how she too was connected to the span of time, how she was part of a continuation of a pattern of life that had preceded her. The emperor's declaration had both reclaimed and restored her to the primordial and eternal standard, weaving its golden thread into destiny. She also knew that, for her people—whose lives and history had been ravaged by enslavement—although their memory of the details of their origins may have been stolen from them, history itself had never forgotten them. The whole truth broke into recognition: sacred threads persist, and to every generation while living on the earth, every great and magical gift that has ever been is available, if only they know to take hold and press it into service. Into the very fabric of our lives, God has woven spun gold.

Brenna slowly became aware of the room, her seat. She blinked, inhaled deeply, and grasped the arms of the chair to bring herself back. Finally, looking up, her eyes asked, *What was that? Where have we been?* The emperor responded with steady-eyed scrutiny and then a recognition that allowed the slight heaving in his breath to settle his chest. Finally, he sat back and folded his hands.

"How are you, my dear?" he asked, continuing the conversation aloud. Brenna inhaled and righted her posture before him.

"I'm OK. I'm fine," Brenna managed, though she was surprised at the truth of it.

"Good. Good," he said, a slight smile dawning. "Do you know what happened to you?"

"Everything happened to me. Everything!" The words rushed from her mouth.

"Do you recall anything from your journey?"

Brenna paused, closed her eyes, and then tilted her head. "Yes, I heard a statement repeated several times: *slow...moma...kada*, or something like that. Yes, slow moma kada. What does it mean?"

"I think you have the sounds but not the syllabication: *Slomo, Makeda*."

"Yes, that is what I heard," she excitedly confirmed.

"Then, my dear, you have heard from the ancestors: Slomo is King Solomon, and Makeda is the Queen of Sheba. Brilliant." He paused before adding, "We will continue this at another time."

Nothing would ever be the same, yet it was as if they were renewing a relationship and continuing a conversation initiated long before. Then the emperor stood, and Brenna stood in turn. She remembered Maya and Bessie. Over an hour had passed.

"Your Majesty, my two companions are still waiting to meet you. I beg your pardon. I completely forgot them."

"Well, then, let us bring them in." He spoke in Amharic, and the two women were escorted in.

The mood changed to the formality of a reception. When the two others joined them, though the familial tone was suspended, the emperor greeted them with warmth. They presented him with the plaque and gifts the Watts Summer Festival had sent. The emperor gave Bessie and Maya golden necklaces each bearing a traditional Ethiopian Coptic cross. Then he handed Brenna an oval green leather case with a gold crown stamped on top. She accepted the box then looked up at him. He nodded, and she opened the tiny latch. It was a gold bracelet. Rich, heavy gold. It had two thick bands joined together by giraffe-tail hair braided with spun gold. Affixed to the front of the bracelet was also a gold crown. He had given her a bracelet exactly like the one he wore on his own wrist. Brenna tried to contain her reeling emotions.

"May I?" She nodded, and an attendant took the case, removed the bracelet, released the clasp, and handed it to His Majesty. Brenna held out her delicate wrist, and the emperor placed the bracelet around it. He held the open ends of the bracelet at her wrist and, with the click of the clasp, somehow sealed her fate.

As the audience continued, Brenna managed to smile and be pleasant despite the fact that the room had receded. The camera flashes and the conversation between the emperor and her companions seemed muffled through cotton. She was still operating on automatic as they said their goodbyes and bowed their final curtsies before the throne. Just as she reached the door, the emperor's voice sliced through her daze.

"Miss Hayes," he called from the throne.

Startled by the call, she turned. With a beckoning of his wrist, he summoned her back to him. She returned and nodded a curtsey. "Yes, Your Majesty?"

"I have a surprise for you."

"But Your Majesty, you have already given me so much," she feebly protested.

"It's someone to meet."

He was standing close, so she leaned in and asked in a hushed tone, "Who?"

He leaned to her ear and also whispered, "It's a surprise." They both laughed. "You will receive a new itinerary at your hotel in the morning. You will like it."

Brenna smiled at him and replied, "Your Majesty, I like you very much. So if you think I will like it, I know I will."

"Let me know."

"I will."

"No. You must give me a report," he said, admonishing her with a smile.

"Then of course I will." Smiling back, she bowed and left.

That evening, Brenna dozed before sleeping, overwhelmed by the events of the day and spinning with images of opulent living that she had not even imagined possible. She fluffed her pillow and turned to the wall. As she nestled to sleep, she heard the phrase repeating: *Where are you from? Where are you from? Where are you from?* Then she heard her own four-year-old voice rehearsing her childhood address: *8762 Maple Avenue, 8762 Maple Avenue, 8762 Maple Avenue.* But with the events of the day, she knew that there was much more to it than that.

Chapter 15

⬡⬡⬡

Prince Yohannes

The next morning, Brenna retrieved the envelope that had been placed under their hotel room door. She found two itineraries: one for her and another for her companions. The morning schedule was the same as before, with the following addition to the afternoon:

4:00 p.m. Meeting with His Royal Highness Prince Yohannes at the offices of the Duke of Harrar.

She saw that Bessie and Maya's itinerary continued on with the rest of the planned activities, while after 4:00 p.m. that day, her new itinerary was blank until their departure, three days away. "What does this mean?" Brenna asked as she showed them the itineraries.

Bessie examined it and laughed. "Well, it looks like the emperor's set you up with this Prince Yohannes. Maybe you're supposed to spend your time with him."

Brenna did not like this. She wondered if the demands of protocol would require her to obey. At breakfast, she quietly asked one of her hosts how old the prince was. They said the prince was eighteen. What did His Majesty expect her to do with a child for two days? Later, her companions, claiming to be tired, tried to weasel out of the meeting with Prince Yohannes.

"We're all going," Brenna said insistently. "We all met the emperor, and we all have it on the new itineraries he sent, so we're all going." Grudgingly, they prepared to go.

They arrived at the offices of the duke of Harrar a few hours later; the garden was so pretty that Brenna would have preferred staying there rather than proceeding to perform her duty. Finally, they approached an elegant paneled suite of offices and were escorted through a door with polished brass letters that read DUKE OF HARRAR in English and Amharic. When they entered, Prince Yohannes was seated at a large mahogany desk, writing.

"Your Highness, your guests have arrived," his secretary announced.

The duke looked up and stood to greet them. He was definitely older than eighteen. Brenna halted briefly then quickly recovered her pace. His eyes were large and dark beside his aquiline Ethiopic nose. His trimmed mustache perched above his parting lips, and deep dimples punctuated a rascally grin. Then there was the matter of the cleft in his chin. He looked Brenna in the eye as he extended his hand. She flushed beneath her civility.

"It's my pleasure to meet you," he said as he took her hand. "Miss Hayes, I presume."

"Yes, the pleasure is mine, Prince Yones."

"Yo-han-nes," he said, correcting her pronunciation. "But my Christian name is John. Yohannes means John in my language. You may call me Prince John, if you like."

"Yo-han-nes," Brenna repeated. He nodded and moved on to greet her companions.

"What is your language called, Prince John?" Maya asked as she shook and held on to his hand with the question. Brenna wondered why Maya pretended not to know.

"It is Amharic, an African Semitic language." He turned and swept his hand toward three upholstered armchairs, and the ladies took seats. He looked back to Brenna.

"Miss Hayes, your first name, Brenna, reminds me of an Amharic name: Brehenna."

"Bre-hen-na. I like it. What does it mean?"

"It means 'light,' or perhaps, 'my light.'"

"How do you spell it?"

"Well, because Amharic has its own alphabet, with the English translation of the sounds, we spell it several ways: Berhane, or Brehenna, or Brehane, to name a few."

That name seemed very familiar to her, and so did he. She kept looking at him. As he charmed Maya and Bessie, she kept looking to see what she had never felt before. Then she was caught. Caught in the web of his features. Caught in the triangulating pleasure of prince, privilege, and promise. She realized her feelings were not new and that somehow she knew him. They had history together. Ancient history. It seemed that she had once burned for this. Something in her told her it was worth it. Burning again. Only this time, she would not burn alone.

Her companions chatted on with the prince while she watched, occasionally nodding and smiling in his direction. Brenna shuddered as a chill and swell of heat passed through her. Then, like star birth, shards of light flashed from her core and quickened the quiescent gift of numinous beauty from its ancient cocoon. Rarely summoned in modern times, still the gift immediately unfurled and rose within the young woman. The full gift caused every dimension of Brenna to sparkle.

Drawn, Prince Yohannes turned to her, and invisible waves of radiance engulfed him. A shiver subdued his grin, a query crossed his brow, and his eyes clicked a quick calculation; he recovered with an offer. "Brehenna—Miss Hayes—I own a hotel here in Addis, the Wabe Shebelle. It has a discotheque, and I would like to give you a party there this evening." He turned and addressed the group, "Yes, I'm giving a party tonight for all of you."

They all agreed.

He stood, and they followed. When Brenna accepted his extended hand, he placed his left hand on top, still looking in her eyes. "It's settled, then. I'll send a car for you at nine." He released her hand. "Ladies, it has been my pleasure to meet you," he said, acknowledging each face. Resting on Brenna again, he added, "Until tonight." She nodded, and they left.

Brenna welcomed the air and light of the outdoors. She needed to get her bearings, but the image of his smile lingered in her mind, along with the warm grasp of his hand. *Brenna, Brenna, watch out for this one.* But something in her was already slipping.

"Oh my God," Maya giggled, "he's so fine!"

Bessie seconded her. "Yeah, fine and rich. A prince and a duke. Girls, y'all better get busy. This one's a catch!" Bessie and Maya laughed and shook their heads. Bessie turned to Brenna.

"Girl, are you hearing me? You can't let this one get away. If you and Maya don't want him, I got nothing against a younger man, especially a rich one," she said with a harrumph.

In the portion of her mind that paid attention to what Bessie was saying, Brenna wondered, *What do they think they have to do with him? He's mine.* She debated with herself. *"Listen to yourself: you don't even know this man."* Yes, I do. *"No you don't."* It seems like I do. *"But you don't; slow down. Don't overvault yourself, or you'll stumble. You'll fall."* OK. But I do know him from a long time ago. *"Maybe so. But you have to get to know him in the now."* Brenna stopped debating herself. *We'll see.*

The excitement of the afternoon and the anticipation of the night sent Brenna straight to bed. She needed rest to recover and refresh. She set the alarm for seven thirty so she would have a whole hour and a half to prepare.

Before Brenna dozed off, Maya, who was occupying herself with writing postcards, asked, "What are you wearing tonight to the party?"

Brenna thought for a second before answering; she decided to tell a little lie. "The red and white skirt and top. It's easy to dance in."

"Yeah, it sure is. OK," Maya said, returning to her writing.

Brenna turned over in the bed, feeling only slightly ruffled for lying. She knew exactly what Maya would wear now. Maya had a habit of trying to copy Brenna's style, and Brenna wasn't too pleased about this. Before they had departed for Africa, Maya had stopped by Brenna's house to get suggestions on what to pack for the trip. Instead of just taking the suggestions, she then went out and bought three duplicate outfits. Maya must have thought it was a cute idea, but Brenna was appalled. Luckily, Brenna had brought a long purple slinky jersey gown. It was a little nothing of a dress, but when she slipped it over her head, the dress glided over each curve, slope, and protuberance that a well-formed twenty-one-year-old beauty queen's body could proffer. She secretly referred to it as her "trouble dress."

After she woke from her nap, she showered, lotioned, powdered, perfumed, and pampered her Afro. She applied her mascara and lipstick, carefully attending to every detail. But she did not remove her robe. As suspected, Maya had chosen to wear the red and white outfit so they would match. Only when they rang the room to inform them that His Highness's car had arrived for them did Brenna spring into action. She dashed into the bathroom. Off went the robe, and in a flash, the purple dress cascaded down her body. Then, around and around her head went the purple and orange print fabric, building an immaculate foot-high gele. The final touch was a pair of dangling earrings. In three minutes she was out, whisking her shawl from the chair and draping it over her shoulders. She confidently led the exit from the room.

As they walked to the elevator, Maya said, "I thought you were wearing this outfit."

"The skirt is dirty," was all Brenna said. It was somewhat true, she thought, not wanting to create a stack of lies. In fact, Maya's copying her outfits had finally worked to her own advantage. Her companion looked prim and proper in her long A-line skirt and blouse, while she herself looked exactly like trouble of the most interesting kind.

They exited the Hilton and were surprised to see Prince Yohannes standing outside the limousine smoking. When the chauffer opened the door, the prince stepped to the rear as they approached. Suddenly, Bessie and Maya both got protocol fever. "Please let Miss Watts go first." They then stood near the prince, while Brenna entered the car first. Then, they wedged themselves strategically between Brenna and Prince Yohannes. *OK*, Brenna thought, *one point for you.*

The Wabe Shebelle Hotel's traditional decor of thatch and gauzy white and colorful local textiles was a sharp contrast to the completely modern discotheque off its lobby. It was precisely like any disco they could find in LA. With large eyes, dark features, and thick, full Afros, their Ethiopian peers were a handsome lot.

Prince John walked to his reserved booth and stood. Again her companions stood beside him as his hand indicated for Miss Watts to enter first. Scooting around the U-shaped curve, Brenna wondered how she was going to manage talking to him across all these people.

Brenna watched the dancers swaying and bobbing to the same R&B records that were hits back home. Here on the other side of the world, they too were dancing the freak and hustle with authentic rhythm. The women were, of course, beautiful, but so too were most of the men.

Brenna noticed both Maya and Bessie striking match after match, but the tiny wooden local matches were unreliable. A small pile of their unsuccessful efforts had gathered in the ashtray. Neither of them smoked. Brenna looked for the prince and noticed an unlit cigarette waving between his fingers as he stood beside the booth, gesturing in conversation.

"Your Highness," Brenna said, just audible enough. He turned and saw that she had extended a small box of matches to him. He saw the efforts of the other women but reached by them and took the box, briefly embracing her fingertips. He nodded a thank-you and smiled. Although he was a prince, he was still a man. It would have been a bit too much if women had had to light his cigarettes for him. Brenna glanced at the other women with a tiny smirk and considered that a successful round for her.

After some time, with the music blaring and the disco ball casting garish starlight around the walls, it was easy to forget that they were in Africa. The same music, the same dances, and much the same spirit of cool courting display enveloped them. Prince Yohannes was just returning to the table when an extra-long Isaac Hayes song began to play. Brenna had strategically removed her shawl in preparation for being asked to dance. A tried and simple plan: she would be asked to dance by one of the other young men who had been staring and hanging around their booth. That would allow the prince plenty of opportunity to notice her figure and be impressed by her movements. She intended to act really interested and friendly with her dance partner to perhaps stir up a little competition.

Just as she predicted, almost immediately, men swooped down on the women seated in their booth. After the respectable limit of time had passed for the men to make their choices, much to her horror, only Brenna remained alone in the booth. No one had asked her to dance. Not wanting to show her shock, she fingered her glass and feigned interest in the dancers, as if it were she who had chosen not to dance.

Prince John sat down in the booth and lit a cigarette. He blew the smoke to the side and asked, "Hey, where did everybody go?" He looked around before adding, "I see no one asked you to dance."

What can I say to that? How could he say it so matter-of-factly? Why is he looking me in the face? She took a sip of her drink just to have something to do in her embarrassment.

"Well then, would you care to dance with me?" he asked.

Brenna thought, *No I don't care to dance a pity dance with you. I prefer to sit here alone at this table looking like a rejected little fool.* She wanted to run, disappear, or at least think of something clever to say. She didn't say what she was thinking; she just managed a simple "OK."

He stood up and took her hand. She rose from the table, and he escorted her deep into the dance floor. He smelled nice and felt good when he held her in his arms. Time changed, records changed, dancing partners around them changed. The tempo changed, but neither really noticed; they just continued to slow dance. Some six or seven records into the dancing, Brenna confirmed his interest in her. He had noticed her. He had wanted to dance with her over and over again. So why, she wondered, had he put her on the spot about no one asking her to dance? Then she realized.

She leaned back so she could look him in the face. "You did that on purpose. You set me up!"

Prince John broke into a smile. "When no one asked you to dance, you should have seen your face." He laughed, and she popped him on his shoulder. "You were so funny, it was worth the effort."

Brenna was relieved to know she had not been rejected. He had left the table and returned just before the long record came on. He had told them not to ask her to dance and had selected that long, slow record. Payback. She stiffened and accepted the distance of the next fast dance. She didn't look at him, even though every move was for him. She let the cha-cha take her away from him until he was forced to follow her around the floor. Follow the swaying of her hips, the subtle bounce of her breast when she raised her arm to turn, her eyes cutting away from him, and the smile she freely gave to everyone except him. He responded during the next slow song by pulling her in, whispering apologies in her ear, and coaxing her body closer to his. She didn't resist much. She had seen him too, moving with confidence on the dance floor.

Just when she was getting comfortable, he said, "You know, I've never danced with a commoner before."

"Well, at least for the next year, I'm a queen."

"Touché. Then, I've never danced with a queen."

They were both quiet after that and just enjoyed the conversation of the dance. They were learning the quiet wordless nuance of each other, the smell, the feel, the synchronization of their moves.

Cautiously, he inched her closer. Brenna stepped back a pace to see his face. Um. Her eyes met just above his lips. She quickly looked up and smiled. "John, I need to sit for a while; my feet are a little tired."

"Of course." He snapped into action. He looked over to a group of men and gave directive nods: one back, then one to the side. He placed his hand to the small of Brenna's back and escorted her off the floor to a somewhat secluded booth.

"What about our booth? Aren't we joining my companions?"

"Look," he said. He stepped back to let her see her companions at their former booth, laughing and flirting, surrounded by admirers. "I think your friends are just fine."

"Me too," Brenna said as she slid in, far enough from him, but not too far. Instead of sitting beside her, Prince John took the seat across the table. A waiter immediately took their order. This time, Brenna ordered Fanta.

"Is that all? Perhaps some Courvoisier?"

"No, thank you. Fanta will be fine. No ice. But chilled if they have it, please." She reached for her compact in her purse. He instructed the waiter, and they were alone at the table.

He watched her quickly examine her face in the small mirror and reach for the small powder puff.

"You don't need it," he said.

"Excuse me?" She looked up to him, puff suspended in the air.

"I said, you don't need it. The makeup. You don't need it. You're quite beautiful without it. Let me see. May I?" He reached across, lifted her chin with his forefinger and thumb, and examined her face, turning it slightly to the left then right.

"See, I'm right," he said, not releasing her face. She looked back into his eyes, trying not to breathe hard and to think of something diverting to say.

"Well, there you have it," she said, borrowing a meaningless but useful expression from one of her friends back home that cut the moment just enough for her to smile, retrieve her chin, and tuck away her compact. She sat back.

"So you like a boring, unadorned face?" she teased him, still wanting to swipe a little powder and lipstick to freshen up.

"Not any face. I confess, some faces could use a little manufactured support. But not yours." He sat back and took out a cigarette. He flicked his lighter then peered back at her with one eye squinting through the smoke.

"Thank you. I guess that's a compliment?"

"Yes, you should take it as such." Though he didn't admit it, he was more concerned with how much nicer her kiss might be with her soft full natural mouth unobstructed by lipstick. He enjoyed the rich undertones of her skin that had been covered by the face powder, now peeking through by candlelight; he wanted to sniff the light mist of perspiration dancing across her skin. But how?

"Have you ever seen a palace?" he softly inquired.

"Of course I have."

"Where?"

"What?" she asked, looking perplexed.

"I said, what palaces have you seen?"

"Well, I've seen your aunt's and grandfather's palaces," she said with a smile.

"But you've never seen mine," he added with an arched brow.

"You're absolutely right. I haven't." She took a sip and looked out at the dancers.

"My palace is very beautiful at night," he practically whispered.

"I'm sure it is, and I'll take your word for it."

"It's something you should really see for yourself," he said, his dimples coaxing her.

"Well, then, perhaps one day I will."

"What do they say in America, 'There's no time like the present?'"

"That's what they say, yes."

And so it went on like this, back and forth, with affection growing beneath, above, and in between the banter.

Chapter 16

Iskista

The next day, Brenna acted as if her blank itinerary was an oversight. After sleeping late, she joined her companions at the theater for an evening of traditional Ethiopian folk music and dance. Mulu, their hostess for the evening, explained that traditional musicians, called *azmaris*, traveled around the country playing music and singing songs, similarly to the African griot or the English bard. Several of them performed that evening with a crudely made lyre called a *krar* and a *masenqo*, a single-stringed violin.

Then, dancers from various regions of Ethiopia joined the musicians, each troupe with their own version of the major traditional dance, the *Iskista*. While West African dance, which Brenna and her friends were familiar with, focused on lower-body movements, Ethiopian traditional dance focused on the upper body. They were captivated by the men and women jerking their shoulders and rocking their upper bodies to the drums and the haunting ancient melodies. As the music grew in intensity, so too did the gyrations and the back-and-forth body communication between the male and female dancers.

The high-energy performance cooled down when Getatchew Kassa and his band performed an Ethiopian ballad of reminiscence called "Tezeta." The song was filled with sweet, poignant longing. Brenna immediately fell in love with it. Almost everything Ethiopian fascinated her. But also there was something inside everything here that made her a little sad.

The concert ended, and they were taken backstage to meet the performers. It was still strange to meet other blacks who did not understand or speak English. How could people with the same family faces of Nathan, Joe, Carolyn, Alice, and Cathy back home not understand English? But they couldn't, nor could Brenna, Maya, and Bessie understand them. Despite appearances, they were different.

They left the theater and went across a small plaza to a reception hall. They feasted on Ethiopian and Western hors d'oeuvres. Brenna asked Rut, their guide, if she could show her how to dance the Iskista. So, after having a snack, several of the young ladies led them off to a terrace to privately instruct them. Someone started the music.

Mulu began their instruction. She showed them how to stand erect. They followed. "Good; keep your chin up. Yes. Now keep your chest high. That's right. Now try to heave your breast up and then drop." She demonstrated, and they followed. "Now do each shoulder in isolation. Good. Now both shoulders together. OK, watch how I do my neck. Good." Bessie, Maya, and Brenna kept practicing and laughing as they tried to get the hang of it. Mulu summoned the other young ladies.

"Watch us first," Mulu told Brenna. A group of eight young women gathered in a circle. Rut jumped into the center. She stood for a second then did a neck-rocking routine that rivaled their no-tion of Egyptian pyramid dancers. She eyed another young woman named Lisbeth in the circle and moved to stand in front of her. A challenge. Lisbeth answered with an arched brow. She stepped forward with a measured heave-roll-drop motion of her breast. Rut responded with a rhythmic four-squared jutting of her neck. Breast roll. Neck jut. Roll. Jut. Roll. Jut. Double roll. Jut, Jut.

They moved to the center of the circle, and Lisbeth stopped and performed a radical shift of her ribcage. Left front right back. Rut tilted her head back then rolled a nod. Lisbeth: right center right. Suddenly, the music sped up, and the two young women broke out in fierce upper-body gyrations. The wildness of the dance was modulated only by the controlled isolation of the movements.

After a while, the music beckoned the men, whose heads first peeked out the windows. They now spilled out onto the terrace. They wanted in, and they got it. Each man stepped to a lady with a small bow then launched into his own version of the dance.

A lithe, handsome performer whom they had met backstage joined the party. Dressed in a white shirt with a shama thrown across his shoulders, he approached Brenna to dance. She looked around and saw that Maya and Bessie were already on the floor. Eyeing her, he popped a rapid sequence of gyrations that moved head-neck-shoulder-back-hip-butt-knees-feet-jump!

"Oh!" Brenna gasped in delight, and she tried a shoulder move of her own. It was really a "Philly dog" movement from her high school dance days. But close enough. Her partner smiled and con-tinued his display. Brenna, a member of a college dance troupe her-self, was quick to catch on to the new moves of the dance from her partner. She danced and glanced around the dance floor to pick up more moves from the other dancing women and then try them for her partner.

Behind her she heard Maya's pleading voice. "Please show me how to do this dance. I know you could teach me." Brenna hoped the man would dance with her companion. Then she heard Maya say, "OK, thank you." And Brenna knew the man had conceded. After a while, she turned to see how Maya was coming along and was shocked to see Prince John dancing with her. He was dancing away and grinning at Maya's inability to get the shoulder moves right. Maya was so pathetic at it that he went to stand behind her, placed a hand on each shoulder, and proceeded to lift them for her. She made a feeble attempt, he manipulated her shoulders again, and they both fell into a laughing hug.

Brenna knew it was all a ploy, since she had seen Maya dancing the Iskista quite well when they had rehearsed a while ago with Mulu. She was flirting with Prince John, and he was grinning back. Brenna turned to her partner, who had been watching her. He looked in her eyes and gave her a conspiratorial nod. He took her hand and gracefully glided to the center of the dance floor. He began several movements that were so fluid and complicated that those on the dance floor nearby began to make way and stand aside to watch. Slyly, he modeled movements for Brenna to replicate. Moves that displayed, in subtle allure, her slender waist, curvaceous hips, long neck, and ample breast. Then he encircled her in the dance. She did not disappoint. They both received applause when the music finished. A slower song started, and her partner held out his hand for another dance.

Just then, Prince John walked up and tapped Brenna's partner on the shoulder. He glanced to his left and recognized the prince with a nod. John smiled and nodded toward the door. The dancer snapped a quick bow to the prince and Brenna and left with a slight billowing of his shama.

"May I?" Prince John asked Brenna.

"Well, I guess so," she said with a smile, "as my partner has fled."

"Do you know this dance?" he asked as he moved toward her.

"A little," she said. A lot better than Maya.

"Good. Dance with me." He stood tall then began to rock in a jerky male version of the Iskista. Brenna replied with isolated neck movements. They kept their eyes on each other. She watched to see if he would be distracted by the other beautiful women dancing nearby. She watched to see if his eyes would scan the room for Maya. No. He was with her now. Only with her. She knew she could get and hold his attention. But she wanted to be of permanent interest to his heart. She knew she was not willing to stay with a man whose attention she had to constantly vie for, even after he was hers. But this was just a beginning, and she knew he was worth the vying.

Perhaps it was secretly imbedded in the Iskista, but his contrived and ratchety movements enticed her, or perhaps it was because the movements were starkly contrasted with the prince's steady gaze and dimpled smile. When she employed the heaved-breast-roll-drop movements, she saw him bite his lower lip and stare at her as he advanced in her direction. She laughed and flirted with her eyes and body. Tonight they cast their lots. On each other they spent the currency of their youth, beauty, and privilege toward the purchase of an enchanted love.

Chapter 17

Night Language

Brenna agreed to let Prince John drive her back to the hotel that evening. He escorted her out to a polished burgundy Trans Am and opened the door.

"Where's your driver?" Brenna asked.

"I'm on my own tonight. This is my car," he said grinning proudly. "I'm a lowrider."

"Really?" Brenna said incredulously, wondering how lowriding, the favorite pastime of young men in her Los Angeles ghetto and barrio, could have made it all the way to the streets of Addis Ababa, Ethiopia.

"Remember, I went to UC Santa Barbara, so I'm a California boy of sorts too."

She stepped back to view the highly polished finish and the rims on the wheels. She noticed that the car looked slightly elevated.

"Lifts?" she asked, still amused.

"Absolutely. Get in. Let me show you." He secured her in the car and dashed to the driver's side. He turned the key, and the souped-up engine growled a deep bass threat. She laughed. Then he reached for a switch, and the front end of the car sloped downward followed by the rear, leaving them nestled only inches from the ground. He hit the switch, and she heard the wheeze of the hydraulics as they lifted the car again. Now in high profile, he gunned the engine, a challenge to any takers—although there were none—and sped off, not leaving skid marks but dust in his wake.

They drove around Addis for a while as he pointed out sights. Finally, he pulled up to a large gate at the end of a high brick wall. "What is this?" Brenna asked.

"It's my house," he responded, and her neck snapped back to the silhouette of the palace.

"Would you like to come in for a minute?" he asked. She looked at him and nodded.

"John, it's beautiful," Brenna whispered. He turned toward the gate.

"Please, I'd like you to call me Yohannes, if you don't mind."

"Yohannes. Yes, of course; I like it. Yohannes, your palace is beautiful."

"I told you, Brehenna. May I call you Brehenna?"

"Yes. I like how you say it. Say it again."

Yohannes signaled to the soldiers stationed at the guard boxes. They bowed then opened the gates and let his car pass. As they moved down the drive, he said again, "Brehenna. Brehenna." He tried out her name on her ears: "Brehenna," he almost whispered. Then he sang, "Bre he he he he he hen na, ba-a-by," to the tune of "Sherry."

Brehenna laughed and looked back toward the house. The grounds were dark, but she could see light from a few rooms in the silhouetted palace. When they parked in the front, someone turned on the exterior lights. Prince Yohannes escorted her up the steps, and the door opened to a large foyer. Hallways and doors opened in each direction; to the left was a wide winding staircase with an intricate wrought-iron balustrade. Someone took her wrap. She kept her purse and turned back to the prince.

"Let's go upstairs," he said as he directed her toward the stairs. Brenna's expression and the slight tilt of her head made him continue. "Oh. There's a ballroom up there," he added, looking her in the eye and taking her hand. "Really, come on, you'll see."

She walked up the stairs with him and was relieved when a servant opened a set of double doors and there was in fact a ballroom. Prince John spoke to the servant, who made a few adjustments to the room and then left them alone.

"Make yourself comfortable," he said, indicating a nearby sofa. "Let me put on some music. What kind of drink can I get for you?"

"A brandy and ginger, please, no ice," Brenna said, satisfied that she was finally twenty-one and could drink with impunity. She had heard an African official order this drink recently, but she had yet to taste it.

Finally sitting next to her on the couch, Prince John lit a cigarette. He sat back smoking and sipping his drink while Brenna drank and swayed to the Dramatics' "Whatcha See Is Whatcha Get." They sat quietly and took their time.

"So, Brehenna, what do you think?" he asked.

"About what?" she asked, looking at him.

"About my house?

"Yohannes, it's great. It's beautiful." They were quiet again.

"Brehenna," he said, reaching over and touching the back of her hand, "you're beautiful."

"Thank you." She faced him and smiled. He moved his hand to the middle of her back.

"You want to dance?" he asked.

Already a little heady from the drink and the pull of the Dells' "Oh, What a Night" she looked away.

"Yohannes, I'm a little scared," she said with a half-smile.

"Of what?" he asked. His brow went up. "Of me? No, no, no." He reached for her hand again and gently kissed it while looking in her eyes.

"May I have another drink?" she asked.

"Of course!" He hopped up and headed to the bar.

"Fanta," she called after him, "or Orangina. Whatever's cold."

He brought the fresh drinks, and they chatted as she sipped. "Stoned Love" played, and she was relieved by its upbeat tempo.

"I saw Diana Ross and the Supremes once," he said. "My grand-father took me with him to Las Vegas a few years ago. We went backstage to meet them."

"Were they pretty?"

"Well, yes, I guess. But they had on so much makeup, you couldn't tell what they really looked like. Gorgeous, all dressed up like that. And they were friendly. I got Diana's number. But I never called."

Brehenna rolled her eyes at his bragging and sipped her soda.

"Hey, do you want to see the rest of my house?"

"Maybe some other time; it's late. I should be going back."

"OK," he said and lit another cigarette. They listened to an Ethiopian record that was playing.

"What's the name of that song?" Brehenna asked.

"'Tezeta.' It's the number-one hit here."

"Yes, I heard it at the theater the other night. What does Te-ze-ta mean?"

"Remembrances. Memories, more like nostalgia."

"I like it." Again, she felt the longing in the singer's voice and in the pleading instruments. Yohannes sat up, moved in very close, took her hand, and held it on his right knee. She looked at him. He smiled. They looked at each other for a long time.

"Brehenna, stay with me tonight?"

"Yohannes, we just met. I can't stay with you tonight."

"Why not?" he asked her profile.

"It's a rule. I don't know you well enough. I just don't do it."

"Is this night special to you?"

"Well, yes. Yes, it is."

Yohannes was quiet for a moment then asked, "So tell me, when you will have the opportunity to spend the night with a prince again?"

Never, probably, Brenna thought, and her mind went searching for counterarguments to sustain her position. "That's a good point." She paused as if to weigh what he'd said. "I confess it has a certain appeal." Then she added, "It's probably a good line too. Does it usually work?" She looked away from his face.

"Usually," Yohannes remarked. He pulled another Roth cigarette from its box. And lit it with his current butt. The smoking filled the silence.

Then in low, slow, deep tones, he continued his plea. Brenna looked straight ahead into the room with only occasional side glances toward him. When he spoke again, it was in French. She translated. It was an embellishment of the same request. She was taken away, not so much by the words but with the images evoked: late-night cafés, hot black coffee, strong unfiltered cigarette smoke, cabarets, and butterfly wings fluttering a rakish appeal through the language.

Abruptly, John sat up and seized the flesh of her upper arm and held it firmly. In German, he barked the same request over her shoulder. The demand of this language shattered the languor of alcohol and the French, snatching her into sobriety with quickened breath and heartbeat. Part of her wanted the forcefulness to override her own reservations and release her from having to decide. Just then, John released her arm and sat back.

His touch returned as gentle strokes then a bare wisp of his fingertips on the back of her taut neck.

"Relax. Sit back," he said coaxingly. "I won't bite." She eased back and heard him add under his breath, "At least not without your permission."

His right arm, already arched over the back of the couch, slid down to capture her in his embrace. She turned to face him. They breathed each other's air. He moved to kiss her lips. Then slowly kissing her once, back, twice, back, a third time, then moving back to look in her eyes. She felt his heart beating against her hand resting on his chest. He moved from her mouth to her right ear. The dark-featured Italian he whispered licked its music against her cheek, and its long-lashed passion held out the weight of its breathy desire as an entitlement. Brenna stood wavering in the gondola of this linguistic pursuit.

Suddenly her mind brimmed with European images: shadowy evenings and dark boudoirs; stilettos, black leather combat boots, lacy garters, and whips; spaghetti dripping in hot red-meat sauce; baskets of sweet ripened fruits leaking from their skins; cheeses and fresh pastry; theatres and whorehouses; museums and naked *David*'s ass; hairy, funky armpits, moans, and laughter; thick down duvets; robust beer and overturned wine bottles; melting candle wax and waning flames; smoldering embers and heady perfume; silk, brocade, and coarse khaki; opera and simple folk songs. Then the long sultry discourse of a single saxophone with the night.

Even so, she did not concede. Then Yohannes spoke again, and everything stilled. This appeal came like clean air and pure water. Surely it was the same appeal finally winding its way back home to his native tongue: Amharic. The sound was not fancy; the words did not dance and flirt. Rather, they walked naked and direct, as a man fresh from the shower heads to his woman in bed.

"Look at me," Yohannes requested in English, and she complied. "I know you think you might regret sleeping with me so soon. But I believe we'll both live to regret it if we don't. I know I will. Please. Trust me. I will never let you regret this night."

The next two days, they went everywhere together. He took her to meet his mother and four brothers. He took her to play cards with his friends. Through his arms, she had entered a dream—a fairyland of palaces and princes. Right at the heart of it all, there he was, handsome, charming, and fun. He drove them around Addis in his customized Trans Am, playing "Stoned Love" over and over. It became their song.

He was trying his best to impress her, and he was succeeding. Through all the glamour, though, she wondered: *Who are you, really?* It might be easy to let the many compelling trappings obscure who he was as a person. So it was in the evenings, when they were finally alone sitting on the couch before the fireplace watching *Star Trek* that she began to feel at home. With him beside her, nothing outside the walls of the palace seemed to matter. She wanted to stay, yet she had an obligation to continue her tour. Those days that had initially seemed like a setup and a curse on her itinerary were now a blessing. Now, the days would definitely not give her enough time.

"Tell me again where your tour is taking you?" Yohannes asked.

"Next, to Kenya and Tanzania, then to Nigeria and Ghana. But I'll be back here in about three weeks, because Ethiopian Airlines is flying me back to Paris, where we connect to TWA."

"You know, I've been to those places. I could tell you all about them."

"OK, good. Tell me."

"Well, first of all, Kenya, especially Nairobi, is very hot. The city has a very English presence, and I find it rather uninteresting. I could show you many great things here in Ethiopia that you would enjoy much better. You really don't have to go at all. You could just stay right here with me."

"Oh, I see, you don't want to tell me about them to *prepare* me for my trip, you want your telling to be in lieu of my trip. I have an obligation to go. You must know, I really would like to stay with you, but I'm still leaving tomorrow."

"In that case, what shall we do on your last night here?"

"Yohannes, it's only my last night, for now. I'll be back." She leaned toward him and kissed his lips. He held her for a full kiss. Then he whispered, "You better. You better come back to me."

"I will. I promise. I'll be back." They kissed and moved into that smoldering private place lovers go and stayed the night.

Chapter 18

There Is a King in Jerusalem

Ancient Ethiopia

Reigning now for seven years, Queen Makeda was delighted to see Tamrin, chief of the royal merchants, enter the chamber. It had been over a year since he had journeyed to the northern and eastern lands to trade the rich woods, incense, gold, textiles, and spices of Ethiopia. Her merchants always returned with much to enhance the lives of the people. They brought greater wealth into the royal coffers, and they also brought wonderful stories of people and places beyond the borders of their imagination. The entire cabinet listened attentively to the long report, but the queen's interest was piqued when he spoke about the great king of Judah known as Slomo King of Peace, King Solomon. Tamrin told of the beauty of the palaces, and especially the Temple on the Mount in Jerusalem that King Solomon had built to the gods. He told of the people's great love for their king and how he ruled with such unsurpassed wisdom and compassion that many foreign rulers came to sit at his feet and learn the ways of Zion. He was thus called the King of Kings.

Years before, when the call had gone out that King Solomon needed particular resources to build the Temple, Ethiopia had sent great quantities of gold, wood, precious stones, and incense. Queen Makeda recalled that he paid great sums for the merchandise. Yet, as she listened now, something mysterious was emerging in the background of what Tamrin spoke of—she was divining something *other* about this king.

Later that evening in a private audience, Queen Makeda asked Tamrin to speak at greater length about King Solomon.

"Your Majesty, most of my dealings were with his men, so it is from them that I heard reports and stories. They say his wisdom is so profound that he has succeeded in uniting two warring kingdoms without any bloodshed. The king is skilled and highly accomplished in every area. He is not only their king but also their high priest, and he is said to be a master of the sacred arts. His armies are quite vast, but I believe it is more out of awe of the king that no one dares challenge his kingdom. On the contrary, rulers from near and far have married their daughters to this same king in order to assure goodwill and permanent alliances with him. He is unlike his father, King David, who was fierce and whose hands ran red with blood. King Solomon reigns in peace. Even his name, Slomo, means 'peace' in their Hebrew language."

Tamrin proceeded to tell the story of the two mothers, both claiming the same child, who came before the king for resolution of the dispute. "They say that after hearing each woman's tearful appeal, the king drew his sword and held it high over the naked infant's stomach and declared to the mothers, 'I shall cut the child in half that each may have an equal share.' One of the mothers ran under the blade and covered the child with her body. She begged the king, deferring to the other woman, 'Please, Your Majesty, she is the mother; let her take the child.' The king spared the child and took him in his arms. Then, without hesitation, he handed the child to the woman who had protected the infant with her own life, saying, 'Take your child and go in peace.'"

Makeda's eyes welled with tears. She quietly smiled and nodded. Tamrin continued with his accounts late into the evening. The queen asked many questions that urged him on. When he concluded, the queen did not turn from the fireplace, where she had stood listening and staring into the flames. Tamrin sat at ease in the long silence of Her Majesty's contemplation. She finally turned to him with a directive: "Take the necessary season to rest yourself and your men. Afterward, begin immediately to organize the royal caravans. I will journey up to Jerusalem to meet this King Solomon and bear witness to the measure of the man."

That night, in Queen Makeda's dream life, she saw visions of a world and realm whose proportion was so enormous, she felt herself backing up great distances in order to behold fully what she faced. She had backed up so far that it was as if she were at the very border of her land, yet still she could not see the full height of what was before her. Suddenly, it was as if she was snatched from her position, and she found herself deposited on the summit of a high mountain. The vision of the world she had been seeking had vanished from her view, until finally she looked down and beheld this new world beneath her own feet.

Chapter 19

The Queen of Sheba

Ancient Jerusalem

Makeda's journey to Jerusalem took months, but it was a passage of wonderment and anticipation. Upon arrival, she was taken to the palace that was to be her home for more than a year. It was well appointed for the queen and her servants. Her bearers were, for a time, relieved of their duties by the servants of the king.

Weeks passed in preparation for her first audience with King Solomon. There was much to do surrounding the organization of the presentation and display of royal gifts. The musicians and dancers rehearsed day and night. Following the week of the king's royal welcome banquets and events, they would be prepared to reciprocate with feasts and entertainment of the highest Ethiopian culture. The queen herself was taken to the Sea of Salt, where the buoyancy of the oily, saturated water effortlessly held her afloat on her back as she surrendered to the sea and smiled at the pristine blue sky that seemed at her fingertips. Her skin was rubbed to glistening with the coarse salts and the rich mud slathered over her nude body as she lay baking in the sun. No health or beauty ritual was spared; even the women who served Solomon's queens and concubines came to minister secret treatments, while her own women gave the final preparations of oils, fragrances, skin art, hair weaving, and wardrobe selections reserved for Ethiopian *candace*s (queens) for centuries and especially refined for their current monarch.

By request, King Solomon's keepers of the traditions sat with Queen Makeda for hours, inundating her with tales of the ancient fiery spirit of Judah. But now, in these times, the people of Jerusalem moved about their daily lives with the serenity that only those accustomed to decades of peace can have. Life in this land was framed by the rituals of religious tradition and moved from holy celebration to holy celebration. They were one family. Everything that Queen Makeda experienced in these weeks added more layers to the image of the king that was being erected in her mind. Who was this generous and beloved father who ruled in peace?

In due course the day arrived. Queen Makeda, flanked by her royal retinue, entered the Grand Reception Hall. Despite the large number of people gathered there, a hush fell over them at the queen's procession. The intricate construction and weight of her formal imperial attire had the designed effect on her carriage: she moved slowly and deliberately. Even her gold crown, though filigreed for lightness, restricted her flexibility, permitting her to only look straight ahead. With her bearing true and in her gilded robes, Queen Makeda glided across the marble floors toward the throne.

King Solomon rose and joined his standing court to receive her as she was announced: "Sole ruling sovereign of the lands of Abyssinia, monarch in high standing of the Order of the House of Ethiopia: Makeda, Queen of Sheba."

The Queen of Sheba stood before King Solomon and curtsied beneath her heavy garments. As it was impossible and ill advised to bow her head, she merely lowered her eyes in obeisance. In turn he nodded and descended the steps to assist her to the seat beside him. In this brief period, he noticed her daintiness. Even beneath her official attire, he saw her slender hands and her long neck, and the lift and fall of her garment at her bust line revealed the curvature of her figure. So too he noticed the rhythmic sway of her robe as she walked, indicative of ample hips. Or so he surmised. Her face was at hand, so he needed to make no approximations.

Her skin was smoothly polished bronze. Light danced on its moist surface. Her features were finely sculpted and softly rounded like a child's, but it was her large clear eyes that reigned over her face. Full silky arching brows and a lush fringe of lashes shaded her brown velvet irises. Eyes that matched her flesh and sparkled with life. One corner of her full sculpted lips tilted up. Her abundant ebony hair was coiled, braided, wrapped, and draped with colored silk ropes, and thin golden strands held diamonds, sapphires, emeralds, and rubies in place. The rich hue of Ethiopian gold adorned her ears and throat and tinkled from her ankles and wrists.

Queen Makeda sat beside King Solomon, and together they watched the royal Ethiopian procession. A warm sweet womanly fragrance overlaid with rich spices and incense beckoned to his nostrils every time she moved. Her voice held the sweetness of the lyre. Effortless charm. Even had she been a peasant, she would have been extraordinary, but she was in fact the queen of a prosperous and vast land. The wealth of the gifts she paraded before him could not be tallied. He saw that her own beauty of feature and carriage was echoed in her people, who were all handsome reflections. Makeda glowed, and he knew everything about her would be magic.

So this was King Solomon, Makeda thought. She was pleased that finally the name had taken on flesh. He was much more handsome and engaging than she had anticipated. She noticed how each performer received his full attention and how he generously laughed and smiled. Everyone seemed included in his grace. He was a lively, wide-spirited man. And his wisdom: *Will he be as wise as the stories have told? How can I weigh his wisdom? To what do I compare it?* Many questions she asked within herself as she enjoyed the spectacle and fullness of this long-awaited day. Yes, they both were pleased, but the growing proportion of the promise ahead left them even more intrigued and far from satisfied. Strong winds stirred in the palace that night. Strong, hot, belligerent winds.

Although Queen Makeda had settled in to much of the Jerusalem way, still each day brought a wealth of experiences and knowledge. She knew this day would be special, because the king had promised her so. They walked together with an entourage until they reached the inner courtyard. King Solomon dismissed his retinue as they approached the steps of the Temple.

"Leave us to enter privately." Everyone dispersed except Makeda and the chief priests. Makeda marveled at the golden Temple doors. They were so massive that she inquired about them.

"King Solomon, Your Majesty, the height and span of these Temple doors leads me to ask if the Nephilim still walk the land of Israel."

"Most certainly not. Those wicked creatures were destroyed by the Great Flood."

"Wicked? In Ethiopia, we do not consider them wicked. To the contrary, we honor their divine parentage. There is even a legend that my ancestry was a progeny of such. My grandmother said that this is what accounts for the remarkable stature of many of the men and women of our house."

"My dear queen," Solomon said in retort, "that is absurd. To even imagine angels imposing themselves on the daughters of the earth is an abomination."

"For whom?" Makeda said. "I have always felt it must have been an honor and remarkable experience for a human woman to conceive with an angel."

"You are a peculiar woman: at times keen in wisdom and discernment, yet at others, you seem so innocent as to border on the foolish."

"That may well be, my honorable host. I will not dispute you in your own land, nor will I mar the reputation of innocence, for she is pure and sound and there is no fault in her. Since my words bear some resemblance to the foolish, I alone assume the blame for them. Let us leave innocence clean."

King Solomon paused to search Makeda's eyes for some hint of her posture. Was she teasing, or being slyly insolent? No. Makeda quietly looked back at him and waited. Solomon extended his hand and guided her with a gently directing arm across her shoulders. "Come. Let us enter into the House of the Lord."

The heavy odor of incense and sacrifice draped the air of the sanctuary. As Makeda passed over the threshold, even before her eyes adjusted to the subdued lighting of the Temple, a fleeting chill blew across her arms, and her hair tickled at the nape of her neck. She knew she was entering the realm of the sacred. She was walking on holy ground.

Makeda asked and received permission to remove her slippers. The golden floor was cool and alive beneath her slender feet. She felt present, connected, vital, and altered. There was a virginal clarity to the architecture of the anteroom, simple and unaffected. Palm trees, open flowers, and beautiful winged infants were carved deeply into the glistening woods of the ceiling and walls.

Her eyes tried to drink in all the sublime grandeur of this sacred hall. Every turn evoked a silent gasp. The craftsmanship was pure artistry on display in its tones and textures: lapis lazuli, onyx, and pure turquoise. Many narrow clerestory windows punctuated the vaulted ceiling so that light streamed in and embellished the silver, bronze, and golden vessels. Gold. *Is there so much gold in all the earth?* Makeda wondered.

Makeda, stunned and transfixed to one spot, was only able to make a slow pivot until she located Solomon in her gaze. Quickly, seeking refuge, really, she approached him. "In this Temple, Your Majesty, which of the gods do you honor with such esteem?"

"It is not a question of which of the gods, dear queen."

"But in our land, we have built scores of temples to honor each of the gods. Do you say, then, that here, in Jerusalem, you are accustomed to honoring all the gods in this one place? That is too difficult to conceive. How is it possible, when all the gods have their own preferences and demands of ritual?"

"No, Queen Makeda, we absolutely do not honor *all the gods* here." Then he proclaimed, "Shema Israel, Adonai Elohenu, Adonai Ehud. Hear, Israel: our God is One God."

Makeda shuddered and cringed, expecting swift retaliation from the blasphemed gods. Nothing came, except the heightened silence and the brightened light. Then, slowly and without notice, her astounded heart opened like a flower in her breast. Although her mind could not encompass this notion of the One God, the echo of the truth of his words resonated with every fiber of her being. It was as if all the shattered pieces of the pantheon of her gods recollected and reconvened themselves into One Grand Singular Omnipotence. Without ever having known, she immediately knew God and realized she had always known.

Time had shifted, and Makeda was in the sacred hour where silence roared and stillness leaped about her. The light cast shadows, and the shadows made obeisance. The air of the chamber visually rippled. Then the petals of her open heart filled. She was enveloped within this sweet presence and drawn into its core. Basking in the radiance of the Everlasting One, Makeda became sweet honey nectar.

There is only One God. Adonai Ehud, Makeda thought, echoing the confirmation in her soul.

Heavenly angels plucked rare instruments tuned to her heart-strings. Warm tears trickled down her lovely face. Makeda surrendered to the rapture of God's love. Over the melody of the lyre came a psalm of such poignant intensity that her quick and brilliant mind toppled. It ceased to add, measure, and judge. It just stood watching—a bystander—a witness to the Holy Spirit.

Her large eyes opened and searched; as if magnetized, they were drawn to the source of the sound. Finally, they rested upon King Solomon kneeling before the golden doors to the Holy of Holies—lyre in hand, face raised, and eyes closed, glorifying the God of Israel, the God of Creation.

Makeda did not know how she had come to be on her knees, or how the cool gold was now kissing her forehead. Yet she felt her inner eye quelled by its coolness, and the wreckage of her mind was restored with an order and peace guided by this transforming revelation. She watched Solomon worship his God. The God of Creation. The God of Avraham, Yitzchak, and Yaakov.

Makeda had never seen a man so in love. Curls lay damp against his temples with the perspiration of his devotion. Her eyes followed a droplet as it stole from behind his ear, slowly coursed down the muscular sinews of his burnished neck, and pooled into moisture in the hair on his shoulder's ridge. The stillness in his soul settled on his face like marble. His eyes were closed, and his Hebrew prayers lifted the smoke of the incense and the light of the candles as escorts to heaven. Candlelight? *Where has the day gone?* Makeda asked herself, but she knew that no day of her life had been better spent. What she needed to know now was how to truly serve the One God who inspired the seamless homage of this mighty and wise

King of Peace. Her bosom heaved a secret stirring. She also wanted to be known, as a woman, by this man. She wanted to taste the sweat of his unmitigated devotion. She closed her eyes and continued to sway to the harmony of the music and the moment.

And for his part, upon returning from being swept up in the spirit of praise, Solomon always took a while to reestablish his bearing. Even now, the journey back was slow. As his awareness returned, he was in a state of wonder, like a newborn. The starkness of the radiance of God that he had just witnessed caused him to squint in adjustment to the flickering amber candlelight of the Temple. To leave the ecstasy of that communion always begged the question: Why return? Throughout this transition, his fingers had never ceased plucking the responsive strings of his lyre. A distant fragrance started to ground him. The fresh fecundity had a name: Queen Makeda. Yes, she had accompanied him here. What manner of woman was she? He recalled witnessing Makeda plunge headlong into the rapture of anointment when he first announced the Shema to her. He felt the heavens rejoice at her return.

How many others over the generations had heard this same proclamation and remained confused or unmoved? Yet her instantaneous recognition caused her to shudder and her eyes to roll back. He had known exactly where she was bound. He had taken immediately to his knees and leaped into his own incessant praying. He had in mind to catch her—no really, to join her in the spirit—as he might on a garden stroll. To his amazement, he did. Never had he found another soul on the inner path of his own divinity. Yet there she was, moving toward the light, wrapped in the harmony of the angelic chorus. His fingers on the lyre echoed the holy sounds as best they could. Makeda was so intent on approaching the Glory that compelled her that she did not see Solomon ahead of her on the path. She walked right through him. In that instant, she was a breeze inside of him, fresh and alive. She felt like him, yet a woman. *What kind of woman is this?*

Then he saw dancing images swaying against the wood panels and gold. He realized it was the shadows she cast by the candlelight. Her tall slim lines were exaggerated. With the strokes of his lyre, he followed the dancer's lead. Mesmerized by the grace and beauty of this phantom formed by shadows, he was slightly startled by the awareness that he had not yet looked on the woman directly.

Solomon was a lover of women. He had loved his mother first and always still. His nurses obliged and spoiled him with sweet, soft indulgences. As a youth, he studied the women he had known—his sister, cousins, and friends. He could read the movement of a brow, the inclination of fingers in conversations, the tempo of the rustle of a garment better than most men could read a scroll or understand a woman's directly spoken word. He was drawn to them. Intrigued, exalted, and sometimes beguiled by them. But for all the women he had known, suddenly he felt he knew nothing of them at all. Makeda held the promise of revealing the essence of woman, without contrivance. Even now, he noticed a slight hesitancy in his heart as his reckless eyes finally feasted directly on Makeda.

He was taken aback by the colors. The candlelight made sorcery against her bronze skin; the gleaming raven locks gathered upon her head, and rebellious curls cascaded wantonly down her shoulders and across her eye. Through the gossamer white Ethiopian fabric, he saw the silhouette of her perfect body undulating to his music.

Solomon added frenzy to the tempo of his instrument just to see how her body would respond. Immediately Makeda stopped, as if snatched out of ecstasy. With a mildly befuddled expression in her large doe eyes, she sought out Solomon.

It was a mistake. He knew it now. No contrivance, no technique, nothing that he had relied on before could he apply to Makeda. *What manner of woman is this?* God has created in her a new thing. Solomon walked toward her. They met with an embrace. She pulled back. Then eye to eye she spoke. "Your God shall be my God, all the days of my life. Teach me the ways of Zion. Ethiopia and I will never depart from them. This is my word and my pledge."

Then in the stillness, hand in hand, they left the Temple.

—∞—

That night, wearied by the impact of the day's revelation, Queen Makeda needed rest. Sleep came immediately, but instead of granting rest, it snatched her into a whirlwind of activity. Bizarre, wild, puzzling images raced through her bedazzled mind. Being a skillful dreamer, Makeda quickly adjusted to her new landscape and set out on what had all the dream signs of a journey.

When the dream finally settled on a destination, Makeda found herself in a cave. A tomb. She could smell the faint, acrid scent of ancient decay. The place was neither lurid nor terrifying; rather, a calm comfort hung on the surprisingly cool wisps of air that swept through the chamber. Makeda watched her dream-self move toward the back of the cave. Her surroundings seemed familiar. Her hand reached up and touched the rough stones of the back wall. She pushed, and the wall gave way. Suddenly a crack of warm sunlight broke the veiled darkness. The wall opened as a door.

She walked out into a bright lush garden. As her sleep mind adjusted to the light, her dream-watcher self was stunned and enticed deeper into this world. Guided by the sound of a waterfall, she passed flowers, trees, foliage, and grass teeming with vivid life. Chirping birds and other creatures' voices decorated the air. Finding the waterfall, Makeda sat on the baby-soft grass and slipped her bare feet into the dancing waters. Soon she was swimming nude. Renewed like a child, she played. Sheeting waters from the falls trumpeted her head and body and drummed away all other sounds.

Then, when Makeda was finally spent, a light gauzy garment appeared in her hand, and she immediately wrapped it about her. Then, instantly dry, she sat on a boulder. She turned and saw a lion watching her: a male lion. With her glance, Makeda stroked his strong legs and muscular back and engaged his searching eyes as he walked toward her. She bent over to receive him, and the mane brushed against her cheek as he came to stand close beside her. Into her ear his hot lion breath whispered, "Makeda, do you recognize me?"

She did not move, but she quietly responded, "Yes."

"Then come with me."

She stood, and together they walked side by side in silence. Suddenly she found herself at the base of a huge mountain. The lion was gone. Time shifted. Now it appeared to be shortly after sunset. It was hard to tell, because of the light from a huge fire atop the mountain. It was as if there was a blazing forge. The mountains spewed smoke, sparks, and ash, while the throng of people below conducted their affairs with the haste and precision of preparation for honored guests. A woman handed her a pitcher, and Makeda joined in by drawing water from a nearby well.

Makeda did not ask questions, but somehow she knew that their preparation and patience would be rewarded. Deep into the night of her dream, a thundering aroused her in time to see a burnished man with thick wild white hair and a glowing countenance bearing etched tablets of luminous stone. At the foot of Mount Sinai, she stood in awe with all the children of Israel—past, present, and future—to receive the commanded law and testimony of God.

Chapter 20

Makeda the Witness

So it was that Queen Makeda learned the ways of Zion. This day she spent in the Hall of Justice observing. She sat behind King Solomon's throne, shielded from view by a lattice partition. She was able to see through the laced wood and hear the issues that concerned the House of Israel. She paid close attention to the interactions between the people and their king as they petitioned him for relief. King Solomon listened to each subject with focused attention and care. Nothing was rushed.

She observed again and again how the initial tremors of a liege humbly standing before his king gave way, first, to the innocent posture of a child imploring a loving father, then to the quiet vulnerability of one speaking in confidence with a friend. Finally, it seemed as if a stronger sinew, one that erects the spine and establishes the head, was infused into them by the wisdom and utter kindness of King Solomon.

Through the long procession of petitioners, Makeda remained fully alert. She knew this was a precious opportunity to see how Wisdom itself would reign. In her observation, Makeda did not attend to every whit and detail of each case; rather, she stood witness to the state and the movement of the spirit of the interaction. There was always a calling out and a calling forth of the soul from each person. Solomon's abiding presence with God, through the power of his word, gave life.

Makeda recalled being a small girl in the throne room of her grandmother, and later her mother. Both queens were considered highly gifted in the art and strategy of rulership and judgment. But, even from the beginning, Makeda's natural inclination was to follow the tones and textures of the audiences and to notice, but not belabor, the content of the requests that she, as a child, could not comprehend.

What she was attuned to, even back then, was a subtle, almost imperceptible, sound seeping from the petitioners— coarse, discordant, wanton bass tones—that would invariably blend with the cool delicate turquoise melody of the wisdom of the throne of the candace. This wisdom judged, healed, and restored with music. Not music in the instrumental sense, but elemental, unsung harmony that caresses, sorts, balances, forgives, and redeems. It is the sound that emanates from the cultured heart of the queen. The state of Ethiopia had always resided in the heart of the queen. Makeda recalled her mother's words: "We, the queens of Ethiopia, must be virgins when we ascend to the throne. Even afterward, when we are married with children, we retain our virginity because it is sheltered in the cloister of the sacred spirit. We do not belong to our husbands; we do not belong even to ourselves. We are hailed and halted only by the will of our gods, who execute the destiny of our people and our land through us."

So too on this day in Jerusalem, Queen Makeda watched and attended. Later, as the afternoon wore on, she closed her eyes and listened to King Solomon conduct the affairs of state. But the pure sound above the fray that she listened for was not there. Gradually she realized that his way of governance was not accessible by means of the subtle harmonies of the lineage of the candace. It was a new way, a way not of sound. *What is it, then?* she thought. She sensed the Presence that Restores, yet she wondered, if not as sound, what other form was it taking? She leaned forward and peered intently into the room. She listened and watched for any subtle indications. Finally, above the head of King Solomon, she saw the faint glow of a spiraling radiance. Particles of dust? Or perhaps the light. As soon as she acknowledged it, the light clarified and sent ambient rays in her direction. Once the veil was removed, her eyes could now see that he, King Solomon himself, was a vessel of the brilliance.

Makeda felt warmth in her belly. When she glanced down, it was as if a light glowed there. So it was here, behind the fragrant sandalwood lattice screen, where she conceived with the spirit of Solomon, a son. She gently stroked her stomach and the ethereal child inside, who would soon be consummated in the flesh.

In this same instant, she knew that a mantle had been passed. After her, Ethiopia would no longer be ruled by queens and the harmonious chorus of their pantheon of ancestral gods but would, by the confirmation of her witness, be ruled first by their son and, following him, a reign of kings under the direct tutelage of the Light: the One.

The world would remark that Ethiopia, once ruled by mighty queens, had conceded its reign to a lineage of great kings to come. But Makeda knew that the move from candace to *negus* (king) was just the form. Really, it was the turn of the flow of destiny from the undulating sounds of the earth to the very fount of the sun. She closed her eyes to ingest the vision through her breathing.

When she finally looked back into the hall, she saw the Great Light streaming down upon the crown of King Solomon's head as he sat upon his throne. Then the heavenly beam passed through the prism of his mind and, with perpendicular angulation, through his eyes, and it arrayed itself as a rainbow, a covenant, anointing the entire House of Judah.

Time passed as Makeda sat in silent awe. Solomon soon appeared behind the screen and inquired, "Are you all right, Queen Makeda?"

"Yes, Your Majesty," she replied softly.

"Good, then. I thought I might have wearied you this long afternoon." He smiled and extended his arm. "Come walk with me, that I may receive your myriad of questions from the day."

A strange look in Makeda's eyes caught him. She held his gaze but did not smile. She finally spoke: "I have no questions today." She took his arm and rose.

Chapter 21

∞≈∞

The Trail of an Angel

After Queen Makeda informed King Solomon that it was time to begin the preparations for her departure, he apprised her that he had ordered a grand feast in her honor. The months of planning had already begun for hosting the ten thousand great men and households of Israel and Judah as well as the kings and rulers of neighboring lands at this grand feast. King Solomon intended that no one of renown would miss the opportunity to behold the majesty of the Queen of Sheba in his company and at his side.

As the time of the feast drew near, the ministrations to the queen intensified, including several days of purification and salt scrubs at the sea until her body gleamed. Her hair was washed multiple times in herbs and spices, as was prescribed by tradition. Then it was oiled, scented, and wrapped and then meticulously arranged and trimmed with gold. She was massaged with precious oils while fragrant incense clouded the steamy chamber. She ate only fresh fruits and vegetables. After feasting on ambrosia, dates, honey, and nuts, their clean sweetness echoed from her breath and pores.

Days before the affair, Queen Makeda spent an evening in a henna circle, where five women decorated her toes, feet, hands, and neck with tattoos. The reddish latticework was intricate but so subtle that it would only be visible to the close eye, the lover's gaze. Lost in the details of their own artistry, the women, unbidden, infused wedding-night designs in their work. No one spoke of this, not even the queen when she viewed the finished canvas of her body. She smiled to herself as possibility perfumed her thoughts that soon the reign of the *virgin* queens of Ethiopia might come to an end. And should this possibly become so, she prepared herself soul, mind, and body for a man—her man, her king, her husband. Solomon.

The night of the grand feast arrived, and Queen Makeda sat for the hours of adornment by her chief dresser, Penayah.

"Majesty, this gift from the king has not yet been opened. Shall I present it?"

The queen nodded. Penayah opened the small box and displayed it before her. Makeda peered in and saw what appeared to be a tiny hill of gold, lying in the center of a purple silk cloth. *What is this?* she wondered as she lifted the item from the box with the tip of her index finger. The gold did not come out in a cluster, but rather was draped over her thin fingers.

"What is this?" she said aloud. She held it out to Penayah.

Gently, Penayah extended both hands and received the article across the tips of her spread fingers. Makeda could see that the gold had been spun into the finest thread, then woven into the most delicate and intricate of patterns. When Penayah held it out fully, she could see clearly that it was a gossamer golden web.

"What is to be done with it? Does he wish it for my hair?" Makeda asked, and her dresser continued to study its length and breadth.

Then finally she responded. "Majesty, I think it is to be worn on your body. See the shape? Allow me to place it."

Makeda consented by erecting her body for adornment. Penayah then wrapped the narrow center of the golden web around the full length of her neck and then allowed it to drape down each arm to midway down the hands. From the fit against the neck, the web spread across the entire span of her bosom in the front and just beyond her shoulder blades behind. There were no claps or connections. The finely spun gold simply clung to the contours and moisture of her bronze skin, like warm honey. Once in place, the gold seemed to be absorbed into the surface of her skin. Makeda extended her left arm in the candlelight and delighted at the magic the golden ornament made of her flesh.

"Penayah, this appears to be an undergarment. Bring my gown." The queen chuckled with her maid as she dressed. The sight of herself in the glass, fully arrayed in royal purple and blue silk, took her aback when she saw the effect of the nearly invisible gold. It made her skin shimmer with a cast of reflected alabaster iridescence from her gown. The golden overlay seemed to broadcast, in the subtlest manner an exaggeration can manage, the simple rise of her bosom with each breath and slightest movement.

"Bewitching," Makeda whispered to her own reflection. *What magician, demon?* she thought. *No, I must meet the angel who has wrought such perfection. What manner of man is this king to provide a woman with this compelling charm and then command her to his presence? For what sake have you provided me this handsome new skin?* She smiled as the genuine innocence of her virginal body conceded to the new movement of the unaffected, subtle nuance and sway of a woman under the direct personal press of masculine intent. They stepped into the corridor to join her waiting entourage.

"Come, ladies; the king awaits."

Chapter 22

The Feast

The great hall was ablaze with candlelight that danced off the rich, dazzling colors of the jewels and costumes of the guests. The walls were decorated with tapestries and purple hangings. Beaded strands of emeralds, rubies, and other precious stones hung and sparkled from the columns and posts. Silver and brass tableware shone on the banquet tables. The head tableware was of polished gold. The room was filled with burning aromatic powders and incense mingled with the smell of roasted meats and highly spiced dishes. Queen Makeda sat with King Solomon at the high table watching their guests eat, drink, parade, and enjoy the festivities and entertainments. But it was the king and queen themselves who were the true focus of interest. They were a stunning couple. Although the people had heard of the Queen of Sheba, they wondered how is it that no one had ever remarked of the blue and purple iridescence of her brown skin.

They were the center of attention, yet the aloofness of the high table still afforded them a certain level of privacy. It was with effort that Solomon kept his focus on the festivities, for his eyes naturally drifted back to the alluring beauty of Makeda. Where most men would resist, he savored the pleasure of being bewitched. He lavished compliments on Makeda and ordered that her dish and cup be ever filled with spicy foods and pungent drinks.

She caught his eye on her and raised a delicate hand to her bosom and asked, "Solomon, where did you find this mysterious gold netting?"

"Do you like it?" he asked.

"But of course. It has a miraculous effect, but I think it may be too subtle to notice," she said teasingly.

"About as subtle as the proportion of your eyes to the rest of your features," he jested as he caught the laughing gaze of her large Ethiopic eyes. "It was my wife Hannah who fashioned it from the silk of golden-orb anansi from the Malagasy Isle," he proudly announced.

"These Malagasy spiders spin gold?"

"Yes. The strands are so delicate that it takes the binding of a score or more to make one thread."

"And how would you know that, Your Majesty?" she said with a smile at the king.

"I ask questions too, my dear. I was fascinated, so I asked Hannah to show me, and she revealed her workings." Solomon touched Makeda's wrist, and the web lightly lifted with his finger.

"Your wife Hannah is an extraordinary woman, for this was not wrought by human hands alone," Makeda concluded as she observed the shimmer on her arm.

"Hannah's father was the goldsmith—a shaman really—who wrought all the Temple gold, and her mother, although a lady of leisure, had an exquisitely fine hand for stitchery. So you see, it is in the blood."

"I would like to meet your Hannah," said Makeda.

"And so you shall. I will send her to you soon. You will enjoy her company." Solomon paused and rested his large hand over hers. "But this night belongs to us."

They laughed, talked, teased, and shared the popular riddles of the day. They welcomed others to their table for conversation and, in due course, came down to walk among the people. They even danced together for the first time.

The evening wore on, and Solomon noticed the subtlest slowing of Makeda's blink. "You grow weary?"

"Never weary of this splendor. Your Majesty, I thank you for this wonderful evening. You honor me greatly. One day I shall host you in Ethiopia, where I hope to set the evening even half as well as you have done here in Zion."

"Thank you, and you are welcomed. It is my pleasure to please you." At that he reached for her hand. "Tonight, Queen Makeda, I have one favor to ask of you."

"By all means," she replied, "ask of me anything. What is your will?"

He paused, looked out upon the grandeur of his hall, then turned to face her. "Tonight, Queen Makeda, stay with me in my chamber."

Makeda searched his eyes but did not speak. She raised a finger, and an attendant filled her goblet. Although she had signaled for water, she tasted wine. Considering her response, she slowly sipped the wine. "Please, take me for a walk," she said.

King Solomon rose and took her hand, and the two headed for the terrace. They promenaded in the cool night air out toward the border of the garden, walking and talking while the guards and the attendants kept their distance. The issue at hand was her maiden-hood and her stipulation that her virginity as an Ethiopian queen remain intact. Finally, she conceded with a bargain.

"Yes, I will accompany you tonight in your chamber, if you agree to not take me by force. Do I have your word?"

"You have my word that I will not take anything from you without your permission. But you must also swear to me that you will not take anything from me without my permission."

"I don't understand: What of your wealth would I have need of taking, in that I too am wealthy?" Makeda asked with a smile.

"A just bargain is sealed only when both sides make an oath," he replied.

"Very well then, I agree: you have my word that I will not take anything from you without your permission." Makeda agreed to the face value of his terms, not suspecting that he had another plan already in place that might sway things to his advantage.

Chapter 23

In the King's Chamber

Makeda awoke in the middle of the night with a parched throat. Finding no pitcher beside her bed, she slipped from the covers and stealthily moved through Solomon's chamber in search of water. She spied a gleaming bowl. *It must have water*, she thought as she made her way to it. Dry. She tiptoed lightly across the cold marble floor farther into the king's chamber.

Solomon lay sleeping upon his huge ebony bed of Ethiopian wood. Makeda passed her hand lightly over the carved foliage and flowers on the foot of the bed so as not to awaken him. Then she spied the golden decanter and goblet sparkling beside his bed. *Water.* She tried to coax moisture from her dehydrated tongue. Noiselessly, she lifted the pitcher and goblet from his bedside and tiptoed back across the room.

All this Solomon observed. For, although he appeared asleep, he was watching everything, undetected, through his thick eyelashes. He had perfected the masking of sleep—though he rarely slept for over three or four hours in a night. But tonight he had to exercise discipline. He wanted to laugh because this young queen, though graceful and quiet, was anything but stealthy. Not laugh—chuckle perhaps. He was aroused.

On her third goblet, Makeda finally felt satiation coating her throat and cooling her feverish head. *Am I becoming ill?* she wondered. She continued sipping and looking over the rim of the goblet at the sleeping king. He was just a hump of luxurious covers, rising and falling ever so slightly. She wondered why the servants, who had been so attentive, had failed to fill all the water vessels in the king's chambers. She was completely unaware that the king had himself ordered them to not fill them, except for the one beside his bed. Or that it was he who had made certain that her dishes at the feast were hot, salty, and spicy and that they served her wine and not water. He had a plan.

Noiselessly, she returned the pitcher and goblet to his bedside then paused to watch him sleep. He slept peacefully. His confident and animated mouth was at rest. The usual furrows between his thick brows were invisible. His burnished hooked nose rested on the pillow. She felt a tenderness toward him that had not surfaced in the presence of his bold carriage. She wanted to touch his beard. Was it soft or prickly? There, the curl at the nape of his neck—the same curl, she was certain, that had originally snagged her attention in the Temple months before. Now it begged to be caressed, and she desired to comply.

She had spent a great deal of time with the wise king—the beloved of God. Now she saw the man, vulnerable, handsome, and virile. Her breath caught in her throat and then proceeded softly but quickened. Makeda knew she needed to leave his bedside, with her thumping heart, scrambling mind, and now her limbs that had grown too heavy to move.

"What are you doing?" King Solomon asked.

"Your Majesty?" she responded, startled.

"What are you doing at my bedside?" His voice was low, deep, and even.

"I was merely drinking water. My throat was parched, and I was feeling feverish."

"Did you ask my permission?"

"For what? To have a drink of water?" Makeda asked incredulously.

Solomon sat upright on the side of the bed, fully awake and eyeing her.

"You have broken your word, my queen. You have taken something from me without my permission."

"But it was only water!"

"And what could be more precious than water?"

Makeda considered it for a moment but had to concede: "You are correct, of course." Then she thought to add, "But perhaps mercy, Your Majesty. Mercy may be more precious than water."

"Yes, mercy. Then I grant you mercy. You are released from your vow." He saw the relief in her eyes.

"Thank you." Makeda did not move.

"Now, will you also grant this humble king mercy and release me from my vow, as I have released you?" He looked into her eyes.

"It is done, then. You are released," she said, quickly agreeing.

"Very well. Thank you." Solomon sat quietly staring at her. "Please, sit here beside me." He patted the bed. She sat, still looking straight ahead. "Now, I am also released to touch you like this?" he whispered and stroked her left cheek. No answer. She felt a wave of heat on her face and neck. His touch was strong yet tender.

"Yes," she answered in suspended time.

"Am I released to stroke your hair like this?" He gently grasped a handful of her heavy luxuriant hair. He looked at her and waited for her response.

"Yes," she sighed. Then she looked him in the eyes and added, "Yes, and you are released from the requirement to ask further permission, if it pleases you."

"Does it also please you, Makeda, my queen?"

"Sir?" The heat was stifling; she could barely breathe.

He stroked her neck again "Do *I* please you?"

"Yes." She exhaled, closed her eyes, and relaxed against his hand.

"Come lay with me, Makeda."

She searched his large sleepy eyes and saw deep stillness and sparks of rising passion. She saw his full relaxed lips beneath his heavy mustache open slightly, revealing his white teeth. Almost a smile.

"I'm troubled, Solomon." She stood from the bed.

"Please. Speak your heart." He stood, joining her.

She gathered and adjusted her nightdress. Facing each other, their eyes became silent, soul-seeking orbs. Solomon felt a flash of fire shoot through his body; he braced himself. He touched the flesh of her arm, and they both felt blue fire flow through their veins. Their hearts and bodies began to merge in the fire's turbulent sea. Makeda fought to have her say. To be heard.

"I am a virgin queen. Ever since my mother's death, I have ruled alone with the counsel of my advisers. I have neither king nor consort. This protects the purity of my reign. I do not lay with men. I sleep alone." She waited.

"I understand very well what you are saying to me, though I cannot imagine the noble men of Ethiopia not succeeding in warming the heart of such a beautiful, wise, and completely enchanting queen. Were you not queen and merely woman—even then, all men would be devoted." He continued to stroke her arm as he spoke. "As for myself, I could get lost somewhere between your eyes and lips. Makeda, surely I would never impose myself on you." He felt her tremble beneath his hand, so he eased back and told a story.

"According to our faith, a man does not select his own wife. You see, before they were born, they were one—one masculine and feminine soul together. Then God called out for one to separate and to step into manifestation; then later He called the other. It is God's great desire and grace that they find each other and reunite on earth. Together they are better than the best of either alone." He noticed the slight parting of her lips. He took her hand and continued.

"When you first entered my palace and our eyes met, I knew you were my wife. You are my wife. Then, in the Temple, your spirit passed through me like a breeze, and you *were* me. I did not understand fully what that meant, but now I am confirmed. In the firmament before our time, we were one soul. I know now that when God called out my name into manifestation, he called me from you—from us." He pulled her into an embrace.

She folded into the confessional of his arms and said, "When Tamrin first uttered your name, even before he embellished it with tales of your wisdom and great deeds, my heart was already conditioned by God to recognize it. *Solomon.* Your name felt like meat in my mouth. King of Peace. I was compelled by God to come." Nestled against his bare chest, she closed her eyes against her tears. Solomon pulled her closer.

"Come," he said, and again they faced each other, holding both hands.

"Makeda," he said, "here, tonight, in my bedchamber, I recognize you as my wife. I declare before the Most High God that you are she. You are the beloved wife of my soul. Makeda, do you accept me as your husband?" He waited, and she felt his hand tremble.

"I have already accepted your God, and the wisdom of the path of worship that is pleasing in His sight. I have already accepted you as my king and my priest. What more could I ask of God but that my king and my priest be also sent as my husband? Yes. Yes. I am honored to accept you as my husband. Yes...yes." They drank heady kisses of prolonged passion's reward: "Yes... yes...yes..."

He brought her again to sit before they should fall. Makeda caught her breath in slow intake. "Wait. Wait, beloved," Makeda said and pulled her hand away. "I have something for you. A gift." She reached for a coiled lock of her hair and unraveled a cord of gold from which a jewel-encrusted ring fell into her hand. Solomon watched as Makeda handed him the ring. He received it. Makeda whispered, inaudibly but perfectly clear to his hearing, naming each set of stones and their significance. The blue stone for writing and numbering, the green stone for the equality of male and female, blood for the red stone, and the reflecting setting of gold symbolizing light.

"How can this be, that you have brought to me the order of the stones in this ring that perfectly coincides with the stones of divination on our breastplates?" He placed the ring on his finger to further solemnize their troth.

"I had anticipated your greatness, but I was not prepared for this revelation: the joy and glory that we will share as husband and wife." Smiles and tears overwhelmed her face.

"Yes, beloved, God has amply prepared you in every dimension." He gently held her aloft to view, keeping the other hand on his aching chest. "I am exploding, Makeda," he said with a laugh and fell back on the bed with her in his arms. She kissed his hairy chest. He held her close on top of him and stroked her body through the silk. She raised herself back to see his eyes and gave him a series of soft kisses.

"My wife, I am humbled by your beauty." He held her face and kissed her mouth fully and at length. "I can no longer contain my passion," he said in a rasp. Makeda managed to part from him and again stood beside the bed. He rolled over onto his elbow to watch her gown cascade to the floor. He groaned and opened his night robe. She slid in beside him and whispered hotly in his ear, "My husband, give me my wedding night."

Tonight, in the royal palace, on the same Temple Mount in Jerusalem where the Presence of God abided in the Ark, this mighty son of David, King Solomon of Israel, and this beautiful Makeda of Ethiopia, Queen of Sheba, consummated their marriage in flesh, fire, and infinity.

Chapter 24

The Radiant Women

King Solomon was right. In the weeks since Queen Makeda had met Hannah, the two had become close companions. This afternoon, while on one of their regular strolls around the palace grounds, when they paused in a cool shady enclave, Hannah nodded, and their attendant lifted the vines. Hannah led Makeda through the hidden mysterious garden gate into the domain of the women. Rare exotic plants posed, and birds strolled about at leisure decked out in the opulent fantasia of nature on full display: peacock, cockatoo, parrots, and every imaginable variety of orchid. The rich, fecund aromas of flowers mixed with wet earth, lush greenery, and heat enfolded the two women in a sensuous embrace.

"There is no luxury denied us. Look there." Hannah pointed to a lovely waterfall splashing into an emerald pool. Several beautiful nude women swam or lounged on the soft grassy knoll. Two servants attended each woman, providing fruits and drinks or brushing and braiding their hair. Makeda watched as a tall, tan, and muscular servant, wearing only a wisp of a cloth over his loins, kneeled beside an ebony beauty massaging her bare body with long and heavy oiled strokes. Some younger women engaged in playful banter. Their chiming laughter mingled with the calling birds and stirring waters. Tinkling finger cymbals and lutes beckoned in the distance.

"We're just in time to see Usha and Semkiyah perform. They're from India." Hannah took Makeda's hand, "Come, they're wonderful!"

The foliage gave way to a marble pavilion in the clearing. Banners of colorful flowing fabric flapped through the air as dozens of women took their seats on couches heaping with overstuffed cushions and pillows. Hugh palm fans ingeniously mounted on pulleys harnessed the shy breezes and directed them across the moist skin of the women. Hannah offered Queen Makeda a lush lavender silk-cushioned couch beside her own lounger. Immediately, their side tables were filled with pitchers of water, wine, and fresh juices and laden with bowls of fruit, nuts, dates, and sweet cakes. Makeda enjoyed her refreshment and carefully scanned this pavilion filled with King Solomon's women.

Moving in closer, Hannah said, "These are the king's concubines. These are the women whom my husband has taken because of his personal choice alone. Most have no families of importance or wealth to negotiate a marriage, as do most wives, but I find these women far more fascinating. Each possesses some rare gift. You'll see. My husband calls them the 'radiant women' and believes they are necessary to his personal well-being and the smooth functioning of the affairs of our land. They are prepared to dance. Watch closely."

Usha entered from the side of the pavilion in a flurry of movement and color. Long streamers of multicolored silk veils swirled rainbows about her as she raced and leaped and twirled amid them. Lithe and delicate, Usha seemed to disappear, leaving the scarves dancing with a life of their own. Hannah pointed out Semkiyah, who led a small band of women seated to the right of the stage playing drums, cymbals, and a whining stringed instrument. The air was scented with the myriad aromas of incense with which each scarf had been smoked. Usha erected the scarves to resemble the majestic mountain ranges above the northern sea at sunset when the light washes them in color. She swirled the blue scarves forth, and they became the gently rippling sea itself. Makeda detected trees, birds, flowers, and various sea and land creatures in Usha's multiple transformations of the scarves. As the tempo of the music mounted, the scarves became a whirlwind, whisking about the entire platform and coming so close as to tap the faces of the women with their hemlines, eliciting a chorus-in-the-round of shrieks and giggles.

After a while, the women began to stand or kneel upright on their cushions with arms extended. Hannah urged Makeda to rise. As Usha's whirlwind spun its ferocity from center stage, an orange scarf flew from its midst. The women in that direction squealed and competed to grab the scarf. The victor, a tall, large-boned beauty, flaunted it then draped it about her bangled arm as the others acknowledged her with ululations and laughter. Then, one by one or two or three at a time, the whirlwind released the scarves to the gleefully grasping women. Once secured, the scarves served as headpieces, face covers, shawls, belts, waist sashes, banners, and streamers as the women joined Usha and became a vibrant sea of dance, song, and laughter.

Makeda and Hannah stood side by side waving their arms and swaying in place. Makeda had looped a purple and a lime scarf around each wrist, while Hannah flung the fuchsia scarf around her neck and let it careen down her back.

Finally, the music stopped, and there stood Usha scarfless and radiant in the center of the pavilion. Her heavy luxuriant hair, steaming with perspiration, clung to her temples and fell to her waist. Her arm thrust upward then swept down to a low curtsy. She grinned at all the women as she breathed deeply to catch her breath. From their momentary preoccupation, perhaps a dozen women emerged center stage, each with a pitcher they could only partially conceal behind their ample hips. Knowingly, Usha began to slowly back up. But she was trapped. So she feigned acquiescence, covering her eyes and cowering, allowing the women to douse her with the cool scented water as ohhhhhs and ahhhhhs filled the air. Usha finally departed the pavilion drenched with water and the unrestrained approval and company of her sisters. The atmosphere finally calmed to jovial camaraderie. This pavilion was filled with enchantment, beauty, excitement, and harmony. This was not only the garden for Solomon's women; the women themselves were King Solomon's garden.

Makeda, Hannah, and the other women had settled into a pleasant hush when they heard a bustling in the area of the pool. Before the activity could gather everyone's attention, Gorfu, chief of the eunuchs scurried to the pavilion with a breathy announcement: "The king is in the garden!" Nothing traveled faster than a eunuch with news. All the attendants joined the women and prepared them for the king's visit.

Within minutes, the pavilion was transformed with the augmentation of furnishings for the king. Queen Makeda, Hannah, and the other women stood as King Solomon approached the steps beaming at his bouquet of beauties. Hannah slipped immediately to his side, encircling his arm with hers and escorting him onto the platform. Solomon turned his attention to her and noted how her wide-toothed smile still elicited joy in his heart. Although she had been his wife for several years now, that smile threw him back to earlier times when she and Yehudit were his wild and favorite daughters. Though it was muted with time, he still felt an old pang for his daughter's hurt and anger at his marriage to Hannah. Since Yehudit's own marriage, she had remained kind and respectful— yet also estranged. They had tried everything to dissuade Hannah, providing the most worthy and noble suitors, sending her abroad, and fervently praying; some of his wives resorted to secret potions. All to no avail. *But here we are*, he thought. He smiled.

"Come, Slomo," Hannah said, using his familial name. "Queen Makeda has joined us. Usha performed her veil dance."

Solomon turned to Makeda as soon as he reached the landing. She caught his eye, smiled, and gently nodded her respect. The king extended a hand, indicating her to be seated on the purple sofa, where he eagerly joined her.

Their refreshments magically appeared courtesy of the immaculately trained staff of Moshe, chief of tables and protocol. Moshe observed his staff moving with elegant efficiency. He flashed back to his favorite words to new apprentices: "It is the highest honor and greatest responsibility to serve the royal house. You have been chosen because of your sensitivity and grace. To fully attend, you must anticipate their needs and move silently to fulfill them. Everything you witness is to be kept within the discretion of your vow, except that which you share with me. And I expect full reports. You are to be absent in your presence and constant in your availability."

It was also true that the men and women who served the royal house must themselves be beautiful. Part of the vast lore attached to the House of King Solomon was that never had there been such beauty gathered under one roof. In those days, it was believed that beyond the pleasant look, beauty could bring the beholder closer to the angels. The people held that the aroma of a beautiful woman could lift one into a state of grace. So traditionally, the most beautiful woman of a village would accompany the priest to the bedside of the dying. The angels would be drawn to both of them and thereby be at hand to receive the deceased kin.

"Queen Makeda, have you enjoyed the garden?" Solomon inquired.

"I am fascinated by everything here. You have created a paradise on earth."

"I am pleased that you like it."

"I joined in the dance of the veils. Usha is extraordinary." Makeda's eyes still flashed with the excitement of her pleasure and exertion.

"Usha's father was a renowned holy man," Hannah added from over the right shoulder of the king, "and her mother came from a lineage of India's skilled temple dancers."

Queen Makeda lifted her brow briefly in acknowledgment. Solomon watched as Makeda's slender fingers encircled the stem of the goblet and caught a glimpse of her full lips as they parted slightly to receive the drink. The smell of her skin wafted to his nostrils, like a book of sweet remembrances.

He extended his gaze to his other flowers gathered on the pavilion as each in her own way vied for his attention. Even among their lovely faces, his mind was drawn back to Makeda. *Has my seed taken hold?* he wondered. *Is my son now being nourished by her ancient blood and royal flesh?* His mind had already begun selecting the traveling party for the journey to Axum to visit this new wife and son in Ethiopia.

Despite his Makeda-centered considerations, Solomon stayed engaged in conversation with the other women. He spoke in quiet tones. An aura of fondness and intimacy permeated the pavilion. Throughout the kingdom, everyone held each of these women in high esteem, believing them to be vessels of sanctity for the royal seed, believing they had become members of the royal household by way of intimacy.

The truth was that, over their lifetimes, many of his women would only experience one night alone with him, some none. King Solomon was their lover in the sense that it was he who provided them with every accommodation. The legacy they each shared in the aftermath of the king's direct personal intervention was to be elevated to a realm of joy and the renewing grace of perpetual ecstasy. Each of these radiant women had been predestined and prepared by God to be brought into this royal household to submit her gifts to His anointed king-priest, Solomon the Lion, and to the entire House of Judah. They were a sorority who astounded many because of their affection and care one for the other, but more so because of the complete absence of jealousy and competition that usually accompanied plural relationships. For each woman had heeded the call of her God—beckoned through King Solomon—so each was covered by a covenant of grace and dwelled in a state of perpetual bliss. In the closest circles, this place was justly called the Garden of God's Graces.

"Have you been shown the garden?" Solomon inquired.

"Not to any extent," Makeda replied. "We came directly to the pavilion for the dance."

"Very well, then," Solomon said. He extended Makeda his hand and added, "Please allow me the honor of showing you."

Makeda accepted his hand, and they rose. "I would be delighted."

She joined him, and they walked down from the pavilion. Solomon turned to Hannah, who was walking on his right, and said, "Please excuse us, Hannah." Solomon touched her shoulder with a staying hand. But without the usual override of his passionate intent, he actually saw the hurt of a daughter in her eyes. In an instant, wisdom revealed his full hand in the matter of Hannah, his daughter/wife, and his heart flinched insight: the two-edged sword of the spirit of violation had already pierced a jagged edge in his soul. Hannah stopped and nodded an injured smile of concession.

Her place of special privileges with Solomon had come naturally. Because she was once held to be a favored daughter, she had been privy to his most unguarded self, along with the genuine trust and acceptance that such a father-daughter bond afforded. She knew him better than any of his women or wives. So, at his staying hand, Hannah's heart tore as if she were a young daughter realizing for the first time that she was forbidden to grow up to marry Father. For her, this was exacerbated by the deep pang in her womb of a woman who had not heeded the wisdom of that admonition. Though he was not her father by birth, she suddenly felt stifled by the claustrophobic shadow of incest. Hannah continued to watch Solomon walking away with Makeda and witnessed a soft amber cloud descend and encircle them, joining the two as one and obscuring her view. He had finally left her, as all fathers must, alone—her next sigh, a humble freedom.

Arm in arm, Solomon and Makeda strolled at leisure in the garden, cooled by the foliage and the flowing waters. He pointed out rare flowers and birds, and she thrilled like a girl in wonderland.

"Tell me, Solomon, where did you find such women as these?"

"They come from all over the kingdom, all over the world."

"Hannah said they each have a special gift and that you call them the radiant women. Please tell me about this."

"Yes. To please you, yes." Solomon stared out as he scanned his memory. "It began years ago, earlier in my reign. I was visiting a southern province one afternoon. I was seated before a huge gathering, and when I looked out over my people, I saw a glint, a spark of light, bright enough to rival the sun. It hovered in one spot. And just as I saw the light, the Archangel Gabriel appeared at my side and whispered into my hearing, 'And the Lord said, *Every time you see a woman who glows like this, you will bring her into your House.*' Then he was gone. I had my men bring me the woman.

"I invited her into my house, and she came. She was just the beginning. We found she had a talent for singing that brought profound peace and joy. Her voice could even placate a wild beast hungry for meat. After her, on rare occasions I would see a woman here or there. She would glow, and I would know to invite her in." Solomon paused in reflection.

"Could others see their radiance?" Makeda asked.

"I do not believe so. But once they were brought in, over time, the household developed a protocol for refining them. Some of the women knew their gift, while others did not, so they sent many gifted people to help identify the gift. They are indeed radiant women. They are much more than subjects. They have brought to our kingdom gifts of song, poetry, music, dance, healing, prophesy, balance, numinous beauty, and magical presence."

"Did you discover why you were told to bring them into your house?"

"I brought them simply because the Lord bid me do so. The Lord need not explain Himself. I can see by the outcomes what manifests when I obey. We have had peace in our realm, and I believe it is in no small part due to the presence of these women in my house."

"How symmetrical is the way of the Lord," Makeda said.

"Well said, my wife. The Symmetry of God. I love it!" Solomon let out a robust laugh and placed his arm around her shoulder, and they continued their stroll through paradise.

Essiebea Hayes 1971 Miss Watts

Receiving the Royal Bracelet

Emperor Haile Selassie holding hand of Essiebea
Hayes, Miss Watts, Jubilee Palace 1972

Ethiopian Royal Family

Chapter 25

Come with Me

Ethiopia, 1972

After weeks of touring four other African countries as VIPs, the sophisticated independence of the two young women started to wane a bit when no one was there to meet them at the airport on their return fight to Addis Ababa. They found their own way to the baggage claim and spotted their heavy bags but not one porter on duty to help. Other than passengers, the airport looked empty. Then, a distinguished-looking middle-aged man in a crisp military uniform approached them.

"Good morning, ladies, may I be of assistance to you?" he asked with a flawless smile.

"Good morning," Brenna replied. "Yes, please, we need help with our bags."

"Please point out your luggage." He walked toward the baggage conveyor, placed their luggage on the floor, and called for another soldier to assist. He returned to the ladies and gave a short bow. "Excuse my manners; let me introduce myself. I am Colonel Getechew." He extended his hand, and in turn they introduced themselves. "May I be of further service?" he inquired. Brenna was surprised, because she had assumed that Prince John had sent him to pick them up from the airport. Bessie, who had departed for America from Ghana, had told them she would place calls home to their parents as well as to Ethiopia confirming their new delayed arrival times. She apparently had not done so.

"Oh," Brenna replied, "we thought His Highness had sent you to pick us up."

"Who?" he asked.

"We are friends of Prince Yohannes. He's expecting us. Would it be possible for you to phone the palace for us?"

"No. I cannot just phone the palace."

"Oh," Brenna responded. "Well, maybe you can assist us through customs and help us get a taxi to the hotel?"

"Yes, I will assist you through customs, but the cabs are probably not running. Everything is closed. It is Easter weekend."

"But Easter has already passed."

"In Ethiopia we go by the Orthodox calendar, so our Easter occurs later than yours. By the way, at which hotel are you staying?"

"Well, when we were here before, we stayed at the Hilton," she said and looked at Maya, who nodded, "so we'll be staying at the Hilton again."

"By all means, I can give you a ride in my car, if it is OK with you?"

The girls looked at each other, and then Maya said, "Thank you, we'd appreciate that very much." With his assistance, they moved quickly through customs, chatting along the way.

"Excuse me," Brenna said, "is there a place in the airport where we could cash traveler's checks?"

"There are several places, but they too are closed for the holiday."

"Is anywhere open today? We need to get some local money."

Seeing the concerned look that crossed her face, he added, "Please allow me to take you to the Hilton for a little breakfast first. There, we can sort this out."

They agreed and hoped they were doing the right thing as they climbed into the back seat of his car. He joined the driver up front. They were relieved when they finally saw the familiar Hilton Hotel sign in the distance.

The driver dropped them off, and the three proceeded to the Hotel café. Although they were still concerned about their diminished funds, he insisted they order a hearty breakfast. The colonel was handsome, friendly, and very pleasant company.

"More coffee?" Brenna asked, and she reached for the pot when he nodded. When she lifted it to pour, the loose sleeve of her blouse fell down her arm, and the bracelet that the emperor had given her became exposed on her forearm. She poured his coffee and returned the pot to the table."

"Excuse me, may I see that, please?" he asked, indicating the bracelet and extending his hand to hold her wrist. He turned it around and saw the seal. He started, then immediately rose from the table.

"Pardon me, ladies. This is the royal seal. I did not know." He stood and bowed deeply to her and became very officious. "I will go make your accommodations immediately and I will arrange your call to the palace." He bowed again and abruptly left.

Speechless, the two ladies looked at each other, then smiled and shrugged, grateful that they would now have a hotel room.

Brenna turned the bracelet and stared at the royal seal. She knew the gift had been beautiful, but now she was discovering its significance. She dabbed her napkin to her lips, then placed it back on her lap. With that gesture, the sleeve of her garment covered her bracelet again.

Maya raised her brow and said, "Do you think you could roll up that sleeve?" They both tossed back their heads with laughter, and Brenna neatly peeled back her sleeves.

⁂

They settled into their hotel suite and relaxed while Brenna awaited a call. Suddenly there was an urgent rapping on the door. She opened the door, and there stood Prince John.

"I thought you weren't coming back," he said, reaching for an embrace. "I thought you went back to America." They hugged and kissed, then walked inside.

"Didn't you get my message from Bessie?" Brenna asked. "She was supposed to call and let you know that we'd be weeks late and give you our new flight information. We were surprised that you didn't have a car at the airport this morning. Thank God for Colonel Getechew."

"No, she did not. Well, anyway, you're here now. That's what matters. Come with me; I have people I want you to see."

"Thank God for the bracelet. Hi, Prince John!" Maya called from the open bedroom door.

"Oh hi, Maya, I thought you two got lost. Welcome back," he said. "I'm going to borrow your friend for a few hours. My secretary, Rhonda Sisay, will be calling soon to take you to lunch. A few people would like to meet you."

"OK, great. Have fun!" Maya said. She smiled back and waved.

"We'll do our best. Ciao." He gently closed the bedroom door, giving Brenna and him some privacy in the living room. When he turned around, she was already walking into his arms and kisses. When the kissing slipped into second gear, he pulled back and looked at her.

"Let's go before I change our destination," he said. She nodded, grabbed her jacket, and dropped her room key into her purse.

"What bracelet was she referring to?" Prince John asked as he started his car.

"You know, this one. The one your grandfather gave me." She held out the dangling bracelet on her wrist. He reached over and turned it around. "OK, now I see. I knew he'd given you the bracelet, but I didn't know that it had the seal."

"Yes, it has a seal. What does it say? What does it mean?"

Prince John continued holding her slender wrist, eyeing the seal. "Well, I think the old man liked you," he said with a grin, "and that's all I'm saying."

"I guess that's all I'm getting, then."

"Oh, I assure you, not *all*." Looking in her eyes, he lifted her hand and kissed it.

"Well, I liked him too. What about you? Do you like me too?" she said teasingly.

"I ain't saying nothin'," he said, shifting to Black English. "I take the fifth." He laughed and pulled away from the curb. In a short while, they were pulling into the driveway of another palace.

They found the prince's aunt Sophia just finishing lunch, so they joined her for coffee. Clearly his aunt adored Yohannes and enjoyed seeing him excited about this young woman—although, Sophia cautioned herself, she had seen him excited a few times before. Still she hoped that this relationship promised some stability and perhaps even family in his life. It certainly didn't hurt that her father had encouraged it.

The two enjoyed sandwiches and sodas as they chatted with his aunt. Brenna knew he was saying more than he was translating, since he kept the older woman laughing. After a while he turned to Brehenna.

"Brehenna," Prince Yohannes said, "do you know what the Pythagorean Theorem is?"

"What do you mean," she asked, "like in math?" She paused a second. "Is it A squared plus B squared equals C squared?"

"See, Aunt, I told you she was smart!" Then he turned back to Brenna. "I knew you'd get it right."

"Yohannes, you need not put the girl on the spot," Aunt Sophia said with a laugh.

"I can't believe you're giving me a math quiz!" Brenna said with a laugh, feeling relieved and pleased that she had actually gotten it right. They spent an hour or so with Aunt Sophia, who was funny and adventurous in her own right. She invited them back to dinner later in the week.

The next stop was his cousin and best friend, Peter Maskel. He and Yohannes had been childhood friends and had also recently returned from attending UC Santa Barbara together, where he kept

John out of getting into too much trouble and still managed to earn his own degree in math.

That evening, when they walked in on a poker game, all the young men rose from their seats as they entered and gave a generous bow to Prince Yohannes, then to her. He readily joined their game, which proceeded to go on well into the night. Brehenna sat near John, glancing at his hand but really enjoying how the guys played with one another. Even though they spoke primarily in Amharic, she knew bluffing in any language.

Yohannes leaned over to secretly reveal his hand to her. Although it meant little, she knew that a hand composed of all face cards must be a good thing. She could smell his hair pomade as he leaned close. He sat back upright, but his right hand rested on her thigh. Through the fabric of the skirt, he could feel the heat and firmness of her long dancer's muscles. From time to time, Brehenna got up to sit with the other young ladies, or to get a drink, or to go to the bathroom—but mainly she liked being near him. With his attention on the game, she could sit back and study him without notice: his profile; the way his mustache and the corners of his mouth were always poised to smile or laugh; his neat, curly hairline; the flutter of his thick lashes as he sized up his opponents and visited his own hand. His hands handling the cards, handling her; she slipped so easily into fantasy.

Suddenly the room was too hot, so she walked out on the balcony and viewed Addis at night. It could not compete with the alluringly garish glitter of LA, but it smelled and felt like home. She had asked herself many times why this place on the other side of the world seemed so familiar to her. She looked back at the people in the room and wondered how they could look so much like family.

Just then she saw Yohannes turn around and, finding her, eagerly beckon her back to his side. Once seated, he showed her his hand again, which to her untutored eye did not seem impressive, but she nodded and smiled. Then she noticed the pot of money on the table. She had never seen that much money in cash outside of a bank, and all this money was up for play. Despite the palaces, hotels, cars, and all the trappings of wealth, it was at this moment when Brenna realized that Yohannes had lots of money. *Prince Yohannes has too many attractions*, she thought with a sigh as she surrendered to the magnetism. She had never created a profile of her dream man. That was a good thing, because she would not have dared to conjure a Prince John. Yohannes—yes, she preferred his real name.

She watched the game for a while longer then leaned over and whispered in his ear, "May we go home soon?"

He quickly played out his cards, won, then reached across the table to collect his winnings. As they walked out, he put his arm around her waist and kissed her cheek. "See, you bring me good luck. I think I'd better keep you around." They drove home to Diana Ross singing "Stoned Love." The remainder of the evening's conversation was not in words.

Chapter 26

A Prince Should Know

The weeks passed quickly, with their affection for each other growing stronger. One afternoon, Prince John invited Brenna and Maya for lunch. He was in great form: happy, joking, teasing, and charming. After coffee, he rose from his seat and buttoned his jacket. "Well, lovely ladies, I must get back to business. But I've made special plans for the evening. Can you both be ready by nine?"

That evening, the two young ladies were excited as they dressed, chatting as comfortably as sisters. Maya smiled and moved in to share the vanity mirror with Brenna, who gave her space. "So how does it feel to date a prince?" Maya asked, eyeing the younger woman's reflection. Then she added, "It's kinda like a fairy tale, you know."

"Yeah, I guess so. I just like him," Brenna said and smiled back.

"I think he really likes you too," Maya said. She fluffed out her big natural.

"Really? You really think so?" Brenna asked while applying her lipstick.

"I'm pretty sure. The man sees you every day, lucky lady. It's not every girl who gets to have a prince and a duke." Maya put her hand on her hip to punctuate her certainty.

"Well, I won't say that I *have* him, yet, but we're sure having fun."

"How much longer do you think we'll be staying in Ethiopia?" Maya asked.

"I don't know; I figure we deserve a little vacation after that grueling trip. Don't you?" Brenna asked.

"Oh, I think you're falling in love and don't want to leave," Maya said teasingly.

"You should know. I remember you and Ted in Tanzania. Miss 'I'm So in Love' you didn't leave. Dr. Mungai had to send a special plane for you from Kenya."

"OK, OK. Well, he was fine. Wasn't he?" She looked all dreamy eyed in the mirror.

"I just hope I'm not falling in love with someone who lives on the other side of the world from me," Brenna said, half-lamenting.

"Don't worry about it. He's also rich, so what's a plane ticket to him? When he wants to see a woman, you can bet he'll send for her." Maya finished her makeup and fluttered her lashes at Brenna. "So, how do I look for our special night out?"

"Great as usual," Brenna said.

"Brenna, I hope you don't mind me joining you two."

"Of course not; besides, he invited us both out tonight. We'll have fun."

"Step back, let me see you," Maya said. Brenna did an exaggerated runway strut-and-turn around the suite.

"So, do you think he'll like it?" Brenna asked, feigning coyness.

"Girl, you know you're beautiful, and that outfit is a killer," Maya said in concession. Then she added, "You know there's nothing worse than a pretty girl begging for compliments."

"Yes, there is—two of them!" They burst into laughter.

The phone rang. Brenna answered. It was Prince John. Something had changed; she could tell by his subdued tone.

"Hey. I'll be by to pick *you* up in half an hour. Will you be ready?"

Brenna noticed what she suspected was an exclusive emphasis on *you*, but she replied, "Yes." Then she added, "We'll be ready. We're both ready now."

She hoped he understood that she did not want to be the one to disappoint Maya after he had so clearly invited her for the evening as well. Prince John was silent on the other end of the phone, and then he closed with, "Well, OK then. I'll come up with something. I'll be there soon."

Brenna did not like the awkwardness of the situation, but he was, after all, a prince; he should know what to do. He did. After he picked them up, they went for a drive around the city. They stopped at the Wabe Shebele bar for drinks with a few of his handsome friends. Brenna kept wondering what the "special plans" would be. It was already after eleven. Finally, John stubbed his cigarette butt in the ashtray and looked at her.

"Let's go," he said, and everyone at the table politely rose with them. Someone brought the ladies' wraps, and off they went. It seemed they were just circling about town for a while, and then they pulled through the gates of his palace. Brenna thought that the driving had been a diversion, perhaps buying time for a surprise party—maybe that was the special plans he had mentioned. They entered the foyer and surrendered their shawls but kept their clutches.

Brenna turned to John and said, "Would you excuse me? I need to go to the bathroom." He nodded.

As Brenna walked down the hallway to the right, she heard John say, "Maya, come over here. I want to show you something."

Brenna scanned herself in the large bathroom mirror and took out her compact, ran the puff over the shine on her face, and reapplied her lipstick. Her eyes looked tired, so she popped a couple of drops of Visine in each eye. She adjusted the turquoise wrap on her head and turned in the mirror as she smoothed her hands over her matching dress.

When she returned, John and Maya were talking and admiring some paintings. Together, they walked up to the second floor, where two servants opened the doors to the ballroom. Brenna prepared to smile and make a casual entrance into the surprise. She was surprised because no one else was there. It was just Prince John, herself, and Maya. The lights were on, but the ballroom was empty. Prince John told the servants to prepare drinks, then walked over to the stereo and selected a few records. Brenna settled into the loveseat. Maya took one of two upholstered winged chairs across from her, and Prince John took the other. The R&B beckoned in the background.

"We went shopping at the *merkado* today," Maya said to Prince John.

"Did you find anything you liked?" he asked.

"Yes. I bought some of the silver crosses."

"What kind of crosses did you get?" He leaned toward her.

"I don't know." She raised her brows and fluttered her lashes.

"What does it look like? Describe the shape," he said encouragingly.

"It's kind of round at the top," she said, demonstrating with animated hands. "Then it has little spiky things sticking out." She grinned and giggled.

"Spiky things"? Maya was a UCLA PhD student, so Brenna wondered why she was trying to sound dumb. She recalled Maya asking the merchant and labeling each distinct cross. If she wasn't mistaken, she remembered the "spiky one" was called something like "lala bela."

"Oh, that's a Lalibela cross," John said. *See.* "It's from an area in the north where churches are carved into the ground. King Lalibela had a vision or a dream in which an angel told him to build these underground churches. So he built twelve connecting churches. They're hundreds of years old and still standing. In fact, they're still fully functional churches."

"Your Highness, that's impressive," Maya said in a chiming voice. "I'd like to visit them."

"So would I," Brenna said, wedging herself back into the conversation. She implored in familiar tones, "Yohannes, do you think we have time for a trip to the north?"

He turned to her smile and said, "Let me see what I can do." Then he rose and walked to the bar. "Can I get you ladies anything?"

They both requested fresh drinks.

For a while they sat sipping, and he sat smoking, while they listened to the music. Brenna still wondered about the special plans he had mentioned earlier. Finally the prince spoke. "I know what I'm going to do tonight," he said. He paused and looked at Brenna with a half smile on his face and a slight squint of his nostril. "I'm going to dance with you," he said to Brenna. Then he turned to Maya and added, "Then I'm going to dance with you. Then back to you, then you!" He grinned with both eyebrows raised. Brenna's eyes snapped toward Maya with a quick shake of her head. But Maya was already busy removing her high-heeled boots, probably to bring her down to John's height. John looked over and gave a little laugh. When he looked back to Brenna, she flashed him a sweetish smile and set her drink down.

"Well, why don't you just dance with Maya, then? I'm a little tired." She added, "I think I'll just go lie down for a while." She stood waiting for John's objection that did not come. Instead, he stood and nodded toward her, approving her exit, and with a sweep of his hand, he motioned for Maya to join him on the dance floor. Before Brenna reached the door, she turned around to see the two of them smiling at each other while dancing the skate. She felt betrayed by them both. She was mad, but she couldn't justify turning around. She was not good at being the jealous, spiteful woman, nor did she believe in being put in a position to have to fight for a man, so she left the room. She didn't like it one bit. But what could she do? She didn't know what to do, so she walked to his bedroom and lay across the bed. Her intention was to think through this situation and weigh her options, but instead she fell asleep.

Later, lying across the prince's bed half-awake, she heard the enticing voice of Aretha Franklin singing "Make It with You." It was a new song, and she liked it, so she snoozed and enjoyed it. It played over and over so many times she found herself memorizing the words. Suddenly, her eyes popped open and she became aware of her surroundings and circumstances. She remembered John and Maya eagerly dancing with each other before she'd left the ballroom. She checked her watch to find that it was 3:00 a.m. *What is going on?* She hastily freshened up in the bathroom and headed down the hall. She reentered the ballroom, and although the lights were dimmed, she could see them at the far end of the room slow dancing. She purposefully bypassed the carpet and walked across the hardwood floor so they could hear the clicking of her heels.

"Don't mind me," she snapped as she walked right past them. "I just came to get something to drink."

Prince John looked up briefly from the nestle of Maya's neck, but neither of them seemed to mind her presence. Brenna felt the sting of hurt and embarrassment and the heat of anger. Quickly, she put ice and Coke in a glass and fled the room. She wanted to curse and cry at the same time. When she returned to the master bedroom, she plopped down on the side of the bed. She wanted to disappear. *Why did he even invite me here if he really wanted to be with Maya? And what did these weeks of affection for me mean? Nothing? A great show? Everyone told me Prince John was a playboy. But don't playboys finally grow up and settle down? And Maya—she was way too eager to step in to my place.* Thoughts and feelings swirled in her head as she sat stunned. No strategies or plans emerged. Eventually, she heard the music change to something fast-paced, and she found herself walking back to the ballroom. This time John was alone in the room, standing by the window smoking. He came toward her.

"Don't ask me where Maya is. She left," John said. Then he added, "Wait here, I'll be right back."

Before she could object, he was gone. Brenna suspected that Maya had not left. From her position in the master bedroom, she would have heard any car leaving the drive. She waited, but John did not come right back. After half an hour, Brenna's mind ignited: *Maya is still here. John is with her. Somewhere in this house, they are...*

She couldn't finish. She walked back to close the doors to the ballroom and turned the key to lock them. She locked him out and took the key. Her face flushed fire in her cheeks. Her movements were slow and deliberate to contain her fury. Her heart hurt, and hot tears poured down her face. *I don't care. I don't care...I don't care.* She shook her head and repeated this over and over. Her mantra started to work. She felt her passion turning to ice and her tears freezing. She could not sit, because the posture might lead to capitulation. So she walked to the back windows overlooking the gardens. She saw the statues and wishes herself to be one. Then she just stared out at the night sky, waiting for the dawn.

Brenna stood all night at the window until the dawn arrived as increments of colored brightness lighting the sky. However subtly, morning had arrived, and she could finally leave his house. His palace. His country. She unlocked the door and pattered barefoot to the master bedroom. The door was ajar, so she peeked in. He was not there. Someone had smoothed the wrinkled bedspread that she had left, but the bed was still made. She hurried to the bathroom and splashed water on her face, gargled, rearranged her clothes, and noiselessly rushed downstairs.

The doorman, who was asleep on the bench in the foyer, jumped up at her approach. Immediately she asked for a car to take her back to the hotel.

"This is not possible without His Highness's permission," he said as if in an announcement.

"Is His Highness still here?" she asked. He walked and opened the front door. Finding his car still in place, he turned back to Brenna and nodded.

"I'm sorry, but I cannot provide a car. You must wait for His Highness."

"Well, would you please call me a taxi?" she asked, staring hard at him.

"I'm sorry, but taxis are not allowed into the palace grounds."

"Well, I guess I'll just have walk out to the streets and get one for myself." She turned around and escaped out the front door before he could block her. Despite his calls, she hurried down the two sets of front stairs then started walking the long cobblestone drive to the guard kiosk. The morning air was fresh and damp. It smelled of sweet flowers from the garden mixed with smoke and the aromas of cooking: butter and spicy berbere pepper. Ethiopia. Then she flinched at the whiff of the distant undertone of open sewage, which reminded her of her current predicament with Prince John.

She tried not to notice the guards as they moved to line up in formation to block the exit. She pretended not to notice, so she paused several times to smell the roses lining the drive. There were six guards, perhaps seven. When she was within twenty feet of them, on command, they all simultaneously pointed beyond her, back toward the palace. She stopped and looked at each one of them. Then a man she knew to be the commander spoke abruptly to her in Amharic. She didn't understand the language, but she knew he was ordering her back to the house.

"I am absolutely *not* going back into that house. I'm going out." Brenna's resolute eyes met his, and her tone was quiet, clear, and determined. She lifted her arm and pointed her finger adamantly toward the street beyond the palace gate. Although she doubted that any of them understood English, she continued to plead her cause. "If you love him so much, you go back." She waved a pointed finger toward them, touched her own heart, and then thumbed behind her. She stood her ground and refused to let the tears that had pooled in her eyes fall, even though her ragged breaths were making her slight body quiver.

Finally, the same senior officer, who knew her as the prince's recent regular companion, commanded the guards, who made a small opening for her to pass out through. It was not permitted, he knew; nobody walked out of the palace grounds—certainly not a lone woman with no driver and no car—especially with no permission. His Highness would not be pleased, but something about her eyes reminded him of his youngest daughter.

Brenna didn't care. She was out. The guards and iron palace gates were behind her now. She walked into the freedom of a new day and crossed the street to start the journey toward her hotel.

Some of the peasants on the street gawked at her and turned to stare. She knew that her evening clothes and proximity to the playboy's palace told something of why she might be alone and unhappily out on the streets so early the morning. She consoled herself with reminders. *Don't worry about the stares. Just keep walking. And just like last night finally ended, this will too. I'll be back in my room in no time. Just keep going.*

She was holding her head high and trying to walk with dignity when someone or something bumped her from behind. She sped up, afraid to look back. Then again: bumps low on her left and right sides simultaneously. She looked down for children but instead saw that she was surrounded by a herd of dirty, musty sheep. They swept her up in their rhythm. Now there she was, bobbing down the street across from his palace, being herded by a flock of sheep.

I must look like a complete fool. She was afraid of the sheep, and all her efforts at composure and dignity failed. She was so humiliated that she wanted to cry, but she couldn't. Bumping along in the little herd, she finally just gave up trying to hold it all together. Suddenly she just burst into laughter. She laughed and laughed. Just like her life right now—she had no control. She was carried away by this ridiculous moment.

Around the corner, Brenna finally hailed a cab. When she arrived back in her hotel room, she immediately called the airport and then home to reschedule her open departure date for Thursday. Emotionally exhausted, she couldn't wait to leave Ethiopia and the disappointment and hurt John had caused her. After she made all her new arrangements, she drifted off to sleep; she was still exhausted from being up all night.

"Brenna? Brenna?" She awoke to Maya's voice. She turned in her direction, expecting to see a gloating, victorious grin. Maya came close with a fretful expression and asked, "What happened to you? We were so concerned."

Brenna's mind snagged on the *we*. *"'We' were so concerned?" Now you're a 'we' with Prince John?* "Yeah, I'm sure you were," Brenna responded through pursed lips.

Maya persisted in telling her story, as if Brenna were interested. "Prince John got really upset when he found out you'd left the palace. He started shouting at me, and then he left. He left me in the palace with no way to get back to the hotel." She went on to tell her how she'd finally called out the window to Prince John's brother Michael, who came to arrange a car.

So, that was her tale of woe. Brenna felt no sympathy, because she knew Maya had been aware of her feelings for John, and she remembered how eagerly Maya had responded to his advances the night before. She wanted to be a better person and feel compassion for her companion's sad face, but she wasn't, and she didn't. The phone rang.

By Maya's response, Brenna could tell it was Maya's fiancé, Cliff, calling from LA. Since Brenna's call, the word must have gotten around to the families about the whereabouts of the young women. When they had not arrived as scheduled, Maya's parents had opened a letter from Tanzania addressed to Maya. Cliff was furious because it was a love letter from a man whom Maya had met there. Her subdued, contrite responses revealed that she would have hell to pay. Brenna reflected on her own overnight hell. *One hell deserves another*, she thought. She turned over and went back to sleep.

Later that morning, Prince John's secretary, Rhonda Sisay, also an African American, called to invite them both to lunch. They accepted and joined her for a light meal and chat. Neither Prince John nor the affairs of the night before were mentioned, until the phone rang.

"It's His Highness," Rhonda announced. "Maya, he wants to speak with you." Rhonda motioned for Maya to take the call in the adjoining room, which she did. Brenna continued to chat with Rhonda, pretending she was unfazed by the fact that John, despite her growing hatred for him, had not asked for her. A few minutes later, Maya returned.

"Brenna, he wants to speak with you now."

"No, thank you," Brenna said. *Seconds? He really thinks I'll answer to seconds?*

"I really think you should take the call," Rhonda said, countering with imploring eyes. "Come on; I'll be with you."

Brenna finally accepted the call.

"Hello, Brenna?" Prince John's cheerful tone came over the line.

Brenna replied flatly, "Yes."

"How are you?"

"Great. How are you?"

"I'm just fine. You know, the Morehouse Men's Choir has a concert at the theater tonight."

"Yes, I've been told."

"Well, I'd certainly like to attend." He was clearly trying to be charming.

"And you should. Doesn't your family have a box at the theater?"

"Yes, of course, but I'd like to go as your guest. Will you invite me?" John asked. Brenna was livid and was poised to say *Hell no* when Rhonda, who was right in her face listening to both sides of the conversation and analyzing every word and expression, covered the mouthpiece of the phone.

"Do you still want to fly out of here on Thursday? Then do what he asks. Just agree," Rhonda said, imploring.

Brenna breathed several times to stabilize her voice for lies and then calmly answered. She said in a false voice, "Of course, Prince Jo—"

"Please, Brehenna," he said in a cooing voice, "call me Yohannes." But it sounded to her like a lying croak.

"Anything you say, Yohannes." She breathed in then slowly exhaled spite before she responded, "I'd love to invite you. Would you be my guest at the concert tomorrow night?"

"Yes. Thank you for the invitation. I'll send the car for you at seven thirty."

She could hear the gloating in his voice. "Thank you, Your Highness; I look forward to it." Brenna hung up the phone after her lie. She smiled at Rhonda, who seemed glad Brenna had taken her advice to be nice to her boss.

Lunch ended shortly after the call. That night, the limo arrived at seven thirty, as scheduled. Brenna begged off the evening, claiming that she did not feel well. Maya attended instead. Brenna never asked, and Maya never said anything, about the concert or the evening. She did not yell or fuss at Maya, because as far as Brenna was concerned, Maya barely existed to her now. And John was shattered, like broken glass. Later, their last night before departure, Brenna answered the phone.

"Brehenna?" It was Prince John.

"Yes?" she replied.

"This is Yohannes." He spoke into silence but continued, "I can't believe you're really leaving in the morning. I need to talk to you."

"It's really late, and I have more packing to do. Sorry. Maybe next time I'm in Ethiopia."

"Well, OK then." He paused and added, "But I still need to speak with you, so I'll join you in the morning on your flight to Paris."

"All right. You know my flight leaves at seven." At this point, she would agree to anything, knowing well that he was too spoiled to get up early enough to make that flight. She would say whatever it took to ensure that he would not impede her departure. Twenty-four hours from now, she would be out of Ethiopia and out of his sphere of influence. She would be free.

"I'll see you in the morning, then. Ciao."

"Goodbye, John." She meant forever.

Chapter 27

In the Sky

Addis to Paris

"Miss Hayes, His Highness will be joining you once the plane reaches altitude," the stewardess said, motioning to indicate a row of empty seats across the aisle.

"His Highness is on board?" Brenna asked, somewhat startled.

"Yes," she said, pointing toward the front of the cabin, "there between the two officers."

Brenna saw the curly top of his head between the military hats. She nodded to the hostess and sighed back into her seat. After the fiasco at the palace the other night, she had hoped to never see him again. But here he was. Maya rose from the window seat to see as well. When she sat back, they looked at each other briefly. Brenna shook her head and turned away.

It was a five-flight hour to Paris. Why was he joining her? Was he actually coming to see Maya? Was he going to try to taunt her all the way? Brenna brushed the concern away by reminding herself that she was on her way home. In just five hours, he would be out of her life.

After a time, Prince John walked back and sat across the aisle from Brenna.

"So, are you feeling better?" He grinned, his cheek and chin punctures on display.

"I'm fine, thank you," she answered, annoyed by the excessive rolling of the Rs in his formerly charming accent.

Smiling and animated, John shared details about the Morehouse Men's Choir concert. It sounded like it was wonderful, and Brenna regretted not seeing her friends, but at least she had seen them in concert at the Cape Coast slave castle in Ghana a few weeks earlier. She knew she could not have suffered John's company the other night. Even now, she tried to ignore him, but Prince John droned on. What had she been doing the past few days? He offered greetings to her from his family members. In Paris, would she have time to visit the Louvre?

Brenna looked ahead as he talked, paying minimal attention and only occasionally glancing in his direction. Seeming amused, Prince John chatted on as if he actually had an enthralled audience. "So you are aware that I must get married soon? Of course you are; you were there at the tea with the princess from Zaire. But how can I tell about all those women? Why do they want me? Because I'm handsome? Wealthy? Duke of a province? How am I to know?"

She turned to study his face, thinking him arrogant beyond belief. *He's a jerk*, she thought. She kept looking. Still, she had to admit, he was fine. OK, he was handsome, wealthy, and a duke. Maybe he wasn't bragging. Maybe he was just stating facts. Then she found herself lost in his features and her thoughts, until his words snagged her attention.

"But I know you really like me. I mean, really like *me*."

Prince John kept talking, apparently oblivious to her incredulous stare. She was struck by his audacity to presume that he knew what she felt. He was very much mistaken. She had to speak. "Wait a minute," Brenna said, interrupting him. He looked at her. "You're mistaken."

"What? You mean you don't like me?" he asked.

"Exactly. That's exactly what I mean. You deserted me for Maya. How could you think I would still like you?" *Keep pressing for a fight, John, and you'll get one.*

"Oh yes, that. It's not what it may have seemed. Come sit beside me. Let me explain."

"No. I don't want to sit by you," Brenna said, raising her cracking voice, "and I don't want to hear your explanation. Just leave me alone."

"Please lower you voice. Come, I really need to speak to you," he whispered and indicated for Brenna to look back. Every head, on both sides of the aisles, was tilted in—listening and watching. She snapped back into her seat. Prince John moved over to the window seat and patted the cushion next to him while he looked at her.

Brenna turned away, then took a deep breath and moved to sit across the aisle. She looked at his hand still resting on the vacant middle seat between them but didn't move closer. She faced him and spoke softly and deliberately: "OK, I'm listening. Go ahead."

"Thank you, Brehenna. I want to explain to you." He nearly sounded sincere. "These last weeks with you, I've loved. But then it started to feel like we were getting too close. Something about you pulls me in," he said, facing the lure of her full lips and the languid sweep of long lashes over her lovely eyes. He glanced away to break the spell.

"The other day when I invited you both out, I had special plans, but they were spoiled because the protests closed the university again. We're having some serious political problems here. I won't go into all that now, but after the plans were cancelled, I had you both at the palace. I thought maybe if I made you jealous, maybe if you got really mad, then you would end it...this thing between us."

"So you thought dancing with Maya and sleeping with Maya would do the trick?" Brenna whispered, but she was furious. "You were right! It did. Next time, just break it off with a girl. You don't have to hurt and humiliate her." She fought back tears by looking up and dabbing beneath her eyes.

"I'm sorry. Really. I didn't mean to hurt you." He reached for her hand. She resisted him taking it but let it rest on top of hers.

"I wanted to get away from you, and I did. But when I did, I realized that it wasn't what I wanted. I really wanted you. I do want you. And for the record, I did not sleep with Maya. I knew you would think I had, but I did not."

He met her disbelieving gaze with a level eye and repeated, "Truly, I did not. And I am sorry for all the changes I took you through." The prince paused and then continued. "Over these last few weeks, I've seen you happy, sad, mad—everything. I couldn't believe you managed to get past my guards. You left me. That's when I knew. You're great. I love *you*. It's you I want for my wife. You *are* my wife." He looked beneath her furrowed brow into her pooling eyes. She let him take her hand.

"I didn't believe you were actually going to leave this morning. I know it is your custom to have an engagement ring, but I didn't have time to fit the ring that once belonged to my grandmother. But let me offer this." He pulled a black-velvet jewelry case from his jacket pocket and opened it. A pair of diamond-encircled emerald earrings twinkled in his palm. He pressed the box in her hand.

"Please accept this as an engagement present, a token, until I ca——"

"Wait, Yohannes!" Brenna cut in. "What are you talking about? Your wife? What?" She couldn't take her eyes off the jewels, and the small case trembled in her hand. They were the most beautiful things she had ever seen. Her other hand went up to cover her mouth. Finally, she closed the box. "I can't do this," Brenna said. She shook her head and tried to hand him back the box. He refused it. They were both quiet for a while. "Are you serious?" she asked.

He looked into her eyes and nodded.

"Then please, Yohannes, take this back." She returned the box. He obliged and placed the case on the seat between them. Again, silence. Then Brenna asked, "There is no divorce in the royal family, right?"

"Right, it's for life," he responded.

"How many wives do you get to have?" She processed his answers with an almost imperceptible shaking of her head.

"Only one," he answered, and another long silence followed. The atmosphere shifted. When the whirlwind of emotions settled, it was Brenna who reached over to take his hand.

"Yohannes Makonnen, you are right. I do like you despite my anger at what you did. I don't know why, but I still like you." She took a deep tremulous breath then added, "I love you." He smiled and squeezed her hand. They both searched each other's faces. He kissed the back of her hand, nodded, then looked back at her.

"Well, Brehenna, will you be my wife?" Waiting, he kept his eyes locked on hers. After a while, her lips began a slow curl at the corner—a tentative smile. She looked away for a few seconds, then looked back at him.

"I do love you, Yohannes," she repeated, "but I can't make a life-time decision like this right now. I just can't. I've been traveling for over two months nonstop. I'm overwhelmed and I'm tired. I don't have one brain cell left that's not exhausted. I can't decide this now."

"What are you saying, Brehenna?"

"I'm saying I can't answer you," she said, searching for right words. "I can't say yes or no to being your wife. I just can't think." He tilted his head and sighed. Their moist hands remained clasped. "Let me get home and rest. I'll think about this, and as soon as I know for sure, I will let you know."

"Well then," he murmured quietly, retrieving his hand and tenting them both under his chin.

"Yohannes, as soon as I know, you'll know." Brehenna nodded her promise.

He took out a cigarette and flicked his lighter. He smoked in silence for a while. "You see, Brehenna, that's what I like about you." He smiled at her again. "Do you know how many women would have taken these, even if they expected to say no later?" He picked up the jewel case and slid it back into his jacket pocket.

"No, I don't know. But if I can't accept the engagement, I can't accept the engagement gift." She shrugged, maybe wishing she could. The earrings were beautiful.

"I love you, and I want you for my wife." His statement was a heart-seeking missive that continued to penetrate her armor and shatter the landscape of her judgment.

"I need to know that we can last together," she replied. Her eyes teared up, but she persisted. "I mean, all that you are, all that I am, and all that we are together, can this be forever? Can children, can a family, stand on this relationship? That's what I have to know for sure in my heart. I do love you. I already know it. Whatever comes, I will always love you, Yohannes. That much is settled."

He opened his arms, and she moved to the seat beside him. They kissed and held each other, both wanting more. Shortly the squeak of the stewardess's carts alerted them of the meal, and they shifted apart to prepare.

Their conversation was easy for the remainder of the flight. Although she was still stunned, Brenna kept up her end of the banter. What was remarkable was that the wall of hurt, anger, and distrust had come completely down. John was his Christian name, but the meaning of his full given name reflected his personage and described the effect he had on many people. He had told her before that his name meant "the borders will bow down." And so, the border to Brenna's heart did just that. They kissed goodbye at the gate in Paris.

Chapter 28

What Just Happened?

California, 1972

*U*pon her return from Africa, Brenna met with the pageant officials, who asked a myriad of questions; most of these she suspected they already had the answers to, because Bessie had returned a whole month before she did with news. Finally, they grilled her about her relationship with the prince. "Is it true that you dated Haile Selassie's grandson? Did he really propose marriage to you? What did you say? Are you engaged now?"

Brenna talked in great detail about the trip, but she just smiled when the subject of Prince John came up. In her interviews, she needed the reporters to help her to fulfill her obligation to the mandate: "We're sending you on this trip to go and come back to tell us how they really feel about us in Africa." Simultaneously, she felt she needed to keep the news about Prince John private, because she still had an important decision to make for herself. But only one national magazine, *Sepia*, approached her for an in-depth interview about her trip. For two hours she shared her African adventures and impressions and answered many questions. Near the end of the interview, Mr. Jones, the reporter, asked her about the prince.

"I'm not at liberty right now to speak about that."

"Oh, it's OK," Mr. Jones said coaxingly. "Whatever you say about that will be off the record. I was wondering, could our magazine have an exclusive interview when you're ready to talk?"

"Well, since you were the only national magazine to show any interest in the story, yes, I'll give you an exclusive."

"Strictly off the record, would you answer just a few questions for me now? When do you think you will be free to talk about your relationship with the royal family?"

"Perhaps, when or if our wedding plans are officially announced by the emperor, then it will definitely be OK to speak," she said, somewhat facetiously, because she had not yet responded to John's proposal.

"So, there is an engagement?" he asked. But Brenna kept looking down and did not answer. Then he added, "Remember, this is off the record, so you can speak freely. I just want to get an idea of the story so I can prepare in advance. Since you've got to go back to school, this may save you the time of a second interview."

"That's true; I will be very busy in my new master's program. It's just important to me that this first article give a full account of my experiences so that Black people will know that we were welcomed and that Africa has not forgotten us. Not at all."

"Tell me a little about the prince. Is he handsome? Intelligent? How did you communicate—does he speak English? How did you meet? Under what circumstances did he propose? Was it romantic?"

"I have your word that this will be off the record, until I say it's OK?"

"Yes, yes, you have my word," he said, nodding. "Tell me about the prince."

Then, as if sharing a confidence with a friend, Brenna recounted the great love of her young life with ardor and enthusiasm. By the time she finished her confidential, off-the-record tale, the reporter had many pages of notes. Mr. Jones gave her his card and asked her to call as soon as the romance could be publicly announced. Brenna thanked him for giving her Africa story and personal story his attention and assured him that he would be the first reporter to know of the official announcement.

———

Brenna spent one whirlwind weekend in Los Angeles before going straight back to school. In six weeks, she succeeded in finishing the final quarter of her senior year. She had already been accepted into a master's degree program that began two weeks after her last final. Exhausted from the Miss Watts' trip and school, she decided to forgo her graduation ceremonies at Stanford and return home to rest.

Over the summer, her schedule remained packed with her graduate studies in education and the final months of her duties as Miss Watts. Two of her pageant prizes came in very handy—the free flights from PSA, and the free car rentals she received from Hertz allowed her to make weekend trips to LA. She also landed a feature role in a movie filmed in Watts. Although she only spoke to John on the phone a few times, she thought of him daily as she sought to know her own heart and confirm her answer to him.

In August, it was time for her to pass the Miss Watts crown on to another young woman. This occasion was the opportunity for her to share in person the fulfillment of the request of those who had sent her to Africa. She wondered how, in the fifteen minutes she was allotted for her farewell as the outgoing queen, she could express the overpowering emotions she had experienced in Africa as an African American finally returning home. How would she explain the many annual ceremonies that took place along the west coast of Africa, where the villagers gathered in droves to offer prayers at ancient slave forts in memory of the ancestors who were taken away and the descendants of those ancestors, that they might be preserved and find their way back home. They prayed for us. Would she also tell of the ways in which Africans embraced and emulated the ways of Black Americans in their music, style, and dress from the images they saw in the latest movies and magazines?

There was much she needed to say and much more she wanted them to feel. Walking across Stanford's quiet summer campus, a sweet song came to Brenna on the evening breeze. She stopped and scribbled down the words and sang it over and over until she reached the tape recorder in her apartment to capture it. By the time she had fully developed this song, she knew she would sing it for her people at the pageant; it would be her gift back to them for their great generosity, kindness, and confidence in her as their Miss Watts.

The stage lighting was subdued as Brenna, dressed in full African regalia, glided toward the microphone and stood washed in the amber spotlight. She heard and felt their affection coming through their applause and ovation. She smiled and loved them right back. She suppressed the emotions creeping up her throat and filling her eyes, because she knew she had to speak and sing.

"Thank you so much…please, please…thank you. Please let me speak…thank you." She waited as they finally settled down. "Thank you." She continued with their attention. "As we all know about our legacy, the truth about our past as Black people has been altered, damaged, denied, or deleted altogether. So a year ago, you told me you were sending me to Africa, on your behalf, to see for myself the truth about how Africa feels about us, and to come back and tell you. So, here I stand before you today to make my report. First, I must say unequivocally: Africa has not forgotten us!" The crowd broke into applause. "I worried about how I could tell you everything. Finally, I wrote a song, which I hope will help you be able to experience what I saw and felt. From my heart, I thank you for the privilege of representing you all over Africa as Miss Watts. This song is my gift to you. May I sing to you?"

"Yeah, yeah, go 'head on, sing it, child, sing yo' song!" rang out among the applause. When they became still, in a tender soprano voice she sang a cappella:

How have you loved me so well?
Loved me so well?
Loved me so well? [Repeat]

When I've been gone,
When I've been gone,
When I've been gone from home...
           so long?

How have you loved me so well,
           Ashanti?
How have you loved me so well,
           Fulani?
How have you loved me so well,
           Kikuyu?

When I've been gone
When I've been gone
When I've been gone from home
           so long?

How do you remember so well?
           Remember so well?
           Remember so well?
           Remember so well?
           [*Repeat*]

When I've been gone,
When I've been gone,
When I've been gone from home
           so long?

I am your mother.
I am your mother

...and I remember so well.

Yes, they've taken you from my breast,
      And since that day
      I've never rest'd
      I've never rest'd

Made you enslaved
      the snap of the whip
      the jab of the knife

But they can never take you out of my life.
      I am your mother.
      I am your mother.

Brenna ended her year as Miss Watts, and the festival went on that year to create the memorable *Wattstax* album. Brenna slipped out of all the excitement and let the new queen have her reign. She went back to school confident in what she was to do next.

In August, just before his birthday, Yohannes received Brehenna's letter. Couched with words from his ancestors' poetry in the Song of Solomon, her response said, "Yes, I will be your wife."

Prince Yohannes smiled and finished the letter. "I knew it, from the beginning. I knew you were mine." He sniffed for her perfume on the pages then pressed his mouth to her lipstick kiss. Finally, he carefully folded the letter and placed it in his breast pocket.

Chapter 29

The Signet

Ancient Jerusalem

The caravan of weary travelers finally reached Gaza, the region of Southern Judea that Solomon had gifted to the Queen of Sheba, Prince Menelik's mother, but the young man was too excited to rest. He and a cadre of his men had set forth to explore. The marketplace was hissing with many dialects and languages. The flamboyant colors of the fruit and fabric embellished the makeshift stalls and merchants hawking their wares. He knew by the aromas on the air that he was no longer among the familiar spices and incense of Ethiopia or Egypt. He recalled the heady lure of oils and perfumes on the women of Misraim and marked Egypt as a place he would one day return to. He scanned this market and took deep breaths of the spicy pungency of his father's land.

Menelik, though aware of the stares and whispers of the people, did not attribute them beyond the intrigue of having an unfamiliar, apparently royal, entourage among them. But the people were puzzled, because he looked like a youthful version of their king; the elders were spreading the word that here was the exact visage of King David, King Solomon's father. Merchants scurried about ordering extravagant displays of their wares and discreetly washing their hands and feet and the faces of their children. The guards were alert, because they had not been notified of an impending royal visit. No one dared approach the young nobleman until a local commander finally stepped forth to inquire of an officer in the prince's guard.

"Please, sir, may we offer our services and know on whom you wait?"

"His Highness Prince Menelik, son of King Solomon and Queen Makeda of Sheba, is come up from our land in the south— Abyssinia," replied the royal guardsman. "He is journeying to Jerusalem to meet his father. Yes, we need your assistance in directing us on to the city." The commander obliged this majestic entourage with lavish overnight hospitality, which also gave him time to expedite a message to his king.

After riding all night and part of the next day, a breathless young messenger knelt before King Solomon. "Your Majesty, one who is, I am told, in the image of your father, our beloved King David, has arrived in the Gaza."

"What is the meaning of this? How is this so? What are his claims?" the king asked, looking at his lords.

"My king, his substantial caravan rests outside the city, and his bearing and attire are regal. Your Majesty, they report that he is your son, en route from Abyssinia to Jerusalem to visit you—his father."

"Makeda," Solomon said to himself. Then he ordered, "Dispatch the royal escorts immediately to the south and hasten back with my son!"

Although many preparations had to be made, the days that it took for Menelik's caravan to arrive seemed too long for the king. Finally his chief returned and said, "Majesty, it is incredible. Still, I cannot believe my own eyes. King David in his youth has returned to us."

"Where is he? Where is my son?" Solomon said, his eyes searching the chamber.

"Just outside the door, sire."

"Bring him in!"

Outside, Menelik's attendants made their final adjustments to his attire and wiped his brow. The doors opened, and he and his men were escorted in. He barely noticed the grandeur of the throne room, as he was struggling to maintain his bearing while trying to catch a glimpse of the king. Finally, his men parted, and he saw the face of his father for the first time. Stunned and pleased, Menelik proceeded to the throne and led his retinue in deep obeisance to the king, his heart fluttering as he held his head low.

"Rise, and let me see your face," the king said. He stood before his throne.

When Menelik looked up, King Solomon saw the eyes, nose, and mouth of his own father. His father's youthful face again stood before him. He searched and saw Makeda in their son's black, luxuriant hair and himself in his shoulders and stature. *My God*, he thought, *to come face to face with oneself, fully grown in the flesh!*

Menelik noticed the king's halting manner and quickly reached inside his garment to bring forth the ring that his mother had sent with him as proof. "Your Majesty, my mother, Queen Makeda of Ethiopia, sends with me a signet." He bowed and extended the ring on his open hand.

Solomon walked down and seized his opened hand and closed it upon the ring. "No, my son, I do not need a signet; you are the living image of my father. Your countenance is the confirmation." He embraced his son. Both closed their eyes to harvest the moment. Then Solomon held Menelik back at arm's length and studied him. Handsome. Strong. Intelligent. In the moisture on his son's lashes, he saw tenderness. Menelik smiled, and his mother's beauty shone on his face. Then, grace ignited the torch of tomorrows, and the radiance of future generations shimmered in his eyes.

They both laughed, and the king turned to his court, arm on his son's shoulder, and said, "This is my son! My firstborn son, Prince Menelik!" Shouts, applause, and music filled the hall. Then, face to face, eye to eye, shoulder to shoulder, father and son talked and dined, laughed and sang, walked and danced, and the sweetness of Makeda's love braided them together by heart.

Chapter 30

The Horsemen

Members of the royal court loved to watch King Solomon and his son Menelik together. For the elders, it was reminiscent of long ago, when Solomon was the shadow of his own father, King David. All that was given by God through generations of blood was apparent, from the definitive Hebraic profile to the nuances of gesture and voice. Solomon and Menelik found themselves walking in step and voicing each other's thoughts. This is what Young David, as Solomon now fondly called his son, had longed for. His thirst for this knowledge, this place, and this spirit was finally being quenched. He was now standing beneath the pinion of his own father's wing.

Had he tarried any longer in Ethiopia, Menelik feared he would have become lost amid the comfort and solace of the Shawl. The rule of the queens was granite demurely veiled in layers of woven gossamer silk. Their delicate hands were elegant in subtlety yet absolute in reign. But now, combined with his observations of his father, he saw that the elements of dominion were the same, but Solomon exhibited a juxtaposition in the presentation of power: contrary to the rule of the queens, kingly rule seemed stark, bare, and audacious. Yet the devastating power of his father was grounded in a spirit that at the core remained kind, being itself humbled by the Awe behind its awesomeness. Menelik knew that only the God of Creation could supply and sanction the power that radiated from his father like a well-stoked hearth.

Their horses blazed as they sped across the hills and valleys of Jerusalem, first father then son taking the lead. Both skilled horsemen and soldiers, they excelled and exceeded each other's high expectations. Their morning runs had become a spectacle. Many rose early to see them ride, weaving in and out like the interplay of destiny and time—mesmerizing and bewitching the mind.

The speeding steeds and men merged into one. Nothing could have made Solomon more proud than the sight of well-earned perspiration coursing from his son's black locks down his neck when they paused to let their horses drink at the well. He watched Menelik soothe and water his stallion with precision and admiration for the beast. King Solomon had longed for such a day, where his every word and gesture would be passed on to his firstborn son, the foundation for the future of the United Kingdoms of Judea and Ethiopia.

He saw himself in his son's muscular stature and in his gestures. Menelik had a quick wit and robust laugh. There was no question about his way with women, for he saw how even some of the most seasoned court courtesans blushed almost innocently in his son's wake. But in quiet moments like this, Solomon felt the stillness of Ethiopia—the serenity of Makeda. Their son was already a priestly man. A king for certain. He was eagerly instructed and informed by all these experiences. Israel held out her heart to young Menelik, and he embraced her.

He is excellent, an excellent son, Makeda, Solomon thought to himself. It seemed almost impossible that over two decades had passed since their first meeting, when she had come with wine, incense, poetry, poultice, veils, and music to set up home deep inside his being. He was her home now, and he provided for her in his daily prayers, encounters, and passions.

Menelik came and stood beside his father. "Tell me something, Father, if I am not too presumptuous." The two moved to sit on boulders in the shade of a cypress.

"Yes?" Solomon gave his permission and waited for his son's question.

"Why did you not come to Ethiopia to see my mother? Or me?" Menelik asked. He quietly exhaled while he watched his father.

"I have never left your mother's side, nor she mine," King Solomon said without hesitation. He continued with a discourse on the spirit and nature of marriage and being one flesh. He had come many times to Ethiopia, for Makeda knew how to summon her king. He knew the Abyssinian highlands and trails by horseback and had spent many hours upon the lake. The sensuous fabric and fragrance of his wife's private rooms lived within him.

Menelik did not speak, but his father saw the puzzled expression cloud his eyes. He stood and offered his son a hand up.

"Stand close; let me show you," he said, and his son moved nearer. "Close your eyes and open your heart. Now, breathe." Menelik obeyed his father. After silent stillness, they both felt the cool morning air softy stir around them. Then Menelik heard a swish like movement of a woman's skirts. Finally, a whiff of natal fragrance came to Menelik's nostrils: the warmth of his mother's scent. His mother was there, not in the ordinary physical sense, but no less completely present. His eyes popped open, and he saw his father smiling. They stood in silence for a long while.

Then Menelik, though hesitant, pressed on. "Were the mystical visitations enough?"

A pained expression crossed his father's face, but he earnestly conceded by saying, "It has sufficed." He turned toward Menelik. "Was it all I would have wanted? No. Look into my eyes, son; you must learn this for a certainty: our lives and our destiny are not ours to make. It is written, and it is so, that the God of Creation, the God of Israel, is the source, substance, and arbiter of our fate." Solomon held his gaze until his son eventually nodded. The king searched the sky and the horizon for words. Then he turned. "Walk with me. I will speak to you of veiled matters."

Menelik stood and walked beside his father along the hilly terrain.

"Yes, with all my heart I wanted to see your mother again and to hold my newborn son. I was forbidden," Solomon said, looking away. Then he turned back and added, "Forbidden by God."

He sighed, and before he continued, Menelik asked, "How so, Father, how so?"

"Shortly after your mother departed, the Archangel Gabriel appeared to me and announced, 'And the Lord said, *You will never see Queen Makeda again in the flesh.*' Then the archangel vanished. I was shocked by the refusal. I spent weeks in supplication and petition. I must have burned a furnace full of incense and sacrificed a herd of animals."

Menelik saw the anguish crease his father's forehead, and then Solomon paused again to communicate face to face with his son.

"I could not come just because I wanted to come it. I did. I wanted to come. But I needed His consent, and He did not give it. Son, it is by our obedience to the will of God that we, our people, and our lands are sustained." Again Solomon picked up his stroll, and Menelik joined him. Quietly, they both studied their view of Jerusalem and the Temple Mount.

"How could the Creator be so unkind?" Menelik asked. His emotions flared at this injustice and the pain of his own years of longing for his father.

"God is not unkind, my son; the Creator is vast." Solomon stated this and studied his son's face with a warming smile. He continued, "God has granted me much. When I was a young man, like yourself, I prayed for one thing only: I prayed for Wisdom. God answered and taught me her ways. I became her servant, and through her tutelage, our people have lived in peace with all nations. I was blessed with her companionship. There is no greater gift to our people than to be ruled by a king whose heart is an instrument of Wisdom's bidding."

"Hear me now, son," the king said almost in a whisper, and Menelik leaned in to his father's aspect. "Our Lady is the Ark of the Covenant and the Mercy Seat that is atop it; this is the reigning throne of Wisdom. Sophia, the spirit of wisdom, is often called such. Can you not see the greater works of the Creator? Even so, beyond all the blessings and great companionship of the spirit of Sophia, one day your mother came into my world. I am he who recognizes Sophia in all her forms. Your mother is the closest I have ever known of an embodiment of Wisdom. Your mother is Sophia clothed in a woman's fineness and flesh. And this same God granted me the priceless privilege of taking her for my wife."

Solomon clutched a hand to his chest and laughed out loud. He looked at his son, grabbed him, and whispered into his mass of curling locks, "And you: God granted me you." His son returned the embrace.

"Yes, God forbade me to come, yet the Archangel Gabriel returned and announced: 'The Lord God has heard your cry: And the Lord said, *You will never see Queen Makeda again in the flesh, but you will see Queen Makeda.*' Then he vanished and left me to puzzle through an angelic conundrum." Solomon noticed his son's furrowed brow and said, "No, son. I was glad. I was relieved, for the Lord had opened a door to a mystery that would allow me to see your mother again, albeit not in the flesh."

"What happened, Father?"

"We did it. Your mother and I, we found a way, a way to spirit travel one to the other. For all these many years, we have done so."

"Father, you speak such beautiful words." Yet he stumbled to find his own. "I am in your story with you. I know it to be true. But Father, I do not understand what it all means."

"Menelik, in that, you have said no small thing. Despite your youth, you are wise. For it is Wisdom to separate what you know from what you understand. Sometimes understanding may follow knowing, but just as often it does not." Abruptly, Solomon turned, brushed the dust from the front of his vest, and proceeded toward the horses.

"Come, Young David, I have something back at the palace to show you," Solomon said eagerly, and Menelik saw that the glint was back in his father's eye.

Chapter 31

Roha

They dismounted upon their return, and the father led the way, waving his groomsmen to the horses. The two barreled down the palace corridors. When they reached the secluded room behind the king's quarters, a breathless hunched servant emerged from the freshly lit chamber in time to receive them. King Solomon stepped inside first then extended his son a beckoning hand. Menelik joined him and felt his father's guiding arm escort him by his shoulder.

Attendants scurried, lighting the remainder of the lamps. Menelik walked in a few steps, then stopped short. Drawn by miniature armature hanging on a wall, he spied a wooden chest beneath it. With tilted head and furrowed brow, he walked over, kneeled, and opened the lid.

Skepticism stalked the witness of his own eyes and hands as the familiarity of the contents of the chest and the entire room enveloped him. "But how could this be?" he wondered aloud. "How could the playroom...from my dreams...be here in Jerusalem?" The wooden carts and lances were tiny but real. Crouching on one knee, carefully moving from item to item, he thoroughly examined the contents. Then Menelik rose and made a measured, 360-degree pivot, slowly revisiting the contents of the chamber. His eyes caught when he spied a thickly draped window in the far corner of the room; he turned to his father and exclaimed, "But if this were really real, then there would not be a window there—but a door."

Although he said nothing, Solomon's expression sent Menelik coursing toward the drape, which he flung back so passionately it whooshed on its rod. There, concealed behind the fabric, was a simple wooden door. Again his eyes snapped back to the tether of his father standing in the middle of the room with his arms folded, watching his son.

Menelik pushed open the door and shouted, "And on the other side would be…" Rushing out, he called, "Roha!" The pony of his youth was not there, but to his left he saw a small empty stable. He stood staring at the weathered but familiar shelter, while his mind swished, ratcheted, and scrambled to realign his reality. Solomon joined him on the patio. As they stood eye to eye, all the years of feeling fatherless, abandoned, and insecure peeled away like a withered protective blister—beneath it, Menelik had transformed.

"But how?" he finally managed to ask. Solomon stood before him and squared his son's shoulders with his hands.

Meeting his eyes, he said to him, "When you were an infant, your mother and I carried you in our spirit. Wherever we were, so too were you. As you grew older and began to know the world for yourself, you placed our travels in the realm of dreams. As you became a young man, you believed them to be fantasies and wishful thinking. Finally, I saw that they had become memories of dreams. My son, I have always been with you in every way permitted. And now, praise be the Holy Name, we are together in the flesh." A wave of emotions shook him, pounded his heart, and shone as delight on his every smiling tooth.

Menelik felt again the spirit of his mother join them, and he knew—the three of them, here in Jerusalem or there in Abyssinia—had always been together. His mended heart softened, lightened, and overflowed his eyes. Father and son embraced as fabricated reality gave way to the hushed presence of astounding truth.

⚬

Later, in his own solitude, his son's pointed questions returned to the king. Why did the Lord forbid him from seeing his beloved Makeda again in the flesh? King Solomon loved women; he genuinely loved them. When he and Makeda met, he already had a score of wives and dozens of concubines. He had expanded the sway of Judah across the earth with matrimonial linkages. But the "radiant women" were brought because of their gifts and the bidding of the Lord.

Although the archangel never stated *why* he was forbidden from seeing Makeda again in the flesh, Solomon himself believed it had something to do with the women. He housed the radiant women in the splendor and comfort of the quarters of his concubines. They were not only exquisitely cultivated in the area of their gifts but also pampered with every pleasure a woman could desire.

King Solomon was not ignorant of his own weaknesses, nor had he forgotten the compromise of his father over coveting another man's wife. He stayed away from other men's wives. He had even stayed away from the radiant women, for years. Then the appeal, the lure, and the promise of a radiant woman began to haunt him. All women were not lit from the inside; the gift of a radiant woman was rarer than the most precious and flawless gemstone. She was one in a multitude of millions. To his eyes, she would glow. Then it became a matter of the flesh. One day the king touched one of them. Just one. *And if you've ever touched the flesh of a radiant woman, well...*

Chapter 32

It Is Time

The months flapped by like a sturdy sail in a steady wind until the time for Menelik's departure drew near. When Menelik finally broached the subject to his father, Solomon waved a dismissal of his son's promise of return to his mother: "Wise as she is, she is still a woman, and a firstborn son is his father's prerogative. I grow old. You will stay here and rule Judah."

"But I have sworn—sworn by my mother's breast that I would return," Menelik said in protest.

"You are a man now," Solomon said. "What business do you have with your mother's breast? This is finished." The matter was concluded.

Menelik did not resume the subject with his father, whose will was likely even stronger than his mother's. Instead, he commanded Tamrin to discreetly begin the preparation for the journey back home, while he continued the rigorous, demanding, and exhilarating course of instruction established by his father.

Tamrin, who owed his primary allegiance to his queen, Makeda, knew the current circumstances required that he present to King Solomon her written words, according to her instructions should an impasse arise. This was his first private audience with the king, and alone—one to one—King Solomon's countenance was almost too awesome to behold. He made sincere obeisance and, with permission from the king, asked to have the chief scribe read Queen Makeda's message. Among the numerous appellations of respect and felicitous greetings, Solomon could hear the fresh cadences of Makeda's language singing across his mind. The royal scribe read:

> Take this young man, our son, anoint him, consecrate him and bless him, and make him king over our country and give him the command that men shall now reign in this land, then send him back in peace. May peace be with the might of thy kingdom, and with thy brilliant wisdom. As for me, I never wished that he should come where thou art, for I feared him staying there. But he pressed me exceedingly, and I then put my trust in the Holy Heavenly Zion, the Tabernacle of the Law of God, that thou wilt not withhold him there in thy sway. Even thy nobles do not wish to return to their own houses by reason of the abundance of wisdom and sustenance which thou givest them, according to their desire. They say, "The table of Solomon is better for us than enjoying and gratifying ourselves in our own houses." And because of this I, through my fear, sought protection so that thou mightest not stablish him with thee, but wouldst send him back to me in peace, without sickness and suffering, in love and in peace, that my heart might rejoice at him having encountered thee.

By the end of the message, the king had fallen into a pensive mood. He kept the letter but dismissed Tamrin without a response. Neither father nor son spoke further of these matters for weeks. Finally, having also been raised in the traditions of Judah, Menelik took advantage of the High Holy Days to confess. "My lord, my father, I know you desire for me to stay here and rule in Israel, but it is impossible for me to forsake my country and my mother. My mother swore me by a bosom oath that I would not remain here but would return to her quickly. She assured me that the Tabernacle of the God of Israel would bless me wheresoever I go or stay. I desired to see thy face, and to hear thy voice, and to receive thy instruction and thy blessing. Now I must depart to my mother, my people, and my duty."

Solomon stared through the eyes of his son and saw no more weighing of the balances his judgement was fixed. He would depart. Betimes, King Solomon gathered his councilors, officers, and the elders of his kingdom and said to them, "My son cannot rescind his vow and consent to dwell here. Come, let us ordain him king of the country of Ethiopia before he departs." After some moments of contemplation, the king continued, "All of you who sit on my right hand and on my left hand, in like manner the eldest of your sons shall sit on his right hand and on his left hand. We will give our firstborn children, and we shall have two kingdoms. I will rule here with you, and my son, with your children, shall reign there, in Ethiopia."

And the priests, and the officers, and the councilors answered him, "As you send your firstborn, so too will we send our firstborn according to your wish. Who can resist the commandment of God and king?" They then made preparations to send their firstborn sons to live forever in Ethiopia.

The time came, and they brought Menelik nigh unto the Holy of Holies and had him hold upon the horns of the altar, and sovereignty was given to him by the mouth of Tzadok the high priest and by the mouth of Benaiah the priest. Then his father, King Solomon, sealed him with the holy oil of anointment of kingship. And when the young man went out from the House of the Lord, they called his name: "David." For the name of a king comes to him by rule of law. And they led him round the city upon the mule of King Solomon, proclaiming: "We have anointed thee from this moment. Long live again the royal father! And the Lord God of Israel shall be unto thee a guide, and the Tabernacle of the Law of God shall ever watch over you. And all your enemies and foes shall be overthrown before thee, and completion and finish shall be with you and your seed."

Then his father, King Solomon, confirmed him by saying, "The blessing of heaven and earth shall be your blessing." And all the congregation of Israel said, "Selah."

From there, Tzadok the priest read to King David II from the commands, laws, and instructions of God. He included the commandments and the reciprocal blessing and curses of the laws of God according to obedience.

Chapter 33

The Court of King David II

The city rejoiced because King Solomon had crowned his son, Menelik, King David II. So the king commanded that the first-born of those who sat on his right and those who sat on his left be sent to Ethiopia to rule at the right and left hands of his own son, King David II. Their rank, ordinance, greatness, and authority shall be unto the sons according to their fathers. So too shall David do unto his nobles as his father to his and order the direction of his kingdom accordingly.

These are the names of the firstborn sons appointed to serve in the royal court of Ethiopia:

Azariah, son of Tzadok, the high priest;
Elyas, son of Ami the archdeacon (the father of Ami was the archdeacon of Nathan the Prophet);
Adram, son of Arderones, leader of the people;
Fankera, son of Soba, scribe of the oxen;
Akonhel, son of Tofel, instructor of the youth;
Samneyas, son of Akitalarn, the recorder;
Firaros, son of Neya, commander of the armed men, chief of the troops;

Lewandros, son of Akire, commander of the recruits;

Fakuten, son of Adray, commander of the sea;

Matan, son of Benyas, chief of the house;

Adaraz, son of Kirem, master of decorations;

Dalakem, son of Matrem, chief of the horse soldiers;

Adaryos, son of Nedros, chief of the foot soldiers;

Awsteran, son of Yodad, bearer of the Glory;

Astarayon, son of Asa, messenger of the palace;

Imi, son of Matatyas, commander of the host;

Makri, son of Abisa, judge of the palace;

Abis, son of Karyos, assessor of tithes and taxes;

Lik Wendeyos, son of Nelenteyos, judge of the assembly;

Karmi, son of Hadneyas, chief of the royal workmen;

Seranyas, son of Akazel, administrator of the king's house.

These are all those who were sent to serve Menelik, David II, King of Ethiopia, son of Solomon, King of Israel, and Makeda, Queen of Sheba. These firstborn sons were sent with Ethiopia's first king to extend and establish there the everlasting and righteous reign of the royal lineage of the House of Judah.

Chapter 34

⊶⊷⊷

Blessed Be

So it was that the great preparations began in earnest for the journey south. Although the young King Menelik found great favor among the firstborn sons who would accompany him back to Ethiopia, Azariah, son of Tzadok the priest, carried the heaviest heart because he would be forsaking the presence of "the Lady," the Ark of the Covenant, toward whom all his hopes had extended to the time when he would replace his own father in the honor of her attendance and care. But now, he was commanded to leave her behind in Jerusalem.

Azariah pined and prayed through restless nights until late one evening, an angel of the Lord appeared to him in a dream and gave him specific instructions. Azariah was to compel the aid of his fellow firstborn sons: Zachariah (son of Benaiah), Elemeyas, Abesa, and Makari. Then they, along with himself and joined by the holy angel, were to engage in a plot to remove the Ark of the Covenant, replace it under its cover with a duplicate, and then take the true Ark with them to Ethiopia. Azariah was firmly admonished not to reveal this design to young King Menelik until a time later to be disclosed. This must not come between father and son. *Thus sayeth the Lord.*

In secret, Azariah informed the others who had been called into this plan by the angel of the Lord. The young king's counselors trembled in their souls, for they knew that if Azariah were false or mistaken, the power of the Ark would utterly destroy them if they entered into the Holy of Holies. She would not be taken, except by her permission. But their love for the Lady and their faith in the sincerity of their high priest, Azariah, compelled them to complicity.

As promised, when the time came, the angel of the Lord joined as an accomplice—opening the golden inner doors, providing invisible coverage of their movements, guiding them every step until Zion was sequestered in one of the common wagons of King Menelik's caravan that was prepared and awaiting the southward journey to her new home in Ethiopia.

The morning of departure had arrived, and King Menelik approached King Solomon for a final word. "Father, pray for me and bless me before I go." King Solomon nodded, for he had already called into attendance the company of his household. His mighty men, his valiant men, his priest, his wives, and his women stood as witness.

King Solomon stood before his son. In his eyes he saw light and promise. He took the holy oil of anointment, and Menelik closed his eyes. King Solomon poured the precious unguent over his son's bowed head. Then the king lifted one hand to the heavens and placed the other on his son. The king's blessing bellowed throughout heaven and earth:

Blessed be the Lord my God who blessed my father David, and who blessed our father Abraham. May He be with you always and bless your seed for all generations. May your blessings extend beyond the vastness of the heavens and the seasons of the earth. May all living creatures submit to your will, and may your will be just. May you live in joy. May you tarry for wisdom and not hasten to a fall. Be whole and not deficient in your character; be peaceful in your heart and perfect in your intention; be gracious and merciful and not subject to vindictiveness nor oppression; be truthful and not slovenly in lies; be not a sinner, but be strong in righteousness; be healthy and robust, and not prone to illness; do not covet perverseness, but stay on your path; be long-suffering and not prone to wrath. And should an adversary think to come against you, he shall be befuddled; and should he turn a hand against thee, that same hand shall be turned into an offering. And my Lady Zion, the holy and heavenly, the Tabernacle of the Law of God, shall be a guide unto thee at all times, a guide in respect of what you should think in your heart and do with your hands. Our Lady Zion shall be your guide. Selah.

King Solomon placed a crown upon young King David II's head. Father and son embraced, and thus blessed, King Menelik of Sheba made obeisance and departed.

Chapter 35

The Journey Home

*E*n route from Jerusalem to Axum, the caravan moved swiftly. Too swiftly. An exhausted King Menelik fell immediately asleep in his carriage and slept deep into the night. He dreamed of flight. He was as an eagle soaring high above a desert oasis. The dream was so vivid he could feel the soft caress of mist above the water as he flew overhead. The feeling of flight was always pleasant to him in his dreams, but this time the feeling held an eerie quality that disturbed him. Aware that he was dreaming, Menelik tried to wake. Although he felt awake, the sensation of the buoyancy of flight remained. He peered through the small window in his carriage and saw that his entire caravan soared three feet above the desert floor of the Negev. They were flying. *Flying?*

Holy men. Priests. Magi. Others. Some, though few, were known to fly. But by what means should this entire caravan be enabled to fly through the night? King Menelik bellowed a command from the window. Eventually, the caravan came to a suspended halt and then settled to the earth. He leaped out of his coach just as his commander had reached the door. His demeanor hurled curses, yet his calm voice asked, "Why are we flying?"

Obviously shaken, the Ethiopian commander addressed his king. "Your Majesty, it is your new chief priest, Azariah, who is able to explain this. May I signal for his escort?" He waited for the king's nod, then signaled a command. He stood beside the king and waited. His men immediately pitched the tent and arranged furnishings for the king's audience. Upon arrival, Azariah was escorted inside to the still-standing king.

King Menelik pivoted to face him and asked, "Azariah, how is it our caravan is flying?"

The sweat gathered like soldiers on the border of his hairline; although the high priest had known this moment was inevitable, bearing the scorn of his king was debilitating. He drew in his breath before speaking. "Your Majesty, I beg your indulgence. This is not heresy. I am responsible. Please forgive me for not informing you earlier. But I was forbidden. We are in fact flying because Our Lady is traveling with us." Azariah dared not look up, though he felt his body retreat in place as the king stepped forward.

"What? You have stolen the Ark from the Temple? From my father? Against the heavens? Who, from hell, are you?" The king hovered over Azariah, breathing with equestrian ferocity in his face. "Look at me!" he roared. Trembling, the priest lifted his face. Silence.

"Please, Majesty," Azariah tentatively ventured in whispered humility, "there are reasons, reasons beyond myself. Please. Allow me to explain."

Menelik, struck by the imprudence of Azariah's words but stayed by the humility of his demeanor, stepped back, folded his arms, and stood braced.

"I had a holy visitation that prompted our extreme act," he stated; he knew the cost of his life. Ignoring the perspiration that swam down his temples, Azariah continued. "I was forbidden to tell you, or to involve you in any way."

"What is happening here?" The king shouted spittle into the priest's face. "Speak straightly to me!"

"Yes, Your Majesty," Azariah said. He gathered his tattered composure and said, "Before the new moon, I had a dream in which an angel of the Lord told me to remove the Ark from the Temple, replace her with a replica, and carry her with us to Ethiopia."

"You have removed Our Lady of Zion from the Temple. Stolen her! You shall die for this. It is sacrilege!" Fury burned red beneath his brown skin.

"I may well die," Azariah said in resignation. He then added, "But I implore you, Majesty, hear me out. I love Our Lady with all my heart, soul, and spirit. I would gladly sacrifice my life for her. But had my actions been false, is it not true that the others and I would have been destroyed when we approached her in the Holy of Holies? She will not be touched except by her own permission. Is not the fact that I am—that we are all—not dead a sign that the direction of the dream was true and not false? The angel instructed me not to involve you. He stated to me, 'King Menelik must not know. This must not come between father and son.'"

"What have you done, Azariah? The king has probably already dispatched his army to capture us! My father built the Temple to house the spirit of God. The Ark has protected Israel through miraculous interventions. You cannot steal Judah's protection. You cannot rob the king of his homage. I do not know you to be arrogant, but the unholy presumption of this act may cost all our lives!"

After a long silence, Azariah spoke. "I am in your hands. I have only my life to offer. If I have here acted outside of accordance with the will of God, then I am no priest. If, in this, I have not discerned His voice and hand in this critical matter, then my life is nothing." Suddenly straightening his back, Azariah pressed on and added, "Your Majesty, you have my oath of loyalty to the laws and ordinances of God and to you and to your father to protect and serve you all the days of my life in the homeland of Ethiopia. I maintain my pledge, inviolate." He did not bow.

The two men stood in thick silence: eye to eye, the young king and his high priest. Menelik breathed deeply to brace his tremulous stance. Outrage ravaged him. Swollen veins marred his forehead and temples. Pain seared the thought of his father's great sorrow and loss on his mind. He searched the heart of Azariah through his eyes. Azariah, for his part, lay bare his naked soul to his king's scrutiny. Face to face, breath to breath, he could feel the heat of his king's mounting wrath.

Then King Menelik's eyes rolled back and closed. Incomprehensible utterances whispered from his lips as his body slowly weaved and bobbed. But the priest understood perfectly. The king was praying. He was invoking the Tzabaoth—the holy warring angels of the Lord, the host of the heavenly army called in to destroy all trespassers with their flaming swords of indignation. The stifled air rippled, cracked, then split in two above them. And there in the rift—the breach in the tent and in the sky—the army of hosts hovered with swords drawn.

They both saw. It was only then that the priest slowly lowered his gaze, bowed his head, and extended his bare neck.

Chapter 36

Until the Lord Says Other

Seemingly, hours passed in suspended time before Menelik and Azariah were released to animation. In fact, it took but a few potent moments for the young king to compose himself and demand to be taken to her.

Without hesitation, Azariah led him to the special common cart that he had had constructed to house the Lady. Menelik winced at the lowly accommodations, then took one more long look at his priest. "Leave us till dawn." The priest bowed and left immediately.

Menelik approached the cart and touched it gently. He opened the door to the wooden compartment that housed the Lady to expose the purple covering. He kneeled and lifted his hands, as he had seen his father do many times before. He opened with a Hebrew prayer. It was a simple blessing and sincere offer of gratitude for the sacred presence of the Tabot. Then, in silence, he stilled himself before the Ark and waited. He could not bring to words the questions and petitions spinning in his mind, so he kept his attention on the beating of this own heart and the blessedness of his proximity to the Lady. In the tranquility of her presence, his bosom began to blossom with a clear, warm, encompassing love. Quietly, the love in his heart flowed from his eyes. He did not know what to do. He must take her back. But how? Menelik's heart ached for his father's inevitable misery once the king realized that they had taken the Ark from its home in Jerusalem. And what of his mother on hearing the news of his betrayal and subsequent death? Just as he bowed to indulge his remorse, the sentiment was brushed aside, and the image of his grieving father dissipated like dust in the wind. In its place was the rustle of a small whirlwind. He tilted his nose toward the sound, and the familiar cadence culled anticipation from his chest.

Menelik opened his eyes; even in the night he could see the whirlwind growing between him and a soft illumination now emanating from the Ark. Without pronouncement, Menelik knew it was the approach of the Archangel Mikael. He rose in the angel's presence. Both parents had taught him that angels preferred one to be upright, so he stood humbly and waited.

Mikael spoke to him for a long span—not in words, but in the way angels actually speak: through images and transportation. Their utterances into the human spirit make direct adjustments. Menelik did not need to change or make up his mind; nor did he have to decide. Menelik's humility and surrender were the potter's clay that the hands of this messenger took and molded to conform to the will of the Lord: *It is His will that the Ark now abide with you in Ethiopia, King David II, grandson of King David of the Covenant legacy.*

This proposition, of his being entrusted with the care of the Ark, astounded Menelik and vacated every notion he had hitherto conceived about the nature of his life's path. Now all was recast, refined, and transformed with this new charge. He was still his mother's child and his father's son; yet in this exchange with this angel, he was quite alone, for he had abandoned himself for shores of spirit quite beyond the reach of parental oversight. It would take centuries for his seed to accomplish that which Menelik took on that day for the sake of his people and in the Name of God.

By dawn, Menelik's weary and radiant spirit was resolved and the priest absolved. He trusted his father's understanding to the Archangel Mikael. Menelik would return home to Ethiopia with a gift of splendor and grace far beyond anything his mother or people could have prayed for, or even dreamed possible.

Presently Menelik, still standing before the Ark, became aware of the haunting music that remained in the wake of the angel's departure. Then, like his father and grandfather before him, King Menelik proceeded to dance with all his might before the Ark of the Covenant of the Lord.

<hr />

For his part, King Solomon, still filled with pride at Menelik's virtues and brilliance, already missed his son. From the balcony, he eyed his kingdom and scanned the canopy of stars that covered it. Abruptly, Tzadok, his chief priest, burst in. "Your Majesty, it is the Ark. I sense that something has happened to the Ark!" Tzadok held his king's gaze. Then he turned and rushed back out the door with King Solomon at his side. Flanked by guards, they hastened to the temple.

They bowed a prayer before the entrance to the Holy of Holies before advancing to the Ark. It rested quietly under its cover. The two men relaxed. It appeared fine. Then Tzadok moved in and touched the fabric of the covering. He looked at the king, and Solomon nodded. When Tzadok lifted the covering, both men gasped at the crude wooden replica beneath. Finally, Tzadok cut the stunned silence. "Our sons. I fear it is our sons who have stolen the Ark."

"What? That is impossible!" *Impossible that the Ark is gone,* the king thought. *Impossible that there are no dead bodies in its wake. Impossible that our sons would dare!* This broke Solomon's heart and ignited his mind with a fiery calm. He summoned the guards. The Temple guards moved swiftly to the door as the two men stepped out. "Send the army to the south and stop the caravan of Prince Menelik. Bring them all back to Jerusalem under heavy guard. Arrest my son and Azariah, son of Tzadok, and bring them to me immediately." Ice coated the king's words.

"Your Majesty?" the chief of guards asked incredulously.

"Do it now. Time is essential. Now!"

The king stalked the hallways to his chamber, waving away his court. In private, he let loose his rage with furious curses and tears. *Who is this trickster son whom Makeda has sent? To woo his father and all Judah, only to steal our most sacred possession?* Finally, he fell to pray and to ask the Lord's forgiveness for failing to protect the Ark of the Covenant, as he had vowed.

The Archangel Mikael appeared before Solomon after he had spent a long while on his knees. "Rise, beloved of the Lord. You have not failed. It is the will of God that the Ark be now in the hands of your firstborn son. Hearken to these words and rise. The Lord has found favor in your son Menelik, and the charge of the Ark of the Covenant is now in his hands. For the sake of this land, the Spirit of the Lord remains seated forever in Jerusalem, but the presence of the Ark will now reside in Judah's southernmost kingdom of Ethiopia. And so it is done. And so it is forever, until the Lord says other."

Chapter 37

The Return of King Menelik

Queen Makeda rushed onto her balcony to catch the sight that had captivated the entire palace. From her vantage point atop the mountain fortress, she held a panoramic view of her capital city. Her eyes, unaccustomed to observing travel at such speed, took time to adjust to the recognition that just on the far north hillside was a flurry of color and dimension—the specter of her son's caravan. *How is he mounting the winds? Whereby has he been granted the ability to fly?* She had heard tales of flight in legend, dreamtime, among the priests, and from the mouth of Solomon. By the Ark, he had said, they were able to sail on the winds. As one who held her breath for the return of her only son and the hope of a piece of the fringe of the outer covering of the Ark, could it be so that his father had granted their son possession of Our Lady herself? Tears overflowed with the joy of her heart's detection that indeed, Ethiopia was now blessed with the presence of God on earth—within the sacred Ark of the Covenant. She turned and commanded, "Prepare the palace for the king. Prepare the Temple. Our Lady has come to Ethiopia. Prepare her house!" Her orders broke the spell, and everyone scattered to establish and order things according to her word.

By the time the queen was dressed and seated upon her throne, Menelik entered the great hall. Dark, handsome, and dusty from travel, he rushed toward his mother but then caught himself to first make obeisance to his queen.

"All honor to Her Royal Majesty, Queen Makeda of Greater Ethiopia and all the Southern Realm of the Kingdom of Judah. I greet you in peace, and with the great tidings and sentiments of the august King Solomon of Jerusalem, in the Holy Name of the God of Israel, shalom."

"Our king has returned, exalted and established in Glory," Queen Makeda proclaimed. She beamed a salute of honor. She then moved quickly down from her throne to greet her son. They fell into the returned traveler's redemptive embrace. "My son, my son," she repeated over and over. Finally their smiling eyes met; the same smile was reflected, mother and son. But in the deep recesses of his eyes, she no longer saw the vestiges of her baby, her boy. He was a man. A respectful difference necessitated an immediate respect and distance in the heart of the queen. "You are well, my son?" Makeda inquired.

"More than well to see your countenance. And you, Mother?"

"My heart has peace at your return." She paused to admire her son and then asked, "Your father has anointed you with the oil of kingship, yes?"

"Yes, Mother. Even more so, he has honored and imbued me with the mighty spirit of his father, and I shall reign as King David II."

"All praises be to the God of Israel," she said and clasped his hand. "Come," she said with a signal to her attendants, eager to pamper her son. "Now eat, rest, and retire yourself from your long journey. Later we will speak. There is much more I long to know."

"There is much more to tell and something even greater to show you," Menelik replied with a weary, radiant smile. "It cannot wait. Come with me now, Mother."

Queen Makeda nodded in agreement, and they eagerly left the Great Hall arm in arm.

From that day, Our Lady, the Holy Ark of the Covenant, came to abide in the highlands of Ethiopia. And the weeks that followed Her arrival were filled with hushed reverence as the people bustled about, eagerly making preparations for the coronation of their first king.

Chapter 38

The Coronation of King Menelik

Long before dawn, the priests had already stoked the fires in the two raised pits that stood on either side of the royal dais atop Mount Makeda. The pavilion, a marble trapezoid against the horizon, came to life with preparations as the people greeted one another and gathered at its base.

The coronation commenced when sets of trumpeters, dressed in white tunics and urbans, walked out to the corners of the pavilion. They wore gold banners across their chests, and the cowls of their shamas were draped over their shoulders and billowed in the light morning breeze. On command, they raised their trumpets and sounded the opening of the ceremony as the multicolored streamers embellishing their horns danced like confetti in the sky. Then a lone priest dressed in full temple regalia walked out and stood center stage. Slowly, he leaned back as he lifted a huge *shofar* and blew a long piercing tone directly into the hearts of the people of the southernmost House of Judah.

The members of the royal entourage took their seats under a turquoise canopy. Next, the princes, captains, and chiefs marched out in formation and stood facing the people. Finally, Queen

Makeda emerged to stand, not at the foot of her throne, but simply to the side in front of the royal family. Even in the shadowy pre-dawn light, the emeralds, diamonds, and inlayed rubies sparkled in the filigreed gold setting of her crown and were coordinated with the shimmering ornamentation of her ceremonial robe. Daybreak cast its amber rose-tinged breath across the backdrop of the final hours of her reign.

The musicians began the lulling rhythm of their traditional anthem beneath the booming voice of the priest consecrating the occasion with prayers. The people rocked and swayed to the ancient sounds. Alert in crisp anticipation, when the music fell silent, the people took a few moments to shuffle into hushed stillness.

Then a solitary figure emerged from behind the mount of the covered throne and walked to the fore of the pavilion. He moved with slow, deliberate grace. His approaching silhouette was as formidable as a huge boulder being rolled by strongmen. A golden breastplate that bore the head of a lion covered his entire chest. His loins were girded with gold cupping and leather straps. Deep purple and blue silk skirted to midway down his thighs. Ceremonial armature hugged the muscular girth of his calves and disappeared into the brazen coverlets that mounted his boots. Diamonds, sapphires, and rubies studded the two gilded sheaths that hung from his sides and housed his weighty swords. A ceremonial cloak of royal blue and spun gold was draped across his broad shoulders. The cape, though held together securely at the neck by a clasp in the shape of a six-pointed star, was cast back by his motion to reveal bronze arms as thick and smooth as the oars of the royal fleet.

The people gasped as one. *Could this be His Highness?* Menelik had not been brought before them since the ceremony that had welcomed him into manhood ten years earlier. Ebony, shoulder-length locks surrounded his squared face. Even from a distance, the people could see the shadow of his thick brows and the grooming of his beard into thick locks that jostled against his breastplate as he advanced toward them. They confirmed that he had the queen's large luminous eyes; but the prominence of his nose and cheeks belonged to the seed of Judah.

When Menelik finally reached the center, he stopped and stood directly below the steps to his covered throne. He slowly turned his head, as if to behold in his gaze each man, woman, and child individually. The priest stepped to his left, while the Queen Mother approached him from the right. Queen Makeda nodded, and Menelik kneeled on the royal stool. His high priest, Azariah, began a succession of prayers over him. The people followed his lead, themselves first bowing facedown to the earth and then remaining on their knees.

They witnessed Menelik, upright on his knees, close his eyes as the priest anointed him with the oil of sovereignty, poured from the same horn used by his father in Jerusalem. Then, step by step, the entire ceremony that King Solomon had performed in Jerusalem to anoint his son to kingship was reenacted here before the House of Judah, forever rooted in Ethiopia.

Drums sounded, and the people rose in response. They heard the snap of fabric as the throne behind Menelik was unveiled. Again they gasped. Although they had anticipated the requisite replacement of the queen's throne of delicately carved ebony inlaid with

ivory and embellished with turquoise stones and filigreed gold—
which, in the memory of even the eldest gathered here, had been
the one throne of all the queens—still they were shocked by the
massive new throne of huge golden carvings and stunned by the
two fierce lion heads protruding from each armrest. The feet of
the throne had thick gilded claws, and the velvet of the seat cushion
was deep crimson. The ceremony proceeded with Queen Makeda
walking over to face her son.

Memories beaded themselves across Menelik's mind at his mother's smile,
and for an instant he felt like a nervous boy again seeking courage in his
mother's eyes. But this time when he entered her gaze, it was different.
The warm magnet that usually drew him into her deep serenity was absent.
Instead Menelik began to feel the pressure of his mother pushing him out of
her eyes. Abruptly she ousted him like a trespasser. He then felt the force of
her gaze move into his own eyes, seeking and pressing him downward into
himself. Although not consciously, he must have resisted, for he could feel the
wrestling between their eyes. Makeda bore down relentlessly on her son. In
her final act of mothering, Makeda backed her son so deeply within himself
that he felt pressed against a wall. Then she stopped, withdrew slightly, and
waited.

Although feeling stunned and abandoned, Menelik did not flee his own
dark place. Something in the shadow of his consciousness drew his attention.
Before he could brace himself, he felt the spread of Sophia, the rush of his
own Wisdom, coursing through his mind and body. The flood pushed his
mother out of his spirit and into the orbit of her own eyes. His entire being
quickened, but he never flinched nor closed his eyes. He was determined to

meet the power and demands of this moment, and indeed of his entire reign, open-eyed and vigilant.

In fact, no words were spoken between mother and son, and only a moment had passed; but in those eye-seconds, a new order had been established. The high priestess brought forth the heavy golden cuff that had been formed from the anointed bracelet of the queens, which Makeda had received at her coronation from her mother, according to custom. The queen placed the cuff in the muscular contour of her son's upper arm and latched the leather clasp.

"The might and magic of this cuff will protect and provide for Your Majesty all the days of your reign. May the legacy of this new reign of kings be glory unto the Lord, world without end."

Then the queen nodded to Azariah, who in turn opened the hinged lid of a jewel-encrusted case and extended the new crown inside to her. Menelik again kneeled and tilted his head slightly forward and braced his neck. Makeda lifted it from the case, lowered the crown atop his locks, and arranged the flaps on either side of his face. Although the crown was cushioned by his thick hair, Menelik still felt its heaviness pressing down on the circumference of his head and the inner padding of the lower rim snugly gripping the flesh of his brow. As he stood to his full crowned height, he saw the flutter of his mother moving to the side.

Makeda bowed her shoulders and head as she backed away from her son, allowing instinct to guide her from behind. Once in place, she stood erect, lifted the delicate crown from her own head, and handed it to her high priestess. She turned and beheld her people in a tender sweeping gaze and then gently led their eyes, with a nod, in the direction of her son.

Ethiopia followed this final subtle command of their beloved queen and let loose with thunderous applause and ululation. *My people. My son. Our king.* Makeda felt the muscles in her long neck finally relax.

King Menelik's crown almost doubled the length of his face and was studded with rows of rubies. A diamond Star of David was inlaid at the center. The velvet flaps attached to the crown were beaded with rubies and pearls that fell from his crown to his shoulders. The people likened the full effect of the raiment of King Menelik to the familiarity of the overflow of Tis Issat Falls, the source of the Blue Nile. The purple, blue, and white fabric rippled about him. Yet, as the sunrise peaked over the hillside behind them, the light hit the rubies across his forehead, sprinted down his locks, and ran along the rubied shaft of the two swords at his sides—and his countenance seemed to stream rivulets of blood.

Menelik slowly took in the panorama of his people. Plentiful as the forest, they were a sea of white strewn with vibrant flowers. Their dark hair and multihued complexions echoed the rich fertility of the earth. Suddenly, all his senses heightened and flooded with the pungent sweetness of the incense, the burnt offerings, the fecundity of the land, and the musky fragrance of life. He heard the drums beating in his blood, and his shoulders and knees conceded to rock to the ancient rhythms. A great gust of energy welled up from his people and crashed over him like a wave, rocking him with its impact. Menelik felt their awe and fear, their hesitation and their hope. Finally, in a sigh, the people yielded to destiny and placed the mantle of their confidence in the hands of their first king. The purity of their hearts and the simplicity of their allegiance to God and to those He divinely appointed cleansed him of ambition, doubt, and arrogance and filled him with humility.

The high priest Azariah moved forward with the scroll of entitlement to announce the list of the royal appellations of kingship. A strong impulse caused Menelik to halt the high priest with a gesture of his hand. Abruptly, Menelik turned and headed directly for the Tabernacle of the Law, which was radiating a pulsating glow that compelled him to draw near. He sped past his mother and the royal family.

Just as he approached the veiled entrance of the Tent, he saw a diaphanous figure waiting outside. The presence of King Solomon was shimmering in the sunrise. His father held back the veil then followed his son into the Tabernacle and on into the inner sanctuary of the Holy of Holies.

The Tabernacle was ablaze. The sky was streaked like purple and orange birds of paradise. Although the earth quaked, the people were locked in place. They looked to the royal family. All the royals stood with their eyes posted on the Tabernacle. Rolling balls of thunder battered their minds and chipped away at their serenity as they all convened their focus on the composure of their former queen.

Finally, King Menelik emerged from the Tabernacle with the essence of his father behind him. Alone, he stalked each of the four comers of the pavilion, at last halting at the center's edge. The illumination of the Ark had swollen and singed his locks bronze and had narrowed his large eyes to slits. Without harm, the gold on his breastplate had molded to his physique—every muscle and sinew revealed. He hovered over his people. God? Animal? Angel? Surely king.

Azariah began to call out his titles as he ascended the six marble steps to his throne:

King Menelik,
Son of Queen Makeda and King Solomon
Elect of God
Keeper of the Faith
Conquering Lion of the Tribe of Judah
His Imperial Majesty
Negusa Negest ze Ethiopia [King of Kings of Ethiopia]
King David II.

King Menelik raised his arms to the heavens with a vow to shelter his people. Scepter in hand, he sat on his throne. The musician-priests let loose the harmonies of the new kingdom. The people fell into ecstasy and danced for the glory of their lives.

Gathered at full sunrise on the dawning of a new day: mother, father, son, and the overvaulting presence of the Holy Spirit.

Ethiopia! Stretch forth your arms to God!

Chapter 39

———⌘———

Harm's Way

Ethiopia, 1973: A Year Later

After Brenna accepted Prince John's proposal, it was still ten months before she completed her graduate program. Letters and phone calls barely sustained them. But at last, it was the next June. Brenna hastily left Stanford with her two degrees in hand and her present and primary hope of being John's wife. She had only been back in Los Angeles for three days when the call came.

"Hello, Brehenna?" It was surely Prince John.

"Yohannes?" she said, her voice smiling.

"Of course, were you expecting someone else?" he asked teasingly.

"Of course, but I guess you'll have to suffice," she said, playing along.

"I have a gift for you," he said as he changed the subject. "A graduation present."

"That's so sweet. Did you send it?"

"No," he said. After a pause he added, "You'll have to come and get it."

"Oh," Brehenna said, a bit confused.

"Are you ready to travel?"

"When?"

"This week. I've already sent your ticket. It's with TWA. Can you leave this Friday?"

"Wow," Brehenna said, catching her breath. "This is a big surprise. OK. I'm coming. What should I do?"

"Just call the airline and arrange your flight, then call me back so I'll know when to collect you at the airport."

"Oh my God, you're not kidding," Brehenna said, perking up.

"No I'm not kidding. Come home. I've been waiting for you all year. Come home."

"OK. Me too. Yes. Yes, yes. I'm coming home. My God, I love you. This is a great gift." Brehenna's voice trailed off and splintered with emotion.

"You're not crying, Brehenna, are you?" Yohannes said, teasingly accusing her.

"No, no, of course not," she said. Then, after her lie, she added, "OK, maybe a little. Happy tears, though."

"Hey, baby, you know it's OK. I'm just teasing. I love you. Come home. Call me."

"I love you too. I'll see you this week. Whatever it takes, I'll be there."

"OK, then, make your arrangement and call."

"Yes, I will. I promise."

"All right then. Ciao."

"Bye." Brehenna sat stunned on the side of her bed. Then she sprang into action, racing to tell her mother of their plans.

———

After spending a week alone together in Addis, Brehenna and Yohannes decided to make their first social appearance as a betrothed couple by accepting an invitation from the women of the family. The day of the affair, Brehenna sang Aretha's "April Fools" and danced around as she dressed.

She picked an Ethiopian dress with lavender trim to wear to the tea that the women of the royal family were giving in her honor. They were going to welcome her into the family as Yohannes's wife-to-be. *It's true*, she thought as she admired herself in the mirror, *she especially looks Ethiopian in traditional clothes*. She wished she was, but in a way, after she married Yohannes, she would be Ethiopian. Ethiopian royalty. Not bad for a girl from Watts and a descendent of enslaved people. She felt a little guilty for feeling ashamed. But didn't the slaves themselves run for freedom when they got the chance? She wanted to escape poverty and the scorn of others who had been born into more. She hoped she would find friends among the women today. She was alone here except for Yohannes. The emperor as her advocate was no small thing, but she rarely saw him. She thought about Yohannes's smile and his habit of tousling her short Afro like she was a little boy. Brehenna floated into the library, where she found Prince Yohannes reading the paper.

"Well, now," he said admiringly, "you'll be a hit today."

"You like it?" she asked with a tilt of her head.

"Absolutely." He stood and walked toward her.

"Thank you, sir!" Brehenna did a little twirl for him. He moved in for a kiss, and she slightly turned him her cheek and added, "My lipstick. I better go; I don't want to keep the ladies waiting." She smiled as they held hands, and he walked her out.

At the car door, he whispered in her ear, "Watch out: some of my cousins are barracudas."

"Well, fortunately I've had to learn to swim with a few sharks," she quipped and kissed him on the cheek.

"Your lipstick," he said to remind her, but he leaned in for a real kiss anyway.

"Oh, well," she said, happily conceding. "I'll fix it in the car." They kissed briefly, and she got in. He waved, and she blew him a kiss from the back window.

Princess Sophia, the emperor's daughter, and Princess Mary, her niece, met Brehenna at the palace steps when she emerged from the car.

"Ta na yis ta leen?"

"In da min a lu." They each greeted her traditionally with light kissing sounds as they alternated cheeks.

"Please come, my dear," said the older princess with genuine warmth. When they entered the salon, at least a dozen other women of the family were seated or moving about the room, chatting,

drinking tea, or nibbling hors d'oeuvres. The women were of varying ages and sizes, but what was consistent among them was the
slenderness of their arms and hands and the fact that their faces
featured either huge luminous eyes or dark gaunt sockets. Those
with both looked haunted. The handshakes were so delicate as to
seem weak, shy, or reticent. Once the women were seated on various chairs and sofas about the room, the questions began.

"So, Miss Hayes, how are you enjoying your engagement with
His Highness?"

"He is one of the more—how do you say…?" another relative
began.

"…spirited young men in our family?" chimed in a second
woman.

"Fine," Brehenna interjected. "Fine. Yohannes is special, isn't
he?"

"I hear the wedding shall be in one year."

"Yes. We don't have an exact date yet. His Majesty will let us
know."

"Of course. There are many plans to be made," a young cousin
added.

"Aunt Sophia," Brehenna said, turning to the elder princess, "Yohannes said I must engage your support for the wedding
plans."

"Oh, you have it, my dear."

"Thank you."

"Miss Hayes, you do plan children, yes? I'm sure Yohannes
would adore having sons."

"We certainly hope for several children."

"We don't raise our own children, you know," a young women remarked.

"What does that mean?" Brehenna asked, turning and setting her tea aside.

"It means you will not need to raise your own children. We have nurses, governesses, and tutors for that. We have many ways that you're probably unaccustomed to."

"I'm sure you're right—perhaps some that I may never become accustomed to. I plan to mother all my children, even with help. I am an educator, after all," Brehenna said to remind them.

Then Princess Mary continued in a soft voice, "There are other duties that will require your attention. Other, more pressing duties," she said with a smile, and several other cousins giggled. Princess Sophia halted Mary with a glance and then spoke quietly but sharply in Amharic. They were silenced. Then she reached over and gently touched the back of Brehenna's hand.

"Pay them no mind. Of course you shall mother your children. Yohannes knows you also have your customs and desires, as a mother and wife, which may differ from ours."

From a distant couch in a high-pitched, gentle tone came a voice. "Miss Hayes, tell us of your family. Who is your father? Tell us of your upbringing."

"My father is deceased, and I'm from a humble background of working people."

"But Yohannes says you are from our lineage?"

"Over the past year, Professor Akele at the university researched my family's genealogy. Although I was familiar with talk of an Ethiopian heritage of some kind from my grandparents, I never heard any specifics."

"They do wondrous things at the university. Especially at Grandfather's bidding," Princess Mary said with a swipe.

"Well, since not one of us was present to witness our conception, we all must rely on the word of our kin to speak our heritage," Brehenna replied.

"Miss Hayes, more tea?" Mulu, their hostess from her previous visit, said to distract her.

"Thank you, Mulu—please." Brehenna accepted and turned her attention to Mulu's round face and sweet smile.

Princess Ruth, another member of the royal family seated near Mary, turned to face Brehenna, and said, "It's not as easy as it may seem, being a member of the royal family."

"The more I learn about duties and responsibilities, it is seeming more difficult, but many of you carry your responsibilities so graciously it's hard to notice."

"There is a lot for you to learn…" Ruth said with a conspiratorial look at Mary.

"I'm certain there is," Brehenna said in agreement.

"And we shall all be pleased to help you." It was the voice from the winged-back chair near the fireside. It was Princess Tenagnework, the emperor's eldest daughter and family matriarch ever since the death of his wife. All eyes turned to her, and many lowered them to their teacups. There was a chill and finality to what she said, as she nodded and gave a dry, even-eyed smile in Brehenna's direction.

Brehenna smiled back and said, "Thank you, Your Highness."

Princess Tenagnework said to the servant, "Please have His Highness join us now."

In a few moments, Prince Yohannes bounded in and made his rounds kissing aunts and cousins as he went. "All the beautiful flowers of Addis gathered in one room," he said in a booming voice as he kissed his eldest aunt's wizened hand and blushing cheek.

"Save that for my sister—you are her pet," said Princess Tenagnework.

"Yes, come here and let me see your handsome face,"Aunt Sophia said, beckoning.

"Now you see all those who have spoiled me," Yohannes said, beaming and grinning at Brehenna; she smiled back and watched him embrace his favorite aunt. As soon as Yohannes had settled in his seat and lit a cigarette, not the servant, but Mary, approached and quietly served him tea. With proprietary precision, she added three spoons of sugar and a slice of lemon; then she looked directly into Brehenna's eyes with an unflinching gaze.

Later that night, Brehenna awoke disorientated. It took her a while to get her bearings. Then she eased from Yohannes's bed, slid into her slippers and robe, and tiptoed across the room. Quietly, she closed the balcony door behind her and walked out to view the sleeping Addis. The night was cool and as pleasant as the sight of the modest city lights. She had not noticed that Yohannes had come out and stood silently by the door until she heard the *zip-click* of his lighter.

"Why are you out of bed?" he asked through smoke. Brehenna turned.

"I had a strange dream. I couldn't get back to sleep. It seemed so real." She turned back to the city.

"Come. Sit over here. Tell me about your dream." He walked over and pulled a chair from the table then sat in the one beside it.

To Brehenna, everything seemed in slow motion as she took her seat. Then a servant appeared with tea service.

"Your Highness?" he inquired at the door. Yohannes gestured, and the tea was served. He watched Brehenna accept the tea and warm her hands with the cup before drinking.

"I thought you might be cold," Yohannes remarked, and then he tried to cover his thoughtfulness by nonchalantly blowing smoke.

"Thank you," she said, speaking to his profile. After several silent sips, Brehenna asked in a tentative, soft voice, "Do you still want to hear my dream?"

"Yes. Sure. Go ahead." He watched her eyes wander then gather a distant focus on the landscape and the activity of her recollecting dream.

"This is a recurring dream. I used to have it a lot when I was young. But I haven't had it for a long time. Anyway, I dreamed I was a little girl, and I was watching my mother weave with an old wooden loom. It all seemed so real. I remember watching her fast fingers and the moving thread. Then I was struggling down a rocky hill toward the water. The sea maybe. I could look down and see my short legs and little shoes. I felt so close to the ground. So I must have been young. It was early in the morning, because I could see the sun rising over the water. I felt happy to see it. The sun. Then I was back with my mother. This dream mother didn't look like my real mother. She was tall and thin. Her eyes were large and soft. She was always smiling and singing to me." Brehenna continued reporting the details of her dream to Yohannes, who sat quietly smoking.

When she was finished, her tale lingered in the air like cotton puffs and golden threads. Neither spoke. What was there to say?

They let their silent separate wonderings disperse in the night air. Although engaged, they were still new lovers who made measured moves and then waited and watched: not to gain advantage or triumph over each other but to exercise the patience to win in love—to dodge what pawns they could in order to spare both king and queen. It was a form of chess designed to save love's kingdom with warm, cushioned, sometimes playful parleys. Tonight, just sitting was all. Eventually, Yohannes took her hand, and they went back into the room to cuddle and let the silent sweetness claim them.

⚬⚬⚬

Weeks later, the couple went on an outing about an hour east of the capital. The landscape grew lush and green, and trees lined the road as they approached Debre Zeit, a local resort town for the wealthy. When they arrived at Fairfield Palace—one of the emperor's vacation homes, named after his wartime home in Bath, England—they found children playing on the lawn.

"Who are all these kids?" Brehenna asked, beaming with excitement.

"Cousins, mainly. Family." He looked at her face. "OK, teacher, I guess you want to join the kids?"

"I do," Brehenna replied, but Yohannes had already turned, held up a hand, and moved toward the racing boys. In seconds, someone kicked the ball to him, and they were off playing soccer. Brehenna watched and laughed, because she had never seen Yohannes, who seemed to love the formality of suits, so full of rough and tumble.

He was on the ground, and his jeans and shirt were already grass stained and dirty.

Cousin Marta walked up to her, laughing. "Bad boys," she said with a chuckle. "That's my husband in the blue shirt—the husky one with the big Afro. I didn't know he could move so swiftly." It seemed the actual boys were laughing from the sidelines as the young men, the princes, took over the soccer game. Brehenna looked from man to man on the field and saw that they were all handsome. Ethiopians were just a handsome people.

"Come, it's hot out," Princess Martha said; she took Brehenna's hand and walked her over to a group of young women on a shaded terrace. Brehenna recognized many of them as they approached her with greetings and kissing gestures. She sat beside Princess Rut and her baby daughter. A servant brought iced tea, which Brehenna gladly accepted. She cooled down and eased in with the women, comfortable despite the fact that they were mostly conversing in Amharic. Their chirping was pleasant on the afternoon breeze. Brehenna knew that one day she too would be fluent enough to effortlessly chime in. But for now, she enjoyed the companionable solitude of a linguistic outsider. She cooed at the chubby girl bouncing in her mother's lap and reached out her hands.

"May I, Rut?" Brehenna asked.

"Ishi," the young mother said. She handed her the child, who came eagerly into her new playmate's arms. The girl was both fluffy and sweet. Brehenna looked back at her mother.

"Kongit," the mother said, offering her daughter's name. "*Kho*ngit," she repeated, stressing the hard K sound.

Shortly, Marta was back at her side, with her delicate hand constantly pushing back curls that stubbornly bounced into her face at every turn.

"Oh, I see you like babies. This one's a beauty. Kongit. Her name means beautiful."

"I love her name!" she said. She turned back to the baby and said, "It's such a pretty name for such a pretty girl. Yes, you are. You're such a *kongit* girl." Brehenna continued to cuddle and bounce the baby.

"Look there, Brehenna," Martha said.

Brehenna could see water over the balcony. She walked with the baby over to the rail.

"That's Lake Bishoftu," Martha said. Brehenna now saw the stunning panoramic view of the landscape and the lake. Foliage and flowers spilled over the terrace, and she saw more vibrant flowers and birds in the garden below. Holding the chubby Kongit on her hip, they shared the sight. Then she heard loud voices and scuffling up the walk.

"The men are back," Martha announced. And they were dirty and sweaty and loud. Yohannes made his way to her.

"I like it, I like it!" he boomed.

"What?" Brehenna asked.

"You and the baby. That looks good to me." He slipped a grubby hand around her thin sundress and kissed her neck. She playfully pushed him away.

"What's wrong, am I too..." He tried to find the English slang. "Funky? Right?"

"That would be exactly right. Don't get that mud on Kongit!" Laughing, she steered the baby away.

"All right all ready." He grabbed for her again, but she was too quick.

"OK, to the showers!" he called to his brother and cousins, also funky, and they all headed inside.

The men had not been gone long when the ladies heard the crunch of car tires on the gravel. Several cars abruptly halted in the driveway. Then there was shouting and the crunch of running feet. Brehenna jumped, for although she couldn't understand the Amharic, she knew trouble was afoot. Several guards appeared out of nowhere and herded the women inside. Rut rushed to retrieve Kongit as Brehenna grabbed the bottle and the diaper bag. They were ushered from the terrace into the salon, where other family members and guests were also huddled. Yohannes and the other men rushed in. Someone was barking orders, and everyone was moving toward the back door. Brehenna was scared and confused. Then, Yohannes was at her side.

"Move quickly. It's trouble, but we'll be all right," he said, but he kept up a steady, anxious exchange with the other men as they all made for the limos and cars that awaited them in the back. Brehenna and Yohannes were the last to pack into the second limo. Just as Brehenna squeezed into the seat, she turned, and Yohannes closed the door behind her. He was not getting into the car. Brehenna jerked to the window; he looked her in the eye and held up his hand to motion something, but she couldn't understand. The car screeched and sped the children and women away.

Back at home, Brehenna stayed downstairs waiting and dozing on the couch. Later that evening, when Prince Yohannes arrived home, she rushed to the door to meet him. He looked haggard but welcomed her embrace. He dismissed his guards, and they headed upstairs. To her demand to know who they were and what had happened, he said they were radicals. Militant troublemakers. No big deal. They took care of everything. There was nothing further for her to worry about. Really.

The passing weeks were uneventful as far as security was concerned. Brehenna often pondered what the royal family must feel being subject to such random attacks. She was a little worried, but she had a man named Colonel Tesfeye to guard her when she went out. She really didn't like having a bodyguard hovering about, watching her every move, but it was a small price to pay for the lovely future she envisioned with Yohannes. One morning, she went out for a trip to the post office and the jeweler. She saw that Colonel Tesfeye had four additional soldiers standing by, whom he insisted must also travel with her.

"John…John, where are you?" Brehenna called as she rushed back to the bedroom.

"Yes? I'm here. What's the matter?" Yohannes hurried from the bathroom, tying his robe and wiping the shaving cream from his cheeks.

"I went out to the car, and the colonel has four bodyguards for me. Four."

"Are you certain they're all traveling with you?"

"I asked if they were all for me, and he said yes. Yohannes, I really don't like having all these people following me around."

"Brehenna, you need the security. That's why you have it. I too have security. We all do."

"I know. But, you've always had it. You're used to it. I understand you all probably need it. I don't need bodyguards. Nobody knows me."

"You can walk around thinking you are anonymous, but believe me, everyone knows who you are."

"But even if they did, I haven't done anything, so why would anyone want to hurt me?"

"Brehenna, it has nothing to do with what you have or haven't done." He took her hand and walked her to the settee. "We need to talk," he said. "The colonel has already reported to Grandfather that people have made threats against your life. It doesn't have to do with you, but more with my family and me. Hurting you would be an act of protest against me—us—the family. You are an easier target, because you are not as mindful of security. Plus you are not yet established in the hearts of the people." He hesitated a moment and added, "I hate to be harsh, but by killing you, they could make a point without arousing the people to protest. It's nothing personal."

"So you're saying that this is real?" Then she conceded soberly, "I'm in real danger."

"Yes, the danger for you is real. So please, be careful as you move about. Allow your guards to stay close and do their jobs. You need to know that Grandfather said that after today, if the colonel has to add any more guards to you, we'll have to send you to a safer place."

"This is scary." She leaned in, and he hugged her to his chest. "Maybe I won't go out, then. You could get someone to shop and do my errands for me, right?"

"I could, but I'm not going to." He pulled back to look at her. "Brehenna, this is our country, our life. My wife cannot become imprisoned in our own home. Go out. Be among the people. You have my most capable guards. You'll be safe."

Brehenna studied his face. "OK, I'll go." Then she added, "But I'll be back early."

"Good. Call me at the office as soon as you get home, OK?"

"OK." They stood.

"Hey, don't look so sad. You'll be fine. Really," Yohannes said reassuringly.

"I'll be fine? *Be* fine? What? If you think I'll be fine, what am I now?" She cocked her head and put a hand on her curvy hip.

At first puzzled by her shift in tone, Yohannes quickly snapped back. "Fine," he said with a smile while sliding his arm around her waist. "Real fine. Beautiful fine." He pulled her to him and whispered in her ear: "Sexy." She pulled back.

"Ah, no you don't. I got to go," she said with a giggle; she wiggled out of his arms and went across the room. She turned back to him when she neared the door, paused, and smiled. "Later. We'll see about this later."

"Count on it," he said. He watched her from behind as she sashayed down the hall.

Several weeks passed, and they were home dining alone. Yohannes slowly leafed through the evening edition of the *Ethiopian Herald*. Across the table, Brehenna haltingly translated the Amharic headline: "STUDENT PROTESTS CONTINUE—UNIVERSITY CLOSES AGAIN."

She sipped her iced tea and compared it with her own experience of annual spring protests at Stanford University, which usually resulted in school closing a few weeks earlier than scheduled. The protesting students, whether the Black Students Union or Students for a Democratic Society, usually got most of their demands met. She assumed that college administrators and trustees at other institutions were as accommodating to their students as was the case at Stanford. She viewed the tragedy of Kent State as a horrible exception. It was a matter of translation. She could barely translate the language of this land and even less so the political and cultural reality looming before her.

The closing of Haile Selassie University this time was portentous, signaling that the ground was shifting beneath the very structure and family to whom she had recently committed her allegiance and future. But Brehenna continued to view the world through the buoyant, cluttered myopia of a young woman whose vision and hands were filled with preparation for her wedding, her new husband, and her new life.

She was daunted by her limited Amharic, so her gaze slid away from the rest of the indecipherable front page. Still, she was somewhat pleased to know that now at least she had been able to read the headline. Her eyes fell on the family crest at the head of her dinner plate. She studied it, only looking up when she then heard the soft bump of the servant's shoulder against the swinging door from the kitchen.

With that, Yohannes set aside the newspaper, and she caught a glimpse of the furrow crossing his brow before it faded and they both straightened for their meal. They ate their salads in silence. When they were finished, the servants quietly removed the plates and replaced them with the main course of beefsteak with a portion of black beans and rice. They began with the small serving of injera and wot, the traditional Ethiopian foods that were served at their table with every meal, including breakfast. Then she watched as Yohannes took a banana from the fruit bowl, cut it in half, peeled it, and then placed slices on top of his hot beans.

Brehenna thought it odd—beans and bananas—but still she reached for the other half of the cut banana and followed his example. She tasted how the sweet banana cooled and rounded out the spicy bean mixture.

He watched her eating it. "It's good, isn't it?" he asked with a smile.

"Surprisingly, yes. I like it," she said, smiling back. They continued enjoying their meal.

Finally, his words slid smoothly across the quiet table. "I have something to tell you. Something you're not going to like."

"Well, what if you don't tell me, then?" Brehenna said.

Yohannes looked across the table with only one corner of his mouth slightly smiling, but his eyes were steady. He continued, "I spoke with Grandfather today, and the colonel reported that he'd had to add two more guards to your detail. Is that so?"

"Yes, there were two more guards this morning. There are six now."

"You do remember what Grandfather said about adding more guards to your detail? Do you remember what this means?"

She looked down at her plate. Her mind slid into a fugue and was unable to acknowledge what she knew it meant. She hoped. Maybe things had changed. "No. What? Tell me again what it means," she asked, barely audible.

"It means you'll be going back home to Los Angeles. You're booked on a flight this coming Thursday morning."

After an awkward pause, he added, "How do they say it in America? 'Well, that's the way the cookie crumbles.'"

Her eyes slashed at him as she jerked her napkin from her lap, slapped it on the table, and began to rise. "That's not funny or clever. Excuse me." The servant barely reached her chair to assist in her departure from the table. Brehenna scurried into the living room. She just wanted to get away from him. To think. What did he mean, "Go back home to Los Angeles"? *This is home*, she thought. *He's my home. Go back to what? This is my life now. He is my husband. This is our home, my family. My people. My country.* Her thoughts scattered like night beetles caught in the light. It had taken her two years to transform her life and reframe her future to this: to envision him as her husband and prepare for having their children; to acculturate herself to Ethiopia; to train for her own duties as a woman in the royal family and the duchess of a province. Then there were the Amharic language studies and learning how to supervise the palace staff. What about all the new family and friends she had met? Slowly she had become accustomed to the emperor being her grandfather as well. She had entered a whole new world. Now this: go back! Her mind was scrambling for some footing—a place to stand. She could not speak. Yohannes followed her into the living room, which was now dark except for the fireplace and a single lamp near a couch.

"Brehenna, come here. Let me talk to you," he said in soothing tones. "Are you angry with me?"

She turned to face him, her eyes glossy with the standing tears she held back. She was afraid to start crying, since very soon there would be no one to console her. She walked cautiously toward him, watching him in case he might hurl another life-shattering curse from his mouth. Reluctantly she came to him, needing to be held. She buried her face between his shoulder and neck. She felt the sting in the back of her sinus and the quivering of her lower jaw, so she nestled closer.

"I'm sorry, sweetheart. I shouldn't have teased you. I meant nothing by it. I didn't know what to say."

"I don't want to go," she whispered into his shoulder. "Please, don't make me go."

He answered her, not from his usual hungry passion but by offering a slow, deliberate kiss that drew her out of her doubt and into his love and longing.

"I don't want you to go. But you are not safe here. Grandfather says you must return to America until we can secure things here."

They walked over and sat on the couch. After a while, Brehenna calmed down. Yohannes got up and put in a videotape of *Star Trek*. The servant brought brandy and coffee, served them, and then left. Again they were alone. Yohannes had his arm around Brehenna as he watched the show, but Brehenna couldn't watch. They now had only two days left. It was not, after all, the beginning of a lifetime together. In anguish, Brehenna did not know how to *not* become his wife, how to undo her new life. She did not know how to be with him just two more days and then be gone.

"What if I spoke to your grandfather? Maybe I could change his mind?"

"No. He is resolved that this is the best way to keep you safe."

"Yohannes, I need to hear you tell me: What do *you* want?"

"Of course, I also want you to be safe," he began thoughtfully. "And I need you here with me. But you will be going back on Thursday. It's settled." He saw the tears moving down her cheeks. "Don't be sad. We'll arrange things here, and I'll send for you." He said this to console her, yet he too wondered if he would ever see her again. So he studied her large eyes and how the fan of her lashes kept them shaded. He recalled the seductive way her lips curled into her private smile. He lifted her chin and peeked under her lowered eyes with a wide grin on his face. Yes, he was forever endeared to her, for even now she couldn't help but smile back. He knew she loved him.

He lowered her beneath him on the couch and stroked the soft flesh of her arm and closed his eyes to preserve the memory in his hand. Deeply, he breathed in the scent of her, and it stirred his appetite. He let himself be mesmerized by the firm swells of her breasts against his chest and the heat of the press of their loins.

Brehenna, on the other hand, held on less to him and more to the hope that one day she would return. She did not want to remember him in detail. She did not know how she could bring him along in her heart yet live without him. She forced her mind to leave their embrace, to look ahead, to begin to construct a vision of an alternate life from the shambles of her dream. Where would she live? Where would she work? Who would she be?

Upstairs in bed, Brehenna swore that she would forget his eyes, his lips, his mustache, his dark curling hair, the view of the back of his body over his shoulder while lying beneath him. She breathed deeply of him so she could remember exactly the smell she was pledging to forget. His eager lust must surely be forgotten. She would forget all of his I love yous and the close, quiet way they slept together. She would forget the beautiful children they would never have. She would forget all of him and the future they had planned together. She vowed to forget everything. She would be forgetting him for the rest of her life.

Chapter 40

The Emissary

In the six months since Brenna's return to LA and the beginning of a new old life, she had secured her first real job as the
first female buyer for a local aircraft company. Now she spent her
days purchasing hardware and taking lunch—actually, dining for
dollars at the best restaurants in Marina del Rey with vendor reps
who sought to maintain contracts with her company and to show
off the company of a beautiful young woman. She found a nice
apartment and a car and was able to purchase fashionable clothes.
She forced herself to accept the mundane routine of her work.
Although she was lauded for her breakthrough into the men-only
club of buyers, her spirit bucked against the tedium of the actual
job itself.

The local news rarely reported events from Ethiopia—or any
other African country for that matter—but from time to time,
she read articles about more student unrest in Addis. She stopped
talking about Prince John and Ethiopia with family or friends, and
they didn't press the issue. Some thought she had been reaching
too high anyway—a girl from Watts trying to be a princess—with

her talk about marrying Haile Selassie's grandson. Get real, girl. Some didn't believe it at all. At this point, Brenna didn't care what they thought. She was just relieved that they hadn't said anything to her. Over the past months, the frequency of John's calls had become sparse, with busyness as his primary excuse. She believed that his interest in her had simply waned, and it hurt. Inside she was shattered. Her big dream love and life hadn't worked out. But she wasn't rich and couldn't indulge the luxury of nursing a broken heart, so she gathered up the pieces and puzzled them back together. Like many of her comrades on the battlefields of love, she padded her wounds with layers of work and muted the hurt with her own busy distractions.

Over the past few months, friends had begun to introduce her to eligible men, and she started dating again. No one in particular captured her interest, and she preferred spending her weekends combing yard sales to find just the right items for her new apartment. Brenna enjoyed planning and preparing meals for herself and sometimes friends. She took classes at the community center in art, flower arranging, and belly dancing. Her philosophy became "Prepare yourself in the downtime"—that being when she did not have a boyfriend. Somewhere within her, she trusted that one day she would have a husband and children. Then she would use everything she had learned in the service of her family.

Early one Saturday morning, Brenna returned from the flower mart with several bundles. She unwrapped her flowers, placed them in a sink filled with cool water, and took out her supplies from the drawer. She turned on the stereo and played a sweet Roberta Flack album. She sang along, not missing a lyric. She danced back into the kitchen fanning a stick of nag champa incense. Brenna sliced the green floral sponge to fit into the several vases and containers she had placed on the counter. Then, while the sponges were soaking in plant food water and a few drops of bleach, she pulled off the excess foliage and snipped the stems of her flowers. Next she positioned fragrant rose-colored stock in a ceramic vase for her bedroom. She pressed several more of the hearty stalks strategically then started draping the delicate, lounging lisianthus to soften the effect.

The phone rang. She danced toward it, swishing the flower in her hand and half-singing with the record. "Hello?" she sang into the phone.

Because of the music and her distracted mind, what she first caught was "...from the imperial palace. His Majesty has a message for Miss Hayes."

"This is Miss Hayes speaking," she said, and her heart skipped.

"Miss Hayes?" the heavily accented voice inquired.

"Yes, this is she. One moment, please, let me turn down the music." She did so. "Yes, hello, I'm back. What is the message?"

"Miss Hayes, an emissary will be arriving in Los Angeles to meet with you and your family. He will bring the message from His Majesty. You are familiar with Dr. Talbot?"

"Who?" she asked.

"Dr. David Talbot, our minister of education."

"Oh, yes," she replied, "he was our host on my first visit to Ethiopia."

"Very well then, expect a call confirming his arrival date."

"OK. Yes, OK, I will expect the call."

"Good. Thank you, Miss Hayes. Goodbye."

Three weeks later, the meeting with Dr. Talbot and his wife took place at Brenna's mother's home. All her siblings were present. It was good to see Dr. Talbot again; he had been such a kind and attentive host while she was in Ethiopia. When he began to speak, everyone grew quiet in anticipation,

"Miss Hayes, His Majesty is concerned about the publicity surrounding your engagement to His Highness. There was a recent magazine article, yes?"

"No, not that I know of," Brenna cautiously replied.

Dr. Talbot removed a document from his briefcase and opened it. She saw a large headshot of herself with the caption "BLACK CINDERELLA FINDS PRINCE CHARMING."

"UPI forwarded this advance copy to His Majesty," Dr. Talbot added, looking her in the face.

Mr. Jones had not kept his promise to hold the story for the formal announcement of her engagement. Brenna felt betrayed and embarrassed. She spoke softly. "Well, I did do the interview, but only on the condition that it would not be released until His Majesty was ready to make the formal announcement. The reporter didn't keep his word." She added with downcast eyes, "I'm sorry if I've caused trouble."

"Well, it could get a bit sticky," Dr. Talbot said. He saw the slight quiver and purse of her lips and added, "But don't worry, my dear, everything is in hand now." He touched Brenna's shoulder. "As an old newsman myself, sometimes it's hard to hold on to a good story. Miss Hayes," he added. She looked up. "Please, no more publicity about this from you, young lady. Agreed?"

"Of course…I mean, of course not. You have my word. No more interviews."

"Very well, then, let's get down to business here." He sat back in the chair to include the rest of the family. "His Majesty has constructed a plan for the marriage to take place privately. And once that is done, he would then announce it as an official proclamation. As such, it would not be subject to speculation or debate. It will be a fait accompli. We are looking to the next six to nine months. We need specific information about how many family and friends are traveling for the wedding. And do you have any family members who wish to stay on to live in Ethiopia?"

Suddenly the living room bustled with excitement and discussion about the wedding and travel plans. What had mainly lived as a fairy tale for most family members, and a lie to some, had just arrived in the flesh to open new vistas for them all. Brenna stole away to her old room and sat on the bed. Just when she had almost convinced herself that her life with Prince John would never happen, the wedding was on. Her heart was beating fast, and the back of her throat was aching. The radical turnaround of events and the sudden resurrection of their love was too overwhelming to hold in, so she rolled over, buried her face in her pillow, and cried.

Through her crying, Brenna heard a soft tapping on the door of her room. She turned, still grasping her pillow. Slowly Dr. Talbot stepped partially through the door.

"May I come in?" he said in his deep soothing voice. Brenna scurried to sit up at the side of her bed, still holding her pillow.

"OK. Come on in," she said with a sniff.

Dr. Talbot stood between the two beds. His presence in her old bedroom made the room seem very small, because prior to this moment, she had only met with him in large offices, palaces, and other extravagant settings.

"May I sit?" he asked.

"I'm sorry. Please, yes." She made room on the bed beside herself. He sat quietly for a few moments while she wiped her eyes and nose with tissues. He waited.

"You see," she felt obliged to explain, "Prince John and I have not talked much lately, so I just thought he'd lost interest in me." Although she tried to hide it, he could feel the trembling of her body as she caught her breath. He took her hand.

"There now," he said to comfort her. "That's one thing you don't have to worry about. It seems His Highness is quite smitten with you."

Brenna looked up. "Really?" She knew she sounded like a little girl.

"Your young man has been quite busy. He's actually taken up his dukeship and is himself running the province—of course, with the help of his cabinet, but he is finally at the helm." He wanted to go on, but he noticed he had lost her attention. "Come now, everything is settled. The main thing is in your favor—in the favor of your marriage."

"And what is that? What is in my favor?"

"His Majesty. His Majesty approves of this marriage. Can you imagine what this will mean for Ethiopian-US relations? What it means for Black Americans? To have a princess in the royal family. A duchess. Maybe even an empress." Brenna saw the beam gleaming in his rheumy, spectacles-magnified eyes. "This is a source of great pride and significance for us all." He was squeezing her hand, which made her recall that he was an American expatriate who had stayed in Ethiopia after being stationed there in World War II.

Brenna sobered under this widened perspective, because she had not yet considered the broader implications for Black people of her relationship with the prince.

"So be careful," he said with a smile. "Many are counting on you."

Surely he meant to reassure her, and despite her understanding nod, she prayed that not one more element would be added to this. His news was good, yes. She was glad, true. Still, she wondered how she would recover from all these twists and turns in the plot of her own life. How to heal from emotional whiplash?

The renewed love and attention of her fiancé helped. A lot. She continued to work over the next few months, but her evenings and weekends were filled with packing and planning. She and Prince Yohannes were talking again on a regular basis. As their impending marriage became imminent, they released their reservations, removed the barriers between their hearts, and let their natural affinity flow, melding two into one.

Chapter 41

Coup

*B*renna had been packing all week; her apartment now resembled a post office, with boxes making a trail to the kitchen or right up the staircase. She hurried upstairs with her glass of wine to catch the bathtub before it overflowed. She turned off the faucet and placed her chilled glass on the ledge of the tub. The warm room was so inviting. She glanced around the bathroom; everything was set: the candles lit, the incense undulating its way up the steam, the bath beads turning the water a clear turquoise. All she needed now was music. Before she reached the stereo in her bedroom, the phone rang. It was Prince John.

"Hello?"

"Brehenna?"

"Hey, sweetheart, I was just thinking about you."

"Hi. What are you doing?"

"I was just getting ready to take a bath."

"Does that mean you're talking to me in the nude?"

"Well, not exactly nude. I have on my robe."

"OK, OK," he said. After a pause he added, "I'm getting sidetracked with that image. I need to tell you something important."

"All right," she said. "I'm listening." She sat on her bed.

"Well, there's good news and bad news. Which do you want to hear first?"

"OK, tell me the good news first."

"You remember that we had a professor working on your genealogy? Well, he thinks he found some of your family members—up in the north. Near Lake Tana. But he's not sure yet."

"Oh my God, that's great! Who'd they find? When will they know for sure?"

"Soon. They said soon. I'm glad you're excited." His voice trailed off, and he took a deep breath. Then his voice sounded strained. "Something's going on right now. We're having more political problems. So, the bad news is, you have to wait before you can come home. Wait until you hear from me again."

"Oh. OK, then. I'll wait."

"Brenna, this is serious—you must not come until I call you back."

"All right, I understand."

"I know you. I don't want to look up and you're calling from Addis airport for the car. I'm serious. Swear to me that you will not come until you hear from me again. Go ahead, Brehenna: swear."

"OK. Prince Yohannes, I swear to you that I will not come home until I hear from you again. I can tell you're serious, so don't worry—I really do swear."

"Good. I have to go now, but I'll call you back within two weeks. OK?"

"OK. I'll be waiting. Everything'll be all right, won't it?"

"Yeah, sure, it's nothing for you to worry about. By the way, I love you."

"By the same way, I love you too, my sweet almost-husband."

"OK. I really do have to go, but I'll call you back. Ciao."

After the call, she put on "Tezeta," their Ethiopian song. Memories. She slipped into the tub, closed her eyes, and let all her senses take her back through the repertoire of wonderful memories she and Yohannes shared. After that, her imagination headed forward, filling their future with love, adventure, and many beautiful children.

Not weeks but days after the call from Prince John, Brenna's mother telephoned early in the morning. "Did you hear the news? There's been a coup in Ethiopia. I think the whole royal family was arrested."

"What?" She was shocked out of sleep.

"Turn on the news," her mother said. Brenna jumped over and turned on the TV. She picked the phone back up.

"Which channel? I can't find it."

"Not the TV, baby, the radio—the news station. That's where I heard it. Have you heard from Prince John again?"

"No, not yet. Ma, let me get to the radio; I'll call you back."

Brenna was stunned. What happened? Finally the radio repeated the report. It was true, then. The emperor? Yohannes? His mother? The whole family arrested? How could this be? It must be a mistake. God, make it be a mistake. Please, God, make it not true. Brenna collapsed to her knees beside her bed and prayed.

She cried and begged and prayed, "Oh God, please let him be OK. Please, God, let him live. Oh, please, please, God, I don't know what to do. Please…please…save him. I don't mean to be selfish, Lord, but please save them all; save the whole family. Turn things around. Make a miracle. Make everything all right again… but if I have only one miracle, please, God, save Prince John. Save Yohannes for me."

Following the report of the coup, she made daily calls to UPI to get an update on the names of the executed. Every day she held her breath, hoping to run their gantlet of familiar names without hearing Prince John's name among the dead.

"Thank you," is all she said before she hung up and turned over to cry on her bed. Every day, she thought they would turn things around, that Prince John would somehow manage to call her. But there was no call, no contact from him. "I'm sorry, God, for sounding so ungrateful; I am grateful that Yohannes is not listed as dead. But God, I'm so sad. Give me strength, God. I need strength to get up, to get through the day. Help me, God. I feel so alone. I feel so lost."

One day while downtown picking up documents at City Hall, Brenna saw Councilman Billy Jones in the hallway. He was their councilman and a family friend. He knew about her engagement to Prince John, so he invited her to his office for a chat. After hearing his consoling words, she explained that she had not received any firsthand news about the family; she asked if there was any way he could help find out how Prince John was doing. He assured her he would see.

A few weeks later, the councilman telephoned her. "I finally reached the secretary of state, who's a friend of mine. He said he would be willing to use his 'good offices' to make inquiries about Prince John for you."

"Oh, great. That's wonderful news!"

"Wait a minute before you get too excited. There is one problem. He said that, although the entire royal family is under house arrest, they seem to only be executing the men who were actually in power. Prince John is a young man who has not been responsible for any political decisions yet, so that is probably why he is still alive. The problem is that having the secretary of state make inquiries on his behalf may signal to his captors that he might be a man of power and influence, and thus a threat. On the other hand, the inquiry may not put him any further in harm's way. The secretary is willing to do it; the decision to proceed or not is up to you."

"Oh. You mean by the secretary just asking, Prince John could be singled out and executed?"

"Yes. That's about the size of it."

"What would you advise?"

"Look, dear, I know you're hurting and anxious to find out about him. The whole situation there seems unstable and volatile."

"I understand what you're saying. Then, tell the secretary, thank you very much for his kindness, but no, do not make the inquiry. I can't jeopardize Prince John's life in any way."

"All right, then. Don't worry. I'll deliver the message. I'm sorry we couldn't be of more help to you."

"Thank you—you have helped me, by making the call on my behalf. If you ever hear anything, no matter how small, please let me know."

"Of course, dear; of course I will."

Chapter 42

Councilman Harris

Weeks passed, then months and years, yet there was no word from John. Over time, hope persisted, as Brenna had never heard even one rumor that John was dead. She no longer talked about him, but she thought of him and prayed for him daily. Something deep in her spirit told her: *You will see Prince John alive again in this lifetime.* So, although she didn't know where or when, she was certain she would see him again. She imagined perhaps one day she might be walking along the streets of Rome and see John coming her way. She imagined he might be with his wife and children. When the two of them greeted each other, she would hug him, shake the hand of his wife as they were introduced, smile, and scrutinize the children's features—hoping to see their father. She would be glad that the promise had come true: she would have seen John alive again. Emotionally, this bit of distance—the invention of the other wife—existed because she dared not even imagine that he would be alive, free, and again with her. Brenna knew how to tuck things away. Some emotions pack neatly like linen, some were hastily thrown on her memory's back shelf, while a precious few others were pushed to the farthest corner of the cellar of her heart. Those she padlocked before tossing the key into the drawer of her mind.

She lived her life. She didn't have the resources to languish in her grief, so she got up each day and went to work, enjoyed family and friends, spent holidays, remembered birthdays, and just carried on. She dated men but didn't pay much attention to them.

Then, one day, almost three years after the coup, she met Rick.

He showed up late at a birthday party that her sister Sharon had given for her boyfriend. Brenna had only recently arrived there from another affair when Darryl, the birthday boy, asked her to get the door. He was looking outside from the upstairs window blinds. "It's Councilman Harris," he said. She opened the door.

"Hi, Councilman Harris," she said, smiling in greeting. "Come in." Although she knew of him, she had never met him. He had succeeded their old family friend Councilman Billy Jones, so he was now in charge of the district where she had grown up and where her mother still lived. She gave him a quick once-over as he stepped inside. He was nice-looking: medium height, light-brown complexion, with a neatly trimmed moustache and beard. She noticed the flecks of gray in his thick curly hair. An older man. He came in bringing the chilly LA November night air. It woke her up.

"Thank you," he said, giving her a broad political grin. "I'm Rick."

"You're welcome. Nice to meet you, Rick. I'm Brenna." She shook his hand.

"Brenna Hayes? So you're Sharon's sister, one of the 'Hayes girls'?" he asked with special emphasis on the Hayes girls.

"I haven't heard it said like that since grade school, but yeah, I'm one of the 'Hayes girls.'"

"Where are you in the order of things?"

"I'm the fourth, and the youngest daughter. Does this mean something to you?"

"Oh, I'm just making conversation. My way of apologizing for bringing in the cold air."

"Thanks. That's thoughtful. But I've warmed back up."

"Just to be sure, why don't you come dance with me?"

"Now? The record's almost over."

"We'll catch the end of this one, then we'll be right on time for the next one." He had already taken her hand, and she was following him onto the dance floor. Since they had both arrived late, by the time they took a break from dancing and got a drink, the party was ending.

"Say, Brenna, I'm really enjoying talking to you. Why don't you come and have coffee with me."

"Well, I don't drink coffee, and it is late. Won't your wife be worried?"

"Not married," he answered.

"Oh."

"Look, you pick the place," he offered. "Somewhere near your house, if you like. Do you like tea?"

"Yes, I do," Brenna replied.

"Me too. See, there's another thing we have in common."

"Now, that's kind of sad," she said, teasing. "OK, Councilman, we're going for tea."

He held the door and said, "I'll follow you."

"OK, it's not too far. Alphy's. West on Manchester. It's on the right, just before the freeway."

"Good, I know the place. I think they're open twenty-four hours."

"All right then, Rick Harris, I'll see you there." She unlocked her car door, and he opened it. She got in; he locked it and secured her inside. He gave a slight salute as she drove off.

Teapot after teapot, and cookie after cookie, they talked for the rest of the night. Rick ate so many cookies that she nicknamed him the Cookie Monster. It didn't deter him from having several more. Finally, when they walked outside, she was surprised to see the sun coming up. Apparently he was someone she could talk to all night. She was making a new friend.

"So, where do you live, Brenna?" he asked, squinting at the sun.

"Not too far from here."

"May I escort you home?"

"Well…no. Thank you, I can manage fine." She started walking to her car. He joined her.

"Perhaps I could have your phone number? I'd like to call you later." He pulled a small pad and pen from his inside pocket and held it out to her with a smile. She looked up at him and took the pad.

"OK," she said, and wrote her number.

"What do you say I take you out later?"

"Later when?"

"Today."

"I have to go home and go to bed. I've been up all night. I'm really not used to staying out all night. We'll see. I need some rest. My eyes are entirely too big to be red."

"OK. I'll call you later. Say about five? Then we could go out to dinner. How does that sound?"

"It sounds fine. First sleep. Then food. I'm so sleepy. I'm probably not making much sense now. Call me at five, and we'll see about dinner then."

"OK, fair enough. Sleep well." Again he secured her in her car. As she pulled off, her wave and smile gave way to a sleepy yawn.

A year after they met, Brenna and Rick Harris were married. One afternoon on their honeymoon in Khartoum, Sudan, Rick returned to their suite following a meeting with an old schoolmate.

"Hi, honey, how was the meeting?" Brenna asked from the chair as she returned the polish brush back to the bottle and slipped her shiny red toenails into her straw thongs.

"It was great. Do you remember me mentioning Ahmed, my roommate from the International House at UCLA?" Rick asked.

"Yeah, I think so. What about him?"

"Well, he's minister of foreign affairs for Sudan now. After graduation, he returned home and is now a member of the government. We had a great time reminiscing about our college days."

"I'm glad. So both of you went into politics?" she asked. He walked over and sat on the bed.

"We spoke about the situation in Ethiopia. Because Sudan still has diplomatic relations with Ethiopia, Ahmed says he could try to arrange for you to meet with Prince John."

"What?" Her casual chatting and straightening of the room came to a halt. "What do you mean?"

"Look, I know you and John never got the chance to say your goodbyes. So why not take this opportunity that's presented itself?"

"But what about you? I'm married to you now. How do you feel about this?"

"I would never have mentioned it if I couldn't handle it. The man is in prison. I understand if you want to have some face-to-face closure with him."

"Wow…Ricky…I don't know what to say."

"Say whatever you feel. We'll go with that. Do you want to try?"

"It feels very scary," Brenna said. She sat next to him, took his hand, and searched his eyes. She inhaled then slowly exhaled. "But OK. Yes, I want us to try." She kept nodding. "Yes, see if he can arrange it."

"OK, then." He patted the top of her hand. "He needs our passports." He rose and walked over to remove them from the room safe. "I'm just going back to drop these off so he can get started. It'll probably take a couple of days."

"Hey!" Brenna called to her new husband before he reached the door. She walked up to him. "You know, Rick, you're some kind of man. Thank you for being so good to me." She leaned in and gave him a warm kiss.

"Hey Partner, you're real easy to be good to. I'll be back soon." He left, and she stood in the doorway watching him walk to the elevator.

Two days later, Rick returned from another meeting with Ahmed. Brenna was on the balcony reading a novel. "Is that you, honey? It's so hot. Do you want a Fanta?" She had already come in and had made her way to the small refrigerator for the cold soda and the glass she had chilled. "How'd it go?"

"Well, Ahmed said there was a problem with your passport." He took the cool glass, gulped down the soda, and then refilled it as he sat in the other chair at the small table. "The representative at the Ethiopian embassy said, and I quote, 'Mr. Harris's wife is persona non grata in Ethiopia and, should she arrive there, she stands to be arrested and imprisoned with the rest of the royal family.'"

"What? I can't believe that I could be arrested! For what? I didn't do anything!" Brenna was shocked. Terrified. How could they target her? She had loved Yohannes, maybe still did, but not enough to join him in prison.

"Hey, baby, I know you didn't. But this is the situation." Rick paused and added, "So what do you want to do?"

"What do you mean, 'What do I want to do'?" she asked.

"Well, do you want to go and try?"

Brenna leaned forward with a furrowed brow and spread her hands palms up. "So these are my choices: go to Ethiopia and get imprisoned with John, or stay here on my honeymoon with you and get dressed for our dinner cruise on the Nile?" She stood, turned, and tilted her head; then, with a hint of a smile and a slightly raised left brow, she walked past him, lifted her black cocktail dress from its hook, and headed for the shower.

"Very well, my Ethiopian princess," Rick said; he smiled to himself as he finished his drink. He watched as his wife's silk robe slinked to the bathroom floor before the door closed.

~~~

A year or so later, the April night air of Los Angeles was warm, so pregnant Brenna, en route again from the ladies' room, stole a few quiet moments from a reception that the councilman and she were giving to view the city from the observation deck of City Hall Tower. Tiny lights sparkled throughout the expanse of the LA basin. It was a low, sprawling city. Brenna loved to look west on a clear night like this one. She could see in the distance where the orderly twinkling neighborhoods ended in a border of streetlights at the silent blackness of the ocean. She was a West Coast girl who cherished having that nothingness always so near. She cozied in her shawl and smiled as the sea and the shoreline spooned under the winking blanket of twilight.

"Excuse me. Mrs. Harris?"

"Yes?" Brenna turned to face the accented voice of the woman who spoke and saw a small delegation of men standing with her.

"Please let me introduce myself; I am Saba Miriam, and we represent the Ethiopian Rights and Welfare Organization. We need your help." Brenna shook each hand and returned their traditional bows.

"What's your concern? How can I help?" Brenna asked.

They explained how many of the Ethiopians who had sought refuge in America after the communist coup in their country five years earlier were now in jeopardy of deportation. This situation was urgent, because they had been given word that a mass deportation would take place. Many feared that upon their return, they and their family members would be in danger of imprisonment, torture, or even death at the hands of the Derg, the shorter name for the Coordinating Committee of the Armed Forces, Police, and Territorial Army that had taken over Ethiopia.

"Please, Mrs. Harris. We have heard that you visited Ethiopia and that you have a sympathetic heart toward our cause. So please ask your husband, the councilman, to intercede on our behalf. It is critical." The two women's eyes locked, and Brenna felt sorrow, urgency, and admiration for the fierceness of Saba's determination.

"Of course. I will bring this to his attention. Please, let's step inside." They all moved back into the reception hall. "I'll introduce you. Then you can request a meeting so you can sit down and explain everything. Wait here."

Brenna found her husband making his rounds. She slid in beside him, took his hand, and greeted their guests. After a few moments, he excused himself and turned to have a private moment with his wife.

"How are you feeling?" he asked as he glanced down to her seven-month-pregnant belly. "Can I get you something to drink? Do you want to sit for a while?"

"Thank you, honey, but I'm fine. But there is a situation I need your help with. Come with me. I want you to meet some people who have arrived—Ethiopians." They moved along the perimeter of the crowd, smiling, shaking hands, hugging, and kissing cheeks, until they reached the delegation standing by the door. This time, one of the men stepped forward first to greet the councilman and introduce their plight. He was well on his way in his explanation and had Rick's full attention when Brenna whispered into her husband's ear. She nodded to the group and again headed for the ladies' room.

On the ride home, Rick explained the politics of their situation and said that they had set a meeting for Monday morning.

"So you're going to help them?"

"These are your people—of course I'll help."

On the drive home that evening, Brenna felt the baby's knee poking her stomach, so she took Rick's hand and placed it on the area. He grinned and kept one hand on her stomach and the other on the wheel for the rest of the way.

Councilman Harris, along with Raymond Roberts, Congresswoman Winters, and others, had founded the Pan African Lobby (PAL) to lobby the legislature on issues regarding Africa and the diaspora. Over the next several months, through many meetings, including one with the president, they helped to secure unofficial asylum: reprieve from mass Ethiopian deportations.

Brenna was overjoyed. Although she could not herself intercede to help John directly, she could get help for his fellow Ethiopians. She thought how life can sometimes turn on its own axis. At the beginning of her relationship with Prince John, it had seemed that she would be the lifelong recipient of great wealth and riches through him. And that, because of her marriage to him, she would be a princess, a duchess, maybe even an empress. But for her part, all she would bring to the marriage was herself. She knew her worth and did not feel she was a small gift; but Prince John also brought himself as well as everything else. She had thought that by birthing their children, it would bring more balance. But no, the axis had spun. Now it was only she who remained free. Free to act and positioned to help.

───

Brenna and Rick brought their six-month-old daughter, whom they named Kongit with them to the affair the Ethiopians were having to celebrate and to honor the couple. They held it at Messob Restaurant, one of many Ethiopian businesses that had established a base on Fairfax Avenue. Rick had hired five Ethiopians on his staff, in various positions. The event was crowded and was full of delicious traditional food and music.

Woizero Debre-Worq, the widow of the former mayor of Addis Ababa, had even brought them a special bottle of vintage *tej*, Ethiopian honey wine. The big surprise came when they unveiled a work of art that contained a mounted wooden carving of the map of Ethiopia with a laminated early baby picture of Kongit smiling from the heart of the country; small replicas of the stone cross churches of Lalibela, the stele at Axum, and a lion's head surrounded the country. They made a toast.

"To Councilman and Mrs. Harris for all their help and support. And to Kongit, our 'little Ethiopia.' Here, Here!"

───

"Alganish, would you put Kongit down for her nap? I need to finish cleaning up this guest list," Brenna called to their Ethiopian au pair. Alganish was a refugee who had fled Ethiopia and now lived with them. Alganish brought the baby over for a hug and kiss from Brehenna before she and the baby went upstairs. Later, as the soft sounds of an Ethiopian lullaby floated down the staircase, Brenna smiled. She was happy that they could provide Alganish with a home as well as expose baby Kongit to both English and Amharic.

The phone rang.

"Hello. May I speak with Mrs. Harris, please?" The formal English came through a heavily accented male voice.

"This is she speaking."

"I have just spoken with your husband, and he gave me your number at home. My name is David Makonnen." The name shocked her. "I don't mean to be impertinent, but do you know my brother, Yohannes Makonnen, Prince John? Are you the Brenna who was engaged to him?"

"Yes, I am," she replied after a long pause through her constricting throat.

"I've been looking for you!" he exclaimed heartily. They talked on. He explained how, whenever he had visited Washington, DC, over the past year, he kept hearing about a Councilman Harris in Los Angeles who was doing so much to help the Ethiopian people. "I always wondered why a councilman way out in Los Angeles would be so helpful to Ethiopians. Then one day someone said his wife's name: Brenna. And I thought, well, maybe. Now, this makes a lot of sense. Perfect sense. I would like to come out to meet you and your husband. I live in Amsterdam now, but I'll be returning to the States in a month or so."

"I'm so happy to hear your voice. I heard you were not at home during the coup, but I had no way of locating you. This is great!" Brenna paused and asked, "How is John?"

"John is well; he is alive. My mother and all my brothers are alive. I am able to be in touch with them through Amnesty International. John is OK." There was a long silence on the line.

"I'm glad. I'm glad to hear it," Brenna said, her voice cracking. "Please excuse me, David, I have to go, but please call Rick to make arrangements for your visit. You are welcome to our home." After she got off the phone, she cried—for so many things.

A month later at their home, Councilman Harris and Brenna opened the front door, and there stood Prince David looking every bit like John: younger, thinner, but surely his brother. Rick welcomed him in with a handshake. The two men had already spent the afternoon together. Brenna embraced Prince David and gave the traditional cheek kisses. Family, friends, constituents, and associates had gathered to welcome him. The reception was a success. They made their point that Prince David could feel at home in Los Angeles. Despite her excellent help, Brenna was still busy as the hostess, monitoring the party. When Prince David asked if he could speak to her privately, she guided him to the library. Finally alone, for a few moments they just sat quietly for a while among the books.

"For several years now, I have been in contact with my family in Ethiopia through Amnesty International. I was able to send word to John about you and the councilman and Kongit. He has asked me to deliver a message to you from him."

"OK," Brenna replied as she eyed him. She took in a deep breath.

"He said to say, and I quote: 'Thank you for loving me enough to continue to love and support my people in my absence.'"

Tears suddenly flooded and fell from Brenna's eyes. Prince David offered his handkerchief and shoulder. Brenna cried, but only for a brief while. She felt the danger of John coming to life again in her heart—not as a memory but in real time. Here sat his brother, looking like him and bringing the first word she had had from him in seven years. She had to go. She was another man's wife, and she felt her heart didn't have the right to those feelings anymore.

"Thank you, David. That means so much to me. Let John know that. Tell him that I continue to pray for him and the whole family." She took his hand. "Come on. Let's go back to the party."

Chapter 43

TOR

Los Angeles, 1984

Brenna lived each day, each year, inside a prayer: a prayer for her family, a prayer for Prince John, a prayer for her people, and a prayer that her life be divinely guided. And it was.

"Hello?" Brenna waited in the silence from the other end, then repeated, "Hello?"

"...Bossin?" asked a gruff voice.

"What? I'm sorry, what did you say?"

"I said boss in?" She could hear the female attitude crackling through the line.

"Oh, you mean is Rick home?" Brenna asked, trying to soothe the waters.

"Yes. That's what I said: Boss in?"

"Sorry, he's not in now. Who's calling?"

"This is Johnnie from the councilman's office."

"Oh hi, Johnnie," Brenna responded. "He won't be home till after four."

"Well, I wanted to ask you something anyway."

"Oh, OK?"

"I just got this here brochure you sent out. About a workshop. Let me see what you call it…yeah, here it is: TOR, the Transformation of Race."

"Yes, that's from me."

"I read it."

"OK…"

"I just want to ask one thing: What kind of bullshit is this?"

Silence.

"It's not," Brenna finally said. "It's a workshop."

"Yeah, but it's a little too deep."

"What do you mean?" Brenna asked.

"This brochure. Look, when you read this, it sounds like something that can really happen. You know, what you say here gets on the inside when you reading it. I mean, this is dangerous. If Black people come to this workshop and you don't deliver—I mean, it could really hurt. See, we can't take being let down like this. Not from this kind of hope."

"I understand what you're saying," Brenna said in acknowledgment.

"Naw, I don't think you do. Listen, Brenna. If you can't really do this, pull it back now. It ain't no shame if you pull it back now. No shame on you. Just take it back, call it off, if you can't deliver."

Brenna closed her eyes and took a deep breath before she spoke. "Johnnie, I hear what you're saying. I really do. Let me say this to you: I can deliver on the things you read in the brochure. People in the workshop will have a chance to 'transform their relationship to race,' as the brochure says. This *can* provide some deep healing of that old wound. So the hope you feel when you read it? It's true, it's real."

"Is that right?"

"Absolutely. And Johnnie, I was purposefully conservative when I wrote the brochure. It's so much more."

"Well, now. If you can do what you're saying, I'll be the first to sign up. The check is in the mail. And I really mean it."

"Great. Got it. You're at the top of the list. Johnnie, I promise you won't regret it."

"OK, then. I'll be there."

"OK."

"Brenna? Thanks."

"You're so welcome. Thank you for hearing me. It's not easy to say what this work is. I look forward to having you in the first public workshop. Really, I'm honored to have you there."

"Well, I'll be there. Bye."

"Thanks, bye."

Alganish came to the door of the breakfast room and looked at Brenna and Rick. "Good evening, sir," she said in greeting to Rick in her halting English; she gave a traditional bow. Then, in Amharic, she told Kongit to come upstairs with her to get ready for bed. She lifted Kongit from her booster seat at the table. Then she ventured in English, "Kiss Mommy and Daddy good night." Kongit walked over to kiss her parents and took Alganish's hand.

"Don't forget my story, Daddy!" Kongit called back.

"I'll be up right after your bath."

"Night, sweetheart."

"Night, Mommy."

"Let's have coffee in the living room; I'll stoke the fire." Rick rose from the table. Brenna nodded and began to clear the dishes. She stacked the dishes on the counter, then turned to pour the percolating coffee into the coffeepot and set the tray. Rick came through the door.

"Hey, partner, can I help?"

"Yeah, you're right on time. Take the tray; I'll bring dessert." Rick lifted the silver coffee service and backed the door open for Brenna, peering over at the goodies.

"Is that Jocelyn's rum cake?"

"Yes it is; she just dropped it by this afternoon. And rest assured, it's really 'drunk,' as Kongit would say. I think Jo drowns these cake in Barbados rum."

"Good, you slice enough for yourself?" Rick said teasingly.

They settled on the couch by the fireplace. Brenna took her coffee, Rick his cake.

"Johnnie called me from the office today."

"Johnny Cochran?"

"No, Johnnie from your staff."

"Yeah, what about?"

"She got the TOR brochure, and it upset her."

"In what way?"

"You know how rough she can be. And you know that I'm a little scared of her. Anyway, she said, 'What kind of bullshit is this?'"

"She wouldn't," Rick said with a chuckle, knowing full well that she would.

"Yes, she did. At first I didn't know what to say. But I understood what she meant. She really felt the possibility of what TOR is. She said that Black people would trust it and feel hope. But she said they would be devastated if it wasn't true. It's like TOR makes people want to let their guard down."

"How do you feel about what she said?"

"I'm OK now. It took me a minute. I didn't expect that kind of reaction."

"You know Johnnie and the mothers of the National Welfare Rights Organization will not hold their tongues when it comes to speaking out for the people. What did you tell her?"

"Well, she told me to take it back. She said, 'Don't do it if you really can't deliver. There's no shame in pulling it back now.' I was really touched by that. How much she cares. I told her that I can't *make* people transform, but I can make sure that their time in the TOR workshop will give them the opportunity to transform themselves."

"What was the upshot?"

"She finally said that if I could really do it, then she'd be there. So she signed up for the workshop."

"Congratulations. I mean, if you got Johnnie, then you'll get them all. She's a staunch sentinel," he said.

"You know, beside the ten of you who came in March, and Ben Ammi in Israel, no one else has ever done TOR. Now I'm asking fifty people to pay money and spend two and a half days in the Transformation of Race workshop," Brenna said.

Silence. Cake. Coffee.

Finally Rick spoke. "It's a bold move, Brenna. But I think you're going to pull it off. I know what I'm still experiencing from TOR, and what the others shared is amazing. Don't worry."

"That's my concern. I'm not worried. I'm the opposite: absolutely confident."

"Yeah, you're absolutely confident in something for which you have little or no evidence, right?"

"Exactly."

"Well, dear, that's called faith."

"That's true. I have faith."

"Remember, Brenna, this whole TOR thing wasn't your idea in the first place. What did you write in your poem?"

"'Coin of the realm'?" she asked.

He nodded. "How did that last line go? 'It's coin that I am and coin I shall be, so Father, spend me.' And the magnificent thing is, He is. God is spending you." Rick raised his arm over the back of the sofa. "Come here."

Brenna slid into his armpit.

"I think the Ethiopian guys on staff should go to TOR too."

"OK, me too. You don't have to be a Black American to have issues about race. I'd be interested in seeing what a TOR shift looks like with them."

"Well, they're in, then. That makes my whole staff. I'm putting them into your capable little hands." He caught her long, slender fingers and played with her wedding rings. He felt they were beginning to grow apart and wondered how long it would be before he wandered too far from home.

"Small but capable, huh?" Brenna smiled as she rested against his chest. They snuggled and watched the fire in silence. She, a little worried about TOR; he, a little sad about them.

"Daddy!" came a little voice from upstairs. "I'm ready!"

"Story time," Rick said, and he gave his wife a quick kiss.

"I'll be up soon," Brenna said, and she moved forward to organize the tray. As she carried the tray back to the kitchen, she assured herself, *I can do it. I can do this workshop.* And where was that aspect of her that had seemed so confident a few minutes ago? Brenna knew that they would all see very soon.

Chapter 44

The Horizon

Dr. Bledsoe, an elderly black physician, stepped into Brenna's path as she walked through the hotel lobby toward the Sunset Room, where the post-TOR workshop breakfast was being held.

"Good morning, Mrs. Harris," Dr. Bledsoe said, tapping the rim of his tan hat.

"Good morning, sir," Brenna said with a smile while tipping her head at an angle.

"Dr. Bledsoe," he said to remind her. "I attended your Transformation of Race workshop. May I have a word with you?"

"Yes, of course, Dr. Bledsoe," she said, noticing his cane. She added, "Would it be OK if we sat for a moment?" He nodded, and they sat in perpendicular proximity on a nearby couch and chair. Dr. Bledsoe spoke about how much he had enjoyed the workshop and, although the workshop took many hours, it didn't seem that long. Fairly quickly, he made his way to his main point.

"Dear," he said, speaking in a quiet Southern voice, "I don't know if you know what you got here. I mean this TOR. I'm from the South, and race has played an important part in my life. It was very hard back then—in time and in the South—for

Negroes—Black people. I remember, starting in my youth, I used to have this recurring vision about race, where I was standing alone in this big grass field in a valley. I would look around, and up on the hill I would see a big foreboding black house. I somehow knew that the house represented race and that one day I would be grown enough and brave enough and strong enough to face it, to enter it. But not then. So, for many years I was on a course of self-improvement. I took every class, seminar, program, or workshop I could that I thought might help me and make me stronger and wiser. From time to time, when I felt particularly strong or able after doing some inner work, I'd bring up the old image of the Black House of Race. I'd be out in the vision of the field again and look up the hill to the black house. I felt there were powerful, malignant forces in that house, and I would stand there and try to measure my newly acquired strength against those forces. Over the years, I've become stronger and stronger. But so far, I've never felt strong enough to enter the house and win the battle.

"Now, here's the thing. This morning, while I was shaving, I thought about the Black House of Race. Then I checked myself. Everything we had done in the workshop had made me feel stronger. Different. So I decided to test it out. I closed my eyes."

Brenna watched as he closed his eyes, took in a deep breath, and opened them again, viewing another world.

He continued. "There I am, standing in the field. I looked around at the tall dry grass blowing around me. I took my time paying close attention to measuring my internal sense of strength and readiness. I felt strong. Alive. Brave. But again, was it enough?

Was I finally strong enough to go in and face the Black House of Race? Was what I got from TOR sufficient to give me this final measure of strength? I decided yes. I think I can do it. Yes, I think I can. I was finally ready. So first, I scanned the fields. Nothing unexpected. Then I let my eyes slowly rise up the slope of the hill. Then, just before I looked at the house, I took a few deep breaths and squared my shoulders. Yes I was ready to enter, ready for battle. Finally, I jerked my head up to face the house." Dr. Bledsoe reenacted his gesture before Brenna, his face looking up as if toward the dreaded place. He held the pose, then his eyes looked aside to her, and he whispered, "When I finally looked up to the house—the house was gone! Completely gone. And I was just standing there alone in the grassy field looking up the hill to see only the horizon and the blue sky!" He turned to Brenna, reached for her hand, and looked her in the eyes.

"My dear girl, I am eighty-two years old, and this is the first morning I woke up knowing that I am a free man. I am a free man." His eyes glistened as he squeezed her hand. "Thank you. Thank you."

Brenna reached with her free arm to hug him. Tears streamed from her eyes.

"You're very welcome. I'm so glad," she spoke into his ear. Then they faced each other again. "Dr. Bledsoe, thank you for your courage." It was in that moment when Brenna knew that all the effort she had made over the past three years developing TOR and all the ridicule she had faced had been worth it. For Dr. Bledsoe to wake up knowing he was a free man after eighty-two years of living—this one testimony alone was worth it.

"Brenna, God's gonna bless you. He's gonna bless you in a big way. Watch for it. Big blessings."

"Thank you. I'm gonna be lookin' out for 'em. I sure am!" Brenna said with a grin, naturally code-shifting into Black English. They both stood. Dr. Bledsoe held out his crooked elbow in her direction.

"Ma'am?" he offered.

"Thank you, sir." She nodded and took his arm.

He escorted her to the breakfast, the essence of gentility. Only this time, the refinement and propriety shone from the inside out.

Chapter 45

❈❈❈

Hope

Los Angeles, 1991

After almost two decades, another coup in Ethiopia ousted the communist Derg, and its leader fled to an Arab state. This was cause for celebration. Cause for hope. The now-sizable Ethiopian community in Los Angeles was hosting its annual Little Ethiopia Summer Festival, and to Brenna's surprise, the organizing committee had invited her to speak. She tried to steer them to her now ex-husband, Councilman Harris, who was retired. But they explained that he had already agreed to speak at one of their other events. This time they wanted to hear her story. They wanted her to share her connection with the Ethiopian people.

Waiting backstage, Brenna felt a jolt when they announced her name. She had never spoken before a large group of Ethiopians, but their enthusiastic applause made her smile. Her gauzy white Ethiopian dress with lilac borders and bodice fluttered in the summer breeze as she made her way to center stage. She settled her notes on the podium and took a moment to look out at the people. She had loved these people, these Ethiopians, all her life. And today, in her own way, she wanted to tell them so.

They had asked to hear her story, and so she told them. She told of that first trip to Africa as Miss Watts when she was just a girl, a young woman. She told of her meeting with Emperor Haile Selassie and his telling her that she was "from the royal lineage of the House of Judah, his house," and that he would have to make the adjustment. She shared that she believed his adjustment came in the form of His Majesty arranging an introduction to his handsome grandson, Prince John. She spoke of their engagement and her return to Ethiopia. She acknowledged that the brutality of the 1974 coup and the harshness of the new regime had forced too many to their graves, to prison, to poverty, and to flee for refuge in other lands. She told of her shared suffering with the imprisonment of her betrothed and the entire family. She told of how overjoyed she was when, in later years, her then husband, Councilman Harris, and the Pan-African Lobby had succeeded in helping secure asylum for the Ethiopians who sought refuge in America.

She told her story and said, "I declare today a new beginning—a season of hope; a season for a renewal of spirit. New opportunity is on the horizon. Can you sense it?" Nods and tentative yeses whispered from the crowd. "Perhaps soon it will be safe to return to Ethiopia. Soon we will reunite with our loved ones." They clapped. "Glorious days are ahead!" Smiling, she waited for their applause to die down. "I would like to close now with a blessing. One used in the ancient Temple days by King Solomon: 'May the Lord bless you and keep you. Cause His face to shine upon you. Be gracious unto you, lift up his countenance unto you, and grant you peace.'" She held her hands in a prayer like gesture and bowed to them.

The emcee, her friend Fakada, joined her at the podium, still clapping with the audience.

"Please, please, let's give Ms. Harris another round of applause." And a fresh round began. Brenna basked in the moment. She was relieved. It felt like a secret she had held in for too long was finally out. She recalled the many times she'd sat in Ethiopian restaurants loving the atmosphere, the music, the food, and the people, but mainly savoring the vestiges of her love for Yohannes. But when she heard them chatting in Amharic with their family and friends, she was always reminded that she was not one of them. She felt the poignant pull of the estranged. But today she was no longer estranged, because finally she had said it. She had spoken her love and claimed Ethiopians as her people—to their face, in public. Brenna smiled, nodded, and turned to leave when the emcee touched her shoulder.

"Please, Brenna, stay for a moment; we have a gift." Brenna inched back toward him, and the audience continued their applause. After a while they quieted, and Fakada spoke again.

"Now, Ms. Harris, we would like to share a token of our love and appreciation for you and all your efforts on our behalf." He gestured to the side, and a man approached with a huge bouquet. The spotlight hit the flowers; Brenna moved toward them, surprised and grinning at their extravagance. They were so beautiful! The audience clapped furiously as she reached to receive them. The audience went silent, and for some reason, the man wouldn't release the flowers.

"Brehenna," said the man, lowering the flowers. She looked to his face and felt the weight of the bouquet in her arms. "Brehenna...

it's me." She searched his eyes and his moving lips, which she could no longer hear. She studied his face to discern his features beyond the years.

"Yohannes?" she ventured, and she instantly knew. The flowers cascaded to their feet with a crash. She could no longer see through her tears. She could no longer breathe. But she could feel his arms encircle her, and she fell into his embrace. She forgot she was in public, in a spotlight, on a stage. In the distance she heard the emcee announce, "Ladies and gentlemen, we are joined on this stage by Prince John: Yohannes Makonnen Duke of Harrar, grandson of His Imperial Majesty Emperor Haile Selassie!"

But for Brehenna, cloaked beneath the scent of her beloved, the roar of the crowd muted to a whisper. And his kiss. After eighteen years, the promise was kept. It was a grand day for these two, who had no present need for hope.

Chapter 46

A Courtyard in Harrar

Ethiopia, 2007

Years later, Brehenna returned to Ethiopia on a tour with the Stanford Alumni Travel Study Club, "Ethiopia: In Search of the Ark of the Covenant." Today they were touring the former Palace of the Duke of Harrar, in the province of Harrar, the very place- which had once been set to be Brehenna's home. Now, it was but a shabby public museum. As Brehenna walked from room to room, her mind reeled from the dissonance caused by the incongruity of the life she and her love had begun here, years ago, and what she now saw before her eyes. She did not know how to *be* here. But her search would not be denied: her soul had compelled her to return to Ethiopia. Her soul could not deny the call to search. For what? She did not know but she knew she had to be here, and here she was.

When Brehenna heard the tour guide directing the group to a display case which exhibited 'original artifacts from the royal family that once lived here', she wanted to scream, *stop!* Her heart was in distress. It felt as if strangers were rummaging through a sacred place- the cemetery of her dreams. She could not move forward, instead she turned and rushed back through the palace and exited into the courtyard. It was dusty, barren, and hot outside. She found shade under a scrawny tree, pulled out her water bottle and drank. As her spirit settled, she looked around the yard and was drawn as if by a cord to one of the deserted bungalows that bordered the courtyard.

She walked into a room that was cool and dark except for the light from a large window covered with a scrolling wrought iron grill. She dusted off an old stool, sat down, and closed her eyes- *Oh Lord, give me strength,* she sighed in her spirit, grateful for the solitude. After a while, she opened her eyes. Then, she noticed that the room seemed to be getting brighter, and somehow newer. A change was slowly transforming the room as light moved from place to place. She followed the movement with her eyes, then stood and pivoted, gaping as the empty pantry shelves began materializing goods until they were fully stocked. She looked out the window toward the palace --and like a wonderland--it too, as well as the entire courtyard, was colorizing as it transformed from black and white to full color.. The paint was now fresh and vibrant on the wooden façade and the yard appeared to landscape itself with lush foliage and blooming flowers. She just stood there staring.

First, she heard their voices, then several small children slowly became visible as they played in the courtyard. Brehenna heard herself thinking of activities *her* children might enjoy inside, away from the heat of the day. She sensed a shift in reality, but *to what?* Suddenly her body felt heavy. She glanced down and saw her own belly—pregnant! *Versions,* came to mind and she wondered, *another version of myself?* Then near her in the room, a woman materialized already busy gathering items from the pantry shelves.

"Elene," Brehenna heard herself saying to the woman, whom she somehow knew was her cook, "make sure you prepare a side dish of sega wot for our guest. The Minister loves beef. Make it extra hot and spicy."

"Should I make cottage cheese for His Highness?" Elene asked in her hushed Amharic tones.

"Yes, please," Brehenna both responded and heard herself respond. Then she felt woozy.

"Your Highness," Elene said, quickly handing her a glass of water and offering a stool.

"Thank you," Brehenna said accepting the water. Normally she would have refused the seat because she liked to keep active, it always made for easier deliveries. But this time she sat, sipped the water, and took several slow deep breaths. She closed her eyes to compose herself. After a while, she sensed another presence inside herself, *Who's here?* An answer: *It's me.* And the me who answered was an echo of her own self –just slightly out of time, out of sync. Simultaneously it dawned on both of them: they were in transition, at an intersection of multiple versions of themselves and multiple realms of reality. Inwardly knowing what was needed, Brehenna, the young duchess, sweetly began receding into the background, inviting the will of Brehenna, her elder self, to the fore. In an instant of déjà vu, Brehenna felt the Emperor again guiding her through the portal of time; but this time she chose to stop and step off. She knew exactly what to do.

Brehenna eagerly looked back out of the window in search of the children. When the eldest, looked up, he looked like a miniature of his father -it was their firstborn, Yohannes! *How can this be?*

She didn't care. She watched her son bend down to show his younger brother... Tefari... how to operate the lever on his dump truck. Gleefully, Tefari caught on, filling and releasing small stones over and over. Yohannes stood proudly watching his brother. A mother's gratitude filled her heart, *my son is kind.*

Then she saw the toddler version of her own daughter, Kongit, rolling a large dusty pink ball back and forth to Alganish, her nurse. Brehenna smiled as chubby legs scurried toward the ball, which rolled past her reach. Yohannes spied the ball and stopped it with his foot, gently tapping it so it rolled back to his sister. When she caught it and picked it up, he clapped and yelled, "Yay, Kongit!" Giggling, she looked at him with unabashed joy. He was her big brother, and that meant everything. Brehenna scanned left and saw the baby boy in a walker. *Her* baby boy, Dawitt, was playing with his nurse, Genet.

Not knowing how long this phenomenon might last, Brehenna rushed out to the courtyard. "Children," she called out, in surprisingly impeccable Amharic, "come to Mommy." Yohannes took Tefari's hand and walked directly to their mother, who had stooped to meet them. First, she hugged her eldest, sniffed him deeply, and then pulled him back to look into his eyes. "I love you, son," she said and again hugged him as he echoed, "I love you too, Mommy." She repeated this with each of her four children. These moments she would cherish forever.

With her heart still humming from this overflow of love, she felt an urgent need to turn toward the palace. She needed to see her husband. Then there he was passing into the doorway, and she loved him anew. Prince Yohannes stopped and looked out at his family. Brehenna stood holding their youngest son on her right hip, with Kongit clinging to her left leg. Princess Brehenna Makonnen, Duchess of Harrar. He grinned at beautiful wife, standing wide-legged in pregnancy, grinning back at him, their eyes making promises they always kept.

Both she and her husband saw it: the flurry of dust on a windless day, a sign of satisfaction in all realms and confirmation of the multiple versions of themselves. Complete and transcendent to time, the magic between them lives on.

"Brehenna, are you ready?" asked Laura their tour guide. "Everyone's boarding the bus. We're going to lunch, now." As Brehenna was called back to the present, she and her young family slowly faded, receding back into their lives in an alternate reality. Brehenna turned to Laura and smiled.

"Yes, I'm ready. I'll be right there." Laura rushed along but Brehenna took her time walking to the gate. When she reached it, she turn back one last time. Brehenna watch and waited. Again she saw a flurry of dust by the palace steps, but this time the dust turned into a small whirlwind that meandered itself across the courtyard. Then it paused right in front of her, twirling like a dervish, and finally dropping, like a curtsy at her feet.

Brehenna thanked her soul for this journey across multiple realms of reality, and multiple versions of life. With access now to all desires met and all prayers answered, she lived the balance of her enchanted life in anticipation and delight.

Epilogue

Woven

I saw a timeless vision in a clear, starless night sky. In the firmament, Destiny sat in a silent colossal tableau weaving at her loom. When the loom began to slowly radiate, Destiny rose, stepped away, and turned to search the heavens. Then, from the northwest and southeast, two thick glowing threads emerged from the blackness. On their own and moving toward each other, they spun and looped like small planes writing in the sky. As they wove themselves together, an additional party of strings surged from the void to engage in the revelry. Destiny and her loom had both vanished from the scene, leaving only the gossamer cloth and a growing multitude of dancing strings wildly weaving themselves into the fabric.

Now the threads gathered to form a colorful border. In a simultaneous bustle, the strings divided themselves like incandescent earthworms cut by an invisible blade and parlayed and do-si-doed into a fine fringe. Then the frenzy of celestial activity ceased. A hush fell upon the earth, and all of Creation halted, gaping skyward.

Above us in the global canopy of night, a scintillating tapestry of celestial luminosity had replaced the moon and stars. Hanging and waving like a heavenly banner, its colors and patterns chronicled the journey of Creation. Before anyone could utter *what the hell*, it was clearly and contrarily heaven on display. Every what, why, or how was consumed in the awesome pervasiveness of this theater of the Divine, made entirely of weather.

There was something so jubilant and celebratory about this phenomenon that it evoked the dawning of a possibility in our collective consciousness that seemed too audacious to even consider. Each soul, reacting as one, looked from side to side before putting an invisible hand over its heart. Me? Could it be? Is it possible that through all the struggling, stumbling, and backsliding through time, in the end...I made it? We made it? Is it conceivable that we are being honored? That this tiny seed of light in us, so far removed from Adam, has in fact won out? Could we have, when all is said and done, actually pleased God?

The weight of the possibility of this acknowledgment humbled us to our knees. After a few seconds of silence, the entire globe erupted in spontaneous applause. Clapping, shouting, ululating, whistling, howling, barking, chirping, neighing, and baying resounded from the earth. The burden of primordial guilt and dread lifted from our shoulders as the beauty in the sky filled the night with the sweetness of grace and the sigh of our redemption.

In terrestrial jubilation, we burst forth in song and dance. The planet rolled and rocked in unabashed relief. Finally, exhausted from exaltation, we paused in silence. In our stillness, we began to feel a faint quaking beneath our feet. We listened with one ear and heard the distant rumble of rapidly approaching thunder. Too soon, the rumble became a deafening roar, booming and hurling its way hastily toward us. Suddenly, the roar was joined by a huge fireball heading from the eastward sky, growing still larger as it advanced. The fireball was heading straight for the dazzling tapestry. The apocalyptic explosion blinded our senses—then utter blackness fell.

Time passed. We trembled, faltered, and barely breathed. Eventually, when sufficient composure had returned to us, we looked up to the sky. It was gone. The Divine Tapestry was destroyed, and with it our fantasy of salvation. The starkness of the silent black night chastened us. The scorching reproach of the remaining heat reversed the ebullient humility that had bended our knees and reduced it to the dense humiliation that now bowed our heads. Were we, after all, as throughout the ages we had dreaded, unworthy children, despised and abandoned by our parents and left alone to fend for ourselves in life?

Bereft now, the shameful tears came freely. For who could see us and testify in this blackness? We all cried. Who was left unjudged to have a testimony? Who was there to testify before? No one. No God. Nothing.

A long while passed. With only the mounting measure of our exhaustion to mark the passage of time, we became aware of this one fact: we were still alive. Out of ancient habit, in our despair we looked up to the mute black sky. We faced heaven with the stunned calm of the condemned who, in the final hour, have no other place to turn. For a long time, spent and empty, we stood facing the abyss.

Then. There in the sky. We may be mistaken. A twinkle? Somehow our eyes were not permanently blinded. It was a twinkle.

A twinkle, then a ripple. Our eyes recalibrated and searched. What is it that we are seeing?

Precisely where the tapestry had been and had disappeared from the sky, something remained. Still glowing and not utterly consumed was a pattern, a faint web, woven of golden threads, still shimmering in the sky. It was holy and beautiful, and not just a sign but our seal.

Not everything will remain, but among us are the Eternals—that and those who are already and will ever be alive in this network of golden luminosity.

To all of this: We are witness.

Yet once more I will shake not only the earth but also the heaven—for the removal of those things which can be shaken, as of created things, so that those things which cannot be shaken may remain (Hebrews 12:26, 27).

SOURCES for writing
Woven into the Fabric

I began writing *Woven into the Fabric* as a memoir. I wanted to capture a series of extraordinary life experiences that, over time, told my story. In large part, Brehenna's story was inspired by my own life. So the sources are all the real experiences and people who have enriched my life, and whose spirits, I hope, echo across the pages. My siblings Catherine, Alice, Nathan (may they rest in peace) and Veronika weathered all the challenges and shared all the joys of our childhood with the courage and determination to make for ourselves better lives. I was "Miss Watts" and Tommy Jacquette and the Watts Summer Festival gave me a glorious trip to Africa in 1972. I met Emperor Haile Selassie who acknowledged me as part of his royal family, and then personally arranged an introduction between his grandson and me. We fell in love. Years later, when Councilman Bob Farrell and I were married, he rallied the support of the Trans Africa Lobby to help prevent the mass deportation of Ethiopians who had sought refuge in America after the 1974 Coup in Ethiopia.

Tsehai Essiebea Farrell

As soon as I decided to write the book, I knew that in the process I wanted to learn to become a novelist. Shortly after my decision, I was accepted into Deena Metzger's Wednesday Night Women Writer's Group where I began to learn the spirit and craft of writing a novel. Among all the wonderful and challenging things I learned from Deena, her admonition to, no matter what happens in your writing, "trust the process" supported me through many strange and mysterious turns of my story.

Here's one example of an odd occurrence that happened while writing this book. The summer following my first year of writers' group, I was off from teaching so I was free to spend mornings at the beach writing. After finishing my writing session one morning, I sat looking out over the ocean and sky. Lulled by the beauty and the lapping of the waves, I heard a woman's voice say, "I am with the creator from the beginning. I am given patterns and sets of living strings. I am Destiny the Weaver." I was so surprised enchanted by the words, I picked up my pencil and pad and wrote them down. They were so potent.

Later in the week when I started writing again, everything was moving quite smoothly, so it took a while for me to realize something significant had changed. For two hours I had been writing my story in the third person. Up until then, it was *my* story and *I* was telling it. But on this day, I had written everything about myself, calling myself *she*. This was odd. When I finished writing for the day I wondered what this shift of narrator might mean. I remembered to- trust the process- and I counted on eventually finding out.

I share this because after the narrator changed, the book left Brehenna's story and opened time to also begin telling the story of the young Makeda, soon to become the Queen of Sheba. Once the story of King Solomon and the Queen of Sheba had merged into the narrative, I realized that I didn't have enough knowledge about these two historic figures nor their time, nor place. Their story was coming through but the writing was different, it felt suspended. How could I anchor their story?

Research. I stopped writing and spent months in UCLA libraries. I have to acknowledge several crucial sources for helping me anchor myself in the right place, time and circumstance to speak life back into the story of King Solomon and the Queen of Sheba. *The Kebra Negast (The Glory of Kings)*, an ancient sacred Ethiopian text, translated into English by E.A. Wallis Budge (1932), gave me the Ethiopian historical and spiritual grounding for understanding the nexus of the relationship between Israel and Ethiopia and the origin of the King Solomon and Queen Makeda of Sheba story. The Bible was also key in the grounding and etching of their story line and language. *The Nag Hammadi Library* opened for me ancient ways of seeing and saying, feeling and knowing. *Sheba: Through the Desert in Search of the Legendary Queen* by Nicholas Clapp and Graham Hancock's, *The Sign and the Seal*, gave me historical anchors for my tale.

When I returned to writing, I eventually became aware of just who the voice was now narrating my book- Destiny. It was she who had taken the helm and I was more than pleased to follow her story. She was transcendent to time and place and privy to the most private thoughts of all the characters. I, the writer, had become a witness. My job was now to see and experience what I was being shown and then to capture it all in language. I became like a tuning fork-I wrote until the writing on the page and what I experienced in my mind's eye resonated with the same vibrational accuracy.

Also essential to realizing this work was the opportunity I took to journeyed back to Ethiopia after 33 years, thanks to the Stanford Alumni Travel Study Club, and our wondrous adventure, *Ethiopia, in Search of the Ark of the Covenant.* I visited and revisited many of the sites in my novel: the ruins of the Queen of Sheba's palace, Emperor Haile Selassie's Jubilee Palace, the Palace of the Duke of Harrar in the province of Harrar, Lake Tana, Tissisat Falls the source of the Blue Nile, Axum and the church where the Ark of the Covenant and its Keeper reside. Addis Ababa's Hilton Hotel and Wabe Shebelle Hotel. Finally, I took a side excursion to Jerusalem to again touch the Western Wall of King Solomon's Temple, just to confirm that these beautiful people in my novel with whom I had spent so many years weaving their tale, were real and their spirits continue to live on.

Other sources who influenced my writing of Woven, over these twenty years, are all the real people who have and continue, even now, to unfold with me in life. Once I mentioned to Deena that I was almost finished writing the book and she asked, "But is the book finished writing you?"

And, just maybe, as a psychic reader once said to me, "You will speak a people back into history."

Acknowledgements

First I wish to thank that voice inside me for guiding me throughout my life and this entire twenty-one year journey of writing *Woven into the Fabric*: Thank you, God. I thank my daughter for living the story with me; and for, in my early years of writing, sharing her mother with the book.

Thank you, Barbara Rhodes for your patience and support and for spending a weekend with me hold up in a Santa Barbara cottage, listening and helping me to me piece together and recount my story before I began writing.

I thank Deena Metzger, my writing teacher, for coaching the writer out of me in the most amazing ways. I thank the women of my "Woven into the Fabric Premiere Book Club": Dr. Barbara Rhodes, Ernestine Henning, Mpingo Griffin, Yeniva Sisay-Sogbeh, Ang Rush, and Maisha Haynes. In the summer of 2007 we spent (at your insistence) four hours per session on four consecutive Tuesdays-a total of sixteen hours- discussing an early draft of the manuscript. Your deep connections and insightful comments about the story encouraged me at a time when my confidence in this journey was waning. The fact that you loved the story and found the writing beautiful gave me the strength to proceed to completion, which at the time I did not know would be another ten years.

I thank my sister Alice for being my first teacher and always believing in me and all the magical things that I shared with you over the years. I'm so glad that you got to read and love the manuscript; but, I am sad that you are not here, in the flesh, to enjoy this portion of the journey with me.

I thank the Stanford Alumni Travel Study Club and Dr. Scott Pearson for our trip to Ethiopia, "In Search of the Ark of the Covenant" which provided me with experiences and insights that undergird my story and my life.

To each of my friends, who cozied up on my living room couch to hear me read chapters aloud, I thank you for your encouragement and your confidence that one day *Woven* would be a book. Thank you Dashanaba King for being a faithful friend.

Barbara and Ernestine, my dear friends, I thank you both for reviewing the final manuscript and giving me your valuable input.

Thank you Angela Perkins for your beautiful artistic rendering of my photo which, I did not know at the time you made me the gift, was destined to be the cover of the book.

Finally, I thank *you reader*, for embarking on this journey with me. And if you love this book, I hope you can feel it loving you right back.

Questions and Topics for Discussion

1. This novel uses two parallel story lines. Discuss the common elements in both.

2. While the backdrop of the story is an epic tale, there is an intimacy in the exploration of the characters' inner worlds and the relationships between them. What does this novel reveal about the inner human dynamic? What does it reveal about relationships (with family ties, between men and women, between men and women and God)?

3. Discuss incidents in the story where the dimension of "common time" is suspended. What did these incidents contribute to the story, and why?

4. Identify and discuss key symbols in the novel. What do you think they represent, and why are they significant?

5. Discuss the major themes in the novel: love, hope, destiny and others.

6. What connections can you identify in the novel that relate to the title, *Woven into the Fabric*?

7. Beyond the fairy-tale elements of the novel, what deep explorations does *Woven into the Fabric* invite you to make?

8. What does the presence of Destiny as the narrator contribute to this novel?

9. Discuss the significance of Brenna's journey in the context of the broader African American journey.

Extend the ending of the novel. What are the best possible outcomes? Why?

24657461R00202

Made in the USA
Columbia, SC
29 August 2018